MAGIC, MOVIES, AND MURDER

BEWITCHER'S BEACH PARANORMAL COZY MYSTERIES
BOOK 1

EMILY FLUKE

ALSO BY EMILY FLUKE

-THE BEWITCHER'S BEACH PARANORMAL COZY MYSTERY SERIES

Be Careful What You Witch For: Prequel to the Bewitcher's Beach Paranormal Cozy Mysteries

Squeaks and Spooks: A Bewitcher's Beach Halloween Companion Novelette

Summoning, Skating, and Skulls: Book 2 (releasing 2024)

Book 3

-GARDEN PARTY GHOSTESS

-THE MARI FABLE MYSTERIES

Death of a Fairy Tale

Kidnapping the Classics

The Pinocchio Project

A Grimm Haunting

Snow Spell's Heartbreak

Book 6 (releasing 2024)

-FOLKLORE FALLS ROMANCE RETELLINGS

Until Theft Do Us Part

Fake Dating's a Beast

Be sure to snag the prequels to both the Mari Fable Mysteries, and the Bewitcher's Beach Paranormal Cozy Mysteries FREE from my newsletter: The Glass Coffin and Be Careful What You Witch For.

https://landing.mailerlite.com/webforms/landing/y4h6c8

"To other 1990s nerds who played outside until the streetlights came on, forgot to rewind their copies of BUFFY THE VAMPIRE SLAYER, and made their crushes a mixtape. And to my sister, who watched GARGOYLES and SONIC THE HEDGEHOG with me."

Oyster Inn

Hair
Salon

Pet
Grooming

Coffee
Shop

Fire
House

Roller Rink
& Diner

Soccer Field

Clinic

Art
Studio

Seashell
Shop

Clothing
Shop

Sunglasses
Shop

Office
Building

Beach

CAST OF CHARACTERS

Noema Wolf (temporary last name. Once werewolves are turned they have no memory of their previous life):

As a werewolf who can smell emotions and a lover of mystery movies, Noema finds herself sniffing out suspects whenever a troublesome visitor upsets her cozy, seaside town. But another case is not what this single mother of four, manager of Mockbuster Video Rental, and playwright needs thrown into her busy schedule.

Halen, Dio, Jovi, and Stevie Wolf:

These four mischievous 'pups' each help their mom solve mysteries or run the video rental shop in their own unique ways. As born werewolves, they don't experience memory loss —but as eight-year-olds, they suffer selective hearing when it comes to following the rules.

Sheriff Sett Lawrence:

This overprotective gargoyle takes life too seriously. His six foot, six inch stony, body with muscular wings and horns, does nothing to match his introverted, patient, and studious personality. But it certainly frightens visitors.

Hattie Sharpe:

This harsh, flapper-girl starlet became a ghost in the height of the Roaring Twenties when her bold attitude landed her the target of a deadly Hollywood stunt. Now, she directs Everland Theater's plays and tells it like it is, no matter how many enemies it creates.

Bette Sharpe:

Hattie's teenage daughter and ghost who babysits the wolf kids, earning money to develop the film in her Kodak camera. What crime will her photograph's capture?

Barney:

The grumpiest fairy you'll ever meet and owner of The Oyster Inn. Unlike their smaller counterparts, pixies, fairies are no different than humans other than delicate wings and their inability to tell a lie.

Chanel Sheen:

As a siren (*not* a mermaid, *thank you very much*) Chanel is the epitome of perfection, and a sea-creature who transforms into the most beautiful-looking human anyone has ever seen. And she's no stranger to shamelessly using glamor to get what she wants, even if its just to barter a higher price for her hand-made shawls.

Cordelia Moyer:

Vampire, fashionista, roller rink waitress, and new mom of

an adopted kindergartener. What could this blood-sucking nocturnal have to hide?

Roman Moyer:

Cordelia's boyfriend and vampire counterpart, turned undead in an epic *Romeo and Juliet*-style love story.

Mae Wildefyre:

Like her husband, Wallace, and other half-dragons, Mae resembles a human but with shiny, scaly skin. Before, when human hunters came after supernatural people, Mae hid with the other half-dragons, shifting herself to appear fully human. Now, she's the center of attention and loving it, until her secrets spread like wildfire.

Vera Fang:

The town's best, and only, real estate agent. Despite her name, she has no fangs, but she makes up for her plainness with pretend accents and designer clothing. Even without fangs, she can get awfully intimidating if you interrupt a house showing.

Piper June:

As an aspiring actress, this shapeshifter pushes beyond the bounds of her shifting abilities and seeks plastic surgery—maybe a little too much plastic surgery. When a lip filler goes wrong, she's ready to take revenge. Or is it all an act?

Dr. Pitt:

While this werebulldog takes care of everyone else in town, who will help him overcome his nerves? What might make this gentle doctor so anxious anyway?

CAST OF CHARACTERS

Cliff Conflick:

The man, the myth, the plastic surgeon. Cliff isn't the nicest guy, but he's got enough money to attract anyone he wants. Unfortunately, no amount of money is enough to stop a curse.

Mayor Fitz Feet:

As if summoned by his name, this short, shiny-headed mayor and volunteer police officer always appears with a cheerful countenance and a glass-half-full attitude. A leader of a town full of rumors, superstitions, and supernatural creatures must stay positive—even when a murder threatens to ruin Bewitcher's Beach's reputation. And his.

Squeaks:

A mouse. Arrogant, intelligent, and adorable, but still just a mouse.

CHAPTER 1
BUTTER OFF DEAD

1997 COASTAL CALIFORNIA

STEAM CURLED from the bag of popcorn I carried down the aisle of brightly colored comedy films. The smell wafted from the wall of new releases to the front of the video rental shop. Buttery goodness filled Mockbuster's every nook and cranny, and I wielded its delicious scent like a weapon against unsuspecting customers.

This was my sneaky little secret and one of my more genius ideas. If people came in to return a video, it served as a reminder that every night could feel like Friday as long as they rented another film. Plus, it gave me an excuse to snack while I worked. I munched on a piece of popcorn and picked up a copy of *The Breakfast Club*.

"Even a Monday feels like the weekend thanks to you," I said to my favorite 80's film. That was the power of stories.

*Speaking of stories...*I gnawed on my lip. My unfinished story for the town's annual play both haunted me and made me giddy. Unfortunately, popcorn was my only idea since writer's block left me stuck with half a script.

I decided a bit of food fuel and browsing the shop's aisles might spark inspiration. All of the movies, from *Clueless* to

Black Beauty, had given me ideas in the past. I snuck a taste of popcorn but didn't get a moment to enjoy the salty crunch. The cheesy cover of an older film, *My Mom's a Werewolf*, caught my eye. Goosebumps prickled over my spine.

How did that stupid movie keep showing up in my shop after I'd sworn I'd chucked it into the trash? I snatched the box off the shelf and peeked inside to verify the accompanying VHS tape. I marched for the door that led to the alley. Because of my werewolf height, an inch or two taller than most human women, I made it across the shop in only a few strides.

I ducked under the staircase that led to the loft, dipped out the side door, and dumped the movie into a pile of empty soda cans. The tape belonged in the trash, buried by wrappers from my kids' snacks and the sticky remnants of a spilled juice box.

As a rule, I didn't carry films that made a mockery of my life. So what if I was both a mom *and* a werewolf? Someday, I'd write a screenplay for Hollywood that gave moms and were-wolves the honor we deserved.

From the doorway, I squinted at the Coca-Cola clock above the blue and yellow *New Releases* sign. Movement caught my eye, and I spied a customer standing at the register. The woman tugged her baseball cap further down on her forehead, creating a shadow across her face.

I hurried to the front and tapped the tape on the counter. "Good choice. *Scream* is good for both a laugh *and* a scare. Perfect with Halloween next month."

"My face is good for a laugh and a scare," the woman muttered to herself, clearly oblivious she was in the presence of a werewolf. My ears picked up the drop of a pin, and the familiar drawl of the stranger's voice piqued my interest.

I readied the register for scanning and looked up to see the face of a famous guitarist on the customer's long-sleeve tee. "I love your shirt."

The woman's permed ringlet curls cascaded around her face as she looked down at her outfit. "Thank you. I got this at a concert."

My jaw dropped. "You've seen Van Halen live?"

The woman nodded. Now that she looked up, I noticed her swollen lips, so large and stretched they looked like painful red balloons. Her striking resemblance to actress Winona Ryder clued me in that she was a shapeshifter. I had heard of shapeshifters struggling between manifestations, but this looked more like an allergic reaction.

"I'm green with envy," I said. "I named one of my sons Halen."

"No way!" She plopped a bag of M&M's on the counter beside the VHS. "That's adorable."

"Yep. Halen, Dio, Jovi, and Stevie. My husband loved metal music, and when you have four kids at once, you need all the help you can get with names." It'd been seven years since his passing, but the mention of him still left my heart skipping.

The woman tried to smile, and the familiarity of her voice nagged at me. Though Bewitcher's Beach was a small town with a secretive and complicated past, newcomers weren't unusual at Mockbuster. With my shop nestled next door to The Oyster Inn, I met many visitors. People who stayed at the hotel ranged from vacationers on a family getaway to newly-weds honeymooning at the beach.

"What brings you to Bewitcher's Beach?" I asked, handing the rental and chocolates to her.

"I have...a score to settle," the woman said with a wink. The tilt of my head must have clued her in on my curiosity. She smirked. "And I never lose."

I didn't have time to sniff out whether she was telling the truth before she thanked me and ducked out the glass door.

Odd. But this town was full of oddities, and that was why I loved it. Still, despite the woman's impeccable taste in music, her presence left prickles on my arms, and I noticed the lingering scent of burnt toast—the smell of regret.

I sneezed and shook my head. "If only I couldn't smell emotions; I wouldn't have to deal with these icky scents."

I glanced from the mouse to the screen. Since the customer had swiped her rental card, the screen showed her name: *Piper June*. I'd heard the name before in gossip around town... involving the police.

I shook off the goosebumps and plopped onto the stool behind the register, ready to partition popcorn into sandwich baggies. The smell usually livened me as much as it did my customers—except for the undead ones.

A tiny mouse, Squeaks, appeared on the ground in front of the register. He skittered past the rental return tub and toward the buttery scent. He hopped onto the register's power cord and climbed up. Once he reached the desktop, the plump, fuzzy mouse stretched up to his hind legs and held his forepaws close to his chest. Squeaks' beady black eyes grew as he stared up at me with eager patience.

I sighed and pulled a piece of popcorn from my daughter's bag. With a palette as picky as Stevie's, she wouldn't eat much anyway. The zebra mouse quickly nibbled the piece and then spun around as if the trick would earn him another treat.

Squeaks' eyes bore into mine until I relented and produced the second piece of popcorn in my fist.

"You win this staring contest. But next time, watch out." I wagged my finger and teased the little pet. His whiskers twitched side to side, challenging me to round two.

"Unless you've got an idea for the play's subplot, I don't have time to make you more popcorn," I said. "I'm 'butter' off dead than missing another theater deadline. Get it? Butter?" I pointed to Squeaks' snack and chuckled at my pun.

The mouse dropped to all fours and nibbled on the rest of his singular piece while I ruminated over the strange woman's words. The last time a troublesome visitor came to town, bikes went missing. The mayor and volunteer police officer, Fitz, had asked me to help sniff out the suspect before half the town lost their bicycles.

Something about Piper's *score to settle* and the fact that she smelled like regret had me wondering if Fitz would request my nose's help down at the station again.

CHAPTER 2
THE CURSE WORD

THE BELL on the door chimed to announce another customer on this slow weekday afternoon. Come tomorrow, vendors and locals alike would swarm Bewitcher's Beach's town square to reserve spots for the fall festival.

Two teenage half-dragons hurried in to giggle over the scantily clad actress on the cover of *Pretty Woman*. Shiny, scaly skin was the only evidence of the teens' magical form to the naked eye. I smiled at them before turning my attention to the notebook.

Just as an idea formed, the bell chimed, and the smell of fresh soil, grass, and wet dogs filled the shop.

Four wild, shouting children tumbled through the door, nearly trampling one another to get to the snacks on the counter.

"Thanks, Mom!" Halen barked. Though fully human at the moment, his voice was lower than most eight-year-olds and always came out twice as loud.

"What're you doing?" Stevie asked. Her messy brown hair with a shock of gray fell into her face. Despite my attempt to fasten it into a ponytail, the length of her never-changing wolf's ears always knocked the hair out of place. Like me, each child carried pieces of their wolf form. Stevie was a mirror of her mommy with large, furry ears, Halen spoke with a bark, and the other two boys always had paws instead of feet.

"Writing," I lied and pointed to the notebook between the register and the row of snack bags. I didn't exactly write much.

"Writing what?" Stevie asked.

"Maybe a western, or a heist, or a romance." Really, it was already written, and I just had a subplot.

"What's ro-mans?" Dio joined the conversation, speaking with popcorn stuffed into both cheeks like a chipmunk.

"Romans," Jovi said as he stabbed the tiny plastic straw into his juice box. "You know, like Hercules?"

Dio shoved his brother, but Jovi was already humming a song from Disney's version of the Greek god's legend.

"Settle down," I said before fixing my eyes on Stevie, the only one with the patience to listen. "Romance is when two people fall in love."

"Ew!" Stevie stuck out her tongue.

"Yeah, I don't want to write it either." I sighed and plopped my chin into my palm.

Halen scratched at the cowlick that made his hair eternally messy. With a hop, his rear end landed on the edge of the desk where he swung his legs hard enough to rock the register.

"Mom likes stories where people stab each other," he said. Then, to demonstrate stabbing, he jutted his arm out to poke Dio's shoulder with the straw from his empty juice box.

While the pack of pups devoured popcorn, I continued browsing. One of my favorite films would eventually spark an idea.

The bell on the door chimed again, announcing the arrival of a human couple, followed by the fairy who ran the seashell shop across town. The backless shirt she wore left space for her wings to flutter. Since she was half the size of the humans, she easily slipped past them and headed for the romance section. I found myself observing customers in hopes of getting character ideas.

Before I knew it, Mockbuster was bursting at the seams with half-dragons, humans, fairies, and shapeshifters. It seemed the locals wanted to get their pick of movie rentals before the weekend brought tourists.

As I helped a shapeshifter find a new release, a ghost phased through the back wall. Her glittery fringe dress and matching headband framed her angular, transparent face. White-blonde hair was cropped to the length of her chin and swished with the shake of her head.

"Script?" Hattie asked.

I cringed. "Not yet. I need to add another character or subplot. It's too short." Though I knew my ghostly neighbor would request the script today, I'd failed her. Now I'd disappointed the woman who both haunted the adjoining building and directed the town's play. Maybe she'd forgive me if she heard about the spooky customer who threw off my focus today.

Hattie pinched the bridge of her nose. "Noema, time is running out."

I spied a customer at the register and headed for the front with Hattie at my heels.

"I know," I said.

"And I will not accept another murder mystery. We need to sell out this year to keep the theater standing."

"I know," I said, arriving at the register. "Cross my heart. It's not a murder mystery."

Hattie folded her arms and silently tapped her see-through foot as I finished the fairy's transaction.

A man with boy-band frosted tips—a hairstyle some might accuse him too old to wear—shuffled to the front desk. He placed a stack of VHS tapes on the desk with a copy of James Cameron's *Alien* at the top.

"Hi. Cliff, right?" I said, trying to remember the name of the man who often came to stay at the Oyster Inn. He'd come for a visit at the beginning of every month for the past three months now. I always remembered repeat renters. The tall doctor always dressed to the nines and walked with a hunch.

Cliff nodded and tossed his thick wallet on the desk. He never failed to flash a hundred-dollar bill even though the stack of videos cost less than twenty dollars to rent. "That's me."

"Good to see you again," I said, though I didn't particularly consider him an acquaintance. He often responded in grunts and had even made a joke at my expense before, saying his ex-wife had the number of a good waxer if I ever wanted hairless ears.

"Hmm," he grunted.

I scanned a bag of popcorn and two Surge sodas, then scooted them back to him. "I need a story idea this good." I held up *The Swan Princess* and turned the case around to show Hattie. "But I swear, subplots are the worst!"

The half-dragon teens snickered, pointed, and gawked at the tape I held up. Red reached Cliff's cheeks, and he grabbed the VHS from my hand.

"That's for my lady," he snapped. "For date night."

"Oh," I said. The faint scent of embarrassment lingered for a moment, and I felt the need to come to his rescue. "There's nothing to feel silly about; it's a classic. I recommend *The Swan Princess* to everyone. I only hope to write something this good once I break my writer's block curse."

"Curse?" Cliff scowled and tucked the videos under his

sweaty arm, standing with more of a hunch now. "I don't take recommendations from witches!"

"But I'm not a witch," I said, my voice trailing off.

His green eyes narrowed, tracing the shape of my head before settling on my gaze again. "Hmm," he huffed. "Could have fooled me. You've got that mischief glow about you."

Before I could respond, he ducked out the door. I wrinkled my nose at the leftover smell of Cliff's emotions. I often avoided catching others' scents, cursing my keen canine nose, because emotions rarely smelled nice. Thankfully, the sour air of embarrassment faded.

"Then I recommend you don't throw around the curse word unless you want a bad reputation." Hattie huffed, growing more impatient with me and my line of customers.

A shapeshifter nodded in agreement as she slid a stack of action films across the desk. According to legend, a curse is the only thing that can undo the mysterious protection spell over Bewitcher's Beach granted to us by an unnamed witch. Because of this, most avoided speaking of curses.

"Now." Hattie phased through the register and pointed to the title of *The Swan Princess* still on the computer's screen. "I think you were absolutely right; a romance is what this town needs. Have the script on the stage by next week."

Next week? My throat tightened. I needed a swig of Diet Dr. Pepper to wash down that shock, though I knew she was right. Fall was coming fast.

With that, Hattie floated across the register and the video stands before vanishing through the back wall and into the adjoining theater.

"Curses." I mumbled the loaded word without thinking. *Oops.*

The shapeshifter gasped and grabbed her films, hurrying away from me.

As I rang up the rest of the afternoon's renters, I plotted a plan to break this block. Tomorrow, while the kids went to a Friday sleepover, I'd walk the town with my notebook and pen and gather inspiration from locals. With that decided, I deserved a fresh bag of popcorn all to myself—and maybe a bite for Squeaks.

CHAPTER 3
SCREEN OF THE CRIME

I PULLED the plug and the screen finally died. The list of movies disappeared as the computer went black, highlighting the dust on the screen. The old desktop register never shut down properly and needed to be replaced soon. I didn't have the patience to wait for the loading hourglass symbol to finish. Instead, I opted to yank the cord from the outlet.

I had a script to finish and only one night without interruptions. Life as a single mother, a business owner, and a playwright didn't come without its stress. I loved every moment, but it took the skill of a balancing act to work around schedules and get the play written. Thankfully, the pups had weekly movie nights with friends from their soccer team.

A tiny shadow crossed the floor. Flickering whiskers tickled my sandaled toes until I knelt and scooped Squeaks into my hand. The red light of the *open* sign shone in his black eyes as he gave me his best sad face.

"I have to unplug it," I explained, knowing Squeaks wanted to curl up by the computer. Like a cat on the hood of a car, he enjoyed soaking in the machine's warmth. "It's a fire hazard."

After hearing Hattie's 1925 Hollywood death story a thousand times, I'd become paranoid about fires. When your ghostly best friend dies in a fire, you learn to take all precautions with unpredictable electronics.

The machine was old, but between soccer cleats and stocking the newest tapes on my shelves, I didn't have the extra funds for a new computer. Besides, my heavy-handed werewolf tendencies didn't do well with the newer, more fragile electronics.

Squeaks squealed and flicked his tail like a whip to get his complaint across.

"I'll keep you warm," I said as I unzipped the fanny pack at my waist and let him crawl inside. He turned around three times and then poked his twitchy nose out of the slit I left open. It was a tight squeeze next to my notebook and pen, but he made do. "There. You can hunt with me."

In my house, the word *hunt* meant a quest for inspiration or a pursuit of magic. That way scary stories of hunters didn't keep Stevie and Jovi up at night. Those who hunted supernaturals were now few and far between since people like us had come out of hiding almost three decades ago. Still, it wasn't an impossibility to cross paths with a zealous supernatural hunter —which was why I lived in Bewitcher's Beach, where legend says the protection spell keeps supernaturals from being attacked.

I slipped out the door and locked it. The *open* sign still glowed through the glass walls. I'd forgotten to flick it off, but I left it for now, eager to get moving.

Though I'd never had a case of writer's block this bad before, I'd hit metaphorical walls with words in the past. Each time, I took to the cobblestone sidewalks of Bewitcher's Beach and hunted for inspiration. The salty smell of the ocean acted like white noise for my sensitive nose and allowed my mind to untangle plot holes.

But this time, I wasn't writing a mystery, so plot holes didn't nag me. Since I struggled creating characters, I planned to close up before the sun set and chat with the evening walkers. Most people, whether vampire, werewolf, gargoyle, fairy, or human, liked to talk about themselves, so it would be a breeze to gather ideas.

The crisp autumn wind beckoned me to step outside onto the sidewalk. The uneven cobblestone used to make me trip and fall, but I'd memorized the worn pathway from Mockbuster to the end of the street and then all the way around. Now I knew every jutting stone and where my feet should land.

A mixture of saltwater, remnants of pumpkin spice from the taffy shop across the street, and damp soil filled my nose. The smell of home.

A home I hoped wasn't infiltrated by another troublesome visitor. Piper had smelled off—regretful—and it nagged the back of my mind.

Hattie's haunting singing voice echoed from behind the theater's double doors. She sang a jazz tune from when she was alive in the 1920s, long before my time—though, of course, I remembered nothing of my life before becoming a werewolf.

I peered through the crack in the door to see the ghost phasing through each row. Tattered red fabric covered the old, worn chairs. She seemed to test the acoustics of the old building as she paused and changed the pitch of her voice several times. Hopefully, she didn't expect me to write a musical for next year's fall festival. If this play did well and sold enough tickets, we'd be able to renovate by adding a second floor of chairs to pull in bigger crowds. And then, eventually, we'd transform Everland's stage into a movie theater.

Squeaks released three shrill chirps to announce his impatience. I pulled my nose from the crack in the door and kept walking. Fairy lights twinkled in the curtained windows of The Oyster Inn. I stepped off the sidewalk and crossed the alley. The inn rivaled Everland Theater in height, both with peaked rooftops of wooden shingles. Everland was one story with a high ceiling to support the acoustics and the small attic at the top where the ghosts, Hattie and her daughter, resided. The inn stood three stories tall and was peppered with dozens of identical windows, all meticulously clean and adorned with twinkling lights and cozy curtains.

I squinted through the front door's window and waved at the fairy who ran the inn. Barney only frowned and went back to collecting dirty champagne flutes from the little bar in the lobby.

Squeaks released a piercing squeal, alerting me to an approaching crowd. I turned to see a group of moms on their nightly power walk. They nearly mowed me down as they refused to slow their pace and flooded the sidewalk around me. Pumping arms punched forward and their feet, from dainty fairy toes to larger half-dragon's shoes and everything in between, moved in a synchronized march. Each woman sported a shiny white pair of sneakers with thick ankle socks.

"Noema!" They spoke all at once. I tried to smile at each person, though I was only acquainted with a few of them from the kids' school.

The selkie leading the group stopped to take a gulp from her water bottle. When the entire group copied her, I found myself trapped in a sea of neon spandex. Squeaks poked out of the fanny pack with my pen between his teeth.

"Pardon," a voice with a French accent said.

I turned to see Vera, a real estate agent who lived in town. It always took an extra second to recognize her since she switched hairstyles and makeup trends faster than the teenagers who shopped at Mockbuster. She squeezed through the group of chatty moms and disappeared into The Oyster Inn.

When the selkie announced she'd had enough water, the group moved on, waving their goodbyes in perfect synchronicity. I spun in the opposite direction and continued my own walk—one where power and pumping arms were replaced by plot ideas and pens.

Two half-dragons approached me with their teeth bared as they smiled sweetly. Mae wore a wig over her small horns, and her husband's hat concealed his.

Wallace smiled at me. "Where's the litter of—"

"I heard you said the 'C' word to a customer!" Mae interrupted her husband's polite question. She released her hold on his hand and slapped her palm to her chest where her fuzzy sweater dipped in a scoop-neck style.

Already? News traveled fast in Bewitcher's Beach.

I stood a little taller and readied my shield against the gossip. When it came to Mae, scandals were as necessary as the fire she breathed. Smoke even emitted from her nose each time she heard about a soccer mom who drank too much wine, or when the sheriff almost arrested me for eavesdropping.

"Well," I started, "that same customer called me a witch, so it was the only natural response." Though that wasn't quite the order of events, Mae didn't need to know every detail.

She opened her mouth, eager for more, but her husband repaid her interruption.

"Do you know what I heard?" he asked, a twinkle in eyes. "I heard my wife make me a promise. If I didn't go to the open house with her, I wouldn't get a slice of her famous mozzarella meatloaf. And I already held up my side of the bargain." He shot Mae a smirk.

She swatted his shoulder. "Okay, okay, you don't have to nag." The flushed red on her cheeks and hint of a smile complemented the smell of love. Love was a combination of joy's citrusy scent with notes of vanilla.

I didn't get a chance to ask about their romantic background, but their playful teasing gave me an idea for a scene with flirting.

Before I knew it, I'd passed Scooby's Dog Grooming and Shaggy's Hair Salon, two places that ate up my monthly budget since the kids needed trims in both wolf and human forms.

At this end of the square, I'd stepped into the town's largest parking lot. A massive milkshake on wheels towered over me as it swayed in the wind. The giant statue tilted to the left under the pressure of the gentle but endless breeze from the shore.

The wind carried the conversations of vendors milling about the town square, scoping out their spot for the biggest event of the year as fall rolled in. I angled my ears to listen.

Past the diner, a familiar friend rolled up to me on skates, smooth as butter on the uneven cobblestone. Cordelia flashed her winning smile, complete with a set of blood-sucking teeth, after waving to her boyfriend. The vampire blew his girlfriend a kiss before cupping their adopted toddler's hand—a story that made their relationship all that more impressive and adorable. The tiny, wobbly young boy smiled up at his father, not the slightest bit deterred by the man's gothic look and sharp teeth.

"Hey, hey," Cordelia said as she zoomed toward me, likely headed for Roller Shakes. As usual, she emerged from her underground home on the other side of town and showed up for the night shift at the diner.

"Cordelia! Can I get your thoughts on something?" I said, a sudden idea flashing into my mind. She had the greatest love story I'd heard in a long time.

Her black hair circled around her shoulders as she came to a sudden halt. "I'll be late if I stop now."

"Go, go!" I waved her on, but she only folded her arms and shrugged.

"Oh, no, girl, if you've got gossip, I'm here for it," she said, plucking a lock of thick hair from where it had stuck to her shiny lips. Her black nail polish glittered against the glow of the streetlights.

"You'll have to see Mae for that," I said. "I'm gossip-less."

Her arms went limp and her head rolled back slightly. A sigh escaped her. "What a disappointment. I was hoping for an excuse to chat, but I've got to run." She skated forward, skillfully dodging each bump in the cobblestone with the thick wheels. "You better come by and entertain me at my shift tonight!"

"Only if you promise to tell me how you met Roman!" I called after her.

Without slowing or turning back, she tossed me two thumbs up, with her arms stretched above her head.

As she skated, Cordelia's arm nearly clotheslined the wide-shouldered sheriff. Of course, a vampire couldn't knock down a stony, six-and-a-half-foot tall gargoyle.

Sheriff Sett tried to dodge, but as always, his heavy body moved too slowly. I cringed at the thwack of her bony wrist against the stony skin of his ribcage. Cordelia shook it off and didn't so much as slow.

Before the sheriff suspected me of eavesdropping, I spun around. He'd threatened to arrest me over it before, knowing my curiosity and character research had pushed me to the bounds of trespassing. Thankfully, he never made good on the threat.

"Noema," he said in a bright voice. "Just the werewolf I wanted to see."

"Yeah?" My cheeks burned. Was it obvious that my evening walk had ulterior motives? I wasn't invading anyone's privacy, but to a stickler of rules like Sett, my hunting bordered on eavesdropping.

To my surprise, the slow-moving gargoyle caught up with me and matched my strides. His rare hint of a smile set me at ease. He wouldn't be friendly if he suspected me of listening in on others' conversations.

"Did you restock the Creme Savers yet?" he asked. "The strawberry flavor?"

Sett could easily snag a bag from the grocery store next to Mockbuster, but he always came in to get the candy from me. I never understood why he didn't take the extra steps to get it a few cents cheaper.

"Not yet; I only have orange," I said.

He nodded in slow motion. "Orange will do. I'll stop by tomorrow. Unfortunately, tonight I have to oversee the vendor contracts for the festival. Better go." He sighed and shook his head as if the vendors had ruined his plans to purchase a bag of candy. His wide brow pinched over deep-set gray eyes that matched his skin. This was his usual expression: serious, focused, furrowed.

When he jogged across the street to the grassy town square, I shook away thoughts of gargoyles and Creme Saver candy, recalling my previous plan—get details on Cordelia's love story. Though I only knew bits and pieces of the vampires' romance, what I remembered was full of drama, sacrifice, and sentimentality. It'd be the perfect inspiration.

Squeaks poked his nose into the air and twisted his head, glaring at me with beady black eyes.

"Don't worry," I said, "we'll finish the walk first." With a plan to break writer's block in place, I allowed my mind to wander.

By the time I made it to the other side of town, I was alone. I squinted at the sight of a few people in the distance, still milling about the town. Like me, they enjoyed a late-night walk, as was common for all nocturnal people from vampires to reapers.

Lost in my thoughts, I hadn't realized how late it'd become. If I wanted to get ideas from Cordelia before I became too tired to think, I needed to get moving. The script wouldn't write itself, and I was well on my way to a successful play—one that'd earn the theater enough money for the big screen. A smile snuck onto my face. I let myself daydream and hurried toward my shop.

As I drew closer, I spotted a large lump outside Mock-buster's door. I grumbled, guessing it was a bag of rentals lazily abandoned on the sidewalk instead of dropped into the return slot. Except, with every step, the lump became less the bag I imagined and more the shape of a person.

My feet moved faster while my heart thumped erratically. Was it superstition, my love for mystery movies, or my overactive imagination that had me expecting the worst?

I squinted, making out the limp figure sprawled on the sidewalk. This was no trick of the imagination. Squeaks released one alarmed squeal after another, while I couldn't so much as breathe. The squeeze in my throat rendered me speechless.

I scanned the trail of VHS tapes scattered over the sidewalk where they'd been haphazardly dropped. My blood turned to ice in my veins.

As sure as the fur on my ears, a body lay face down in front of my shop.

CHAPTER 4
CURSED CINEMA

THE OCEAN BREEZE blew Cliff's hair into his frozen face. Despite the fresh scent of saltwater clearing the air, I only needed one sniff to tell me he wasn't passed out drunk.

Cliff was dead.

Though I did catch a whiff of rich, heavy alcohol, like red wine, from his drool along with pungent lingering fear around his body.

"How?" I breathed and bit back a scream. My gaze darted over the VHS tapes that littered the ground. How did Cliff end up this way, and right outside the rental shop?

The movies he'd rented were scattered over the cobblestone, surrounding him like a summoning circle. Or what I guessed a summoning circle would look like.

I gave my shoulders a wiggle, shaking off the thought. Too many hours spent writing mysteries had turned me into a superstitious conspiracy theorist. This poor man had likely suffered a natural death. Sudden, but natural.

"Natural," I repeated, trying to calm my pounding heart. Cliff wasn't a friendly man, but he didn't deserve a lonely end on the sidewalk in the dark.

I backed into the shop, making for the telephone. Who should I call first? The doctor or the cop? I scrambled to dial the police station. Nervously, I reached for a VHS tape on the desk. I absentmindedly began spinning the reels with a finger from my free hand.

Movement caught my eye and drew my attention through the giant windowed walls. Triton, the gangly human who ran the taffy shop, jogged toward Cliff's body. An older couple stopped to gawk, and even a shapeshifter kid, currently in the form of an octopus, balanced on his tentacles nearby. The shapeshifter stared while he munched on a hard-boiled egg.

"How can I help?" Sett answered on the other end of the line. An offer of help was how he always responded to anyone, at any given time.

"It's Noema. Come to Mockbuster ASAP, someone's... dead." Superstition raged within me. What had caused a healthy man I saw only hours before to collapse outside my shop?

My heart battered against my ribcage as if it couldn't decide whether to leap from my chest or stop completely—the way Cliff's heart had.

Sett promised a quick arrival, and I slammed the phone against the receiver. Without thinking, I grabbed the VHS tape and clutched it to my chest like a security blanket.

In the two minutes it took me to call the sheriff, the crowd doubled. I stumbled outside, freezing between Mockbuster and the body. The shop's door hit my butt as it swung closed. It seemed to nudge me forward, encouraging me to identify the strange smells lingering around the body.

Did Cliff know he was dying, and that was where the smell of fear came from? Then why would he waste time returning rental videos rather than seeking medical help? And what had caused the weird bitter smell I didn't recognize?

People formed a circle around the body, and my nose prickled with the scents of dozens of new emotions. My senses went into overdrive. I observed every detail of the situation down to the salt that seasoned the yolk of the shapeshifter's egg. Smells overlapped one another, ranging from the sharp sting of fear's ammonia to the minty scent of curiosity.

I scanned the scene, noting the sweat stains on his collar and the slippers on his feet. Cliff died clutching *The Swan Princess*'s case, while the other videos had slipped from his hold.

Sett marched toward Mockbuster, clawed hands in the pockets of his thick blue coat. Despite his stony expression, I spied the crack that creased the skin between his eyes. His leathery wings spread out around his thick frame, making way for him through the gawkers, gasping old men, and gossiping soccer moms.

"After my walk, I found him here," I explained, pointing at the body. "He reeks of fear and...something else I've never smelled before."

Sett nodded, crouching to get a good look at Cliff. He pulled out his pager and sent a message to the volunteer police officer at the station. I tried not to read the tiny, blocky text on the screen, but it was impossible when he stood right in front of me.

Fitz, a coroner is needed on site.

"I've called for backup," he said before leaning closer to me and speaking under his breath. "Did you see or hear anything else when you found him? I know you..." He gestured as if to coax the suggestion out of me. "You *hear* things sometimes."

The veiled accusation in his question wasn't lost on me. He suspected me of poking my nose where it didn't belong, or rather my ears. My jaw dropped again. "I don't eavesdrop!"

The arch of his eyebrow twitched ever so slightly. "Maybe

not, but I imagine with hearing as sharp as yours, you can't help but..." Sett's voice trailed off, but I heard the suggestion as clearly as if he'd shouted it. Slowly, he straightened and crossed his arms. As friendly as we were, somehow we always ended up at odds.

"What? I can't help getting myself into trouble?" I asked. My blood boiled and my muscles tensed, ready to rage out in full wolf form.

He'd said it before, calling my investigation of the bicycle thief a "troublesome risk for an innocent citizen such as yourself."

"I didn't mean—" He huffed, forcing air through his nose. "Noema, it's my job to ask questions and get answers. That's how I keep people safe."

"I'm perfectly safe," I insisted. I folded my arms across my chest, unfolding again only to wave my hand at the victim. "Shouldn't you be investigating?"

"Not until the coroner arrives," he said, eyeing me. "*Do* you know anything?"

"No!" It was a knee-jerk response and a lie. I opened my mouth to explain but thought better of revealing Cliff's irritation when I'd embarrassed him for renting a cartoon romance.

The flicker of my ears revealed how desperately I held back from shifting into my werewolf self and running from all these smells.

The corner of my eye caught sight of Mae's scaly arms sweeping back and forth as she bustled up to the curb.

"Oh no!" She slapped her claws to her chest, wrinkling her floral blouse. "Noema, what did you do?"

My heart flip flopped. "M-me?" I asked. "What do you mean?"

Mae gestured at the body. "Wallace and I just passed Cliff on our walk. He was looking everywhere for you. He said your videos made him sick and he was going to demand that you fix him and undo the curse."

Curse? From flip-flop to drop, my heart slammed into the pit of my stomach.

Mae continued while the crowd leaned in to catch every word. "He said 'she told me Mockbuster sends a curse to everyone who doesn't rewind their tapes.' And that's a direct quote!" The half-dragon nodded.

Gasps rippled through fairy, werefox, and human alike.

"A curse is the only thing that can break through Bewitcher's Beach's protection spell," a pixie—a fairy with a smaller body but more magic—squeaked. Her wings tittered with nervous energy as people nodded in agreement.

Fear tightened my throat.

"And he died holding a video!" A voice in the back added. More nodding heads made the crowd look like an undulating wave, threatening to crash on the shore and sweep me away if I got too close.

"Did you ever threaten the victim?" Sett asked, folding his arms in a mirror of my defensive stance.

"No, I swear!" I grimaced, peering at the victim's body by my feet.

The coroner along with the volunteer police officer, Fitz, had finally arrived. Thankfully, they distracted the sheriff while I got a moment to breathe. Sett always gave his full attention to Fitz since the short, bald man was also the mayor of Bewitcher's Beach.

Voices overlapped as conversations buzzed. People threw around theories about his death like a football, bouncing possibilities off of one another.

It was all too much. I released a slow breath and tried to calm my raging heartbeat...until I caught the quiet conversation between the sheriff and the coroner.

"Time of death," the coroner said, "is between seven and eight."

I leaned back and glanced at the clock on the wall in Mockbuster. Cliff had only died half an hour ago.

The coroner, who was still crouched over the victim's body, pointed to the dried drool. I pricked my ears, turning them forward to catch his words. "...indicates an allergic reaction or possible poison."

A gasp slipped from me. Poison? Was that the strange, bitter smell that came from Cliff's drool? Sometimes memories that came with a smell clued me in on the source of the scent. This icky smell reminded me of fertilizer. It sparked thoughts of gardens, grass, or maybe bug spray. I couldn't put my nose on it. What would plants have to do with Cliff's death?

"Could a curse cause him to choke?" Mae asked, confident that the coroner would include her in official police business.

He only clenched his jaw shut and glanced at Sett.

Fitz raised his hand, which didn't even reach my shoulder. "Ma'am, let us do our job."

The act of avoidance said enough, and the crowd, who hinged on his answer, burst into a dozen conversations at once. Nervous energy buzzed, and I clutched the VHS tape tighter to my sternum.

The curse theory had slipped, and the damage was done. What must they think of me?

The soccer moms arched their eyebrows. Triton raked his bony fingers through his shaggy hair. An elderly man nearly popped a blood vessel with his eyeballs bugged so wide. Even the octopus boy who'd shoved the rest of the egg into his cheeks stopped munching.

Each gawker shared one thing in common. They all stared forward, their gazes past me and fixed on the blinking, neon *open* sign that hung in Mockbuster's window. It flickered two more times before going dark.

An omen.

I shook my head. *Superstitions be darned.* The only curse on the rental shop was the belief of a curse...on the rental shop. I definitely didn't hurt people who didn't rewind their video tapes, unless late fees counted.

"Do you think watching the videos is where the curse gets you, or can it happen at rental?" A soccer mom asked Mae.

The half-dragon only shrugged. "Goodness, don't shoot the messenger. I never meant to suggest it was *real*. I'm only repeating what Cliff said."

I sucked in a breath and interjected. "There's no curse. It's not real. He must have eaten a bad salad or something. I smell something bitter like a plant or—"

"Real or not, I'm returning my tapes right now." The older man elbowed his way out of the crowd. Once free, he scurried down the street to the neighborhood at the edge of town.

Most of the onlookers shuffled uncomfortably now, backing away from the building that housed both the shop and the theater.

The theater! Not only would such rumors hurt my business, but they had the power to smash my dreams as a playwright too.

The coroner and police worked together to whisk away the victim's body. Sett made his rounds, double-checking if anybody had witnessed Cliff's demise. Once satisfied, he marched up to me.

Without a body to gawk at, the crowd dispersed. Townspeople continued their Saturday night strolls. Some headed for a greasy dinner at the diner in Roller Shakes. Others resumed their walks. If only I could do the same and continue my plans for the night, but I stared helplessly at the shape of a body outlined in chalk. The poor man's end left my stomach twisted with sadness.

The gargoyle grabbed the pen tucked by his horn and tapped it against a clipboard. "You know I need to ask you a few questions."

"Of course," I said, ready to defend myself. I explained the night's events. Sett nodded along and scribbled notes so messy I couldn't decipher even one letter. Fitz stood by on his tiptoes to see Sett's clipboard. His shiny bald head barely reached Sett's elbow.

"Make note of the plant smell," Fitz said as he pointed to the scribbles. Sett arched an eyebrow down at him but quickly adjusted his face before the mayor caught sight of it. "Noema sniffed out the serial bicycle thief last year and closed the case for us. If she smells something that can help us here, we can wrap this up before superstitions affect attendance at the fall festival."

While that was true, I had no intention of getting involved with official police business. Sett nearly arrested me for sneaking around to catch the thief last year. I didn't have time to help in an investigation, much less waste in a jail cell. Especially if this curse rumor and superstitions hurt my business.

Sett grunted but didn't dare argue with Fitz. I sniffed, expecting to smell the mild odor of gasoline, the scent of impatience and irritation. I rarely smelled Sett's emotions, but I tried anyway.

"No, thank you," I said. "I'm busy enough with the shop, and the pups, and the play I'm writing."

"That's too bad," Fitz said with a shake of his head. "With quick answers, we can nip this curse drama in the bud. We don't need any negative news about shops in town right before the big festival."

I cringed. The mayor was right. If mention of curses or

poison or death got out, it could deter visitors and locals alike from the boost of business that the fall festival gave Bewitcher's Beach. As much as I didn't want to get involved, I might be able to get answers quickly and clear the air before Cliff's crazy accusations grew legs. Besides, helping with the investigation would help prove that I didn't curse or hurt Cliff.

"You don't believe the um..." I glanced at the dark *open* sign through Mockbuster's large glass walls. "You're not worried about the curse?"

"Bah!" Fitz waved his hand as if to clear the air between us. "I believe in what I can see with my own two eyes. Curses are all speculation just to stir up drama in my book. Anywho, I'm off." He patted Sett's arm and said he needed to return to the station and wrap up paperwork. "Think about offering your skills, will ya, Noema?" He tapped his nose and then hopped off the curb. I smiled and promised I would.

If I could find a way to multitask writing, working, momming, and investigating, I'd be happy to help.

Left alone now, Sett eyed me.

"I can't argue with the mayor," he said, "but I really don't think this is a good idea. Your methods with the bicycle thief investigation broke all kinds of rules, and, more importantly, I wouldn't want you in any danger in case this turns out to be foul play."

Between the gargoyle's horns, I spied an older man shuffling along the sidewalk. He balanced a tower of VHS tapes, tall enough to block his view.

"Noema, are you thinking what I think you're thinking?" Sett asked.

I frowned. The silly superstition had officially sunk its teeth into my customers. More seriously, who had told Cliff I cursed my videos? I needed answers. Maybe I could help like Fitz wanted but avoid dealing with Sett's slow process and judgmental stares. I could manage a bit of research on the side and out of the sheriff's way while still finishing the romance plot in the play.

After adjusting my gaze to fall on the man in front of me, I quickly forced a smile.

"Unless it's about a kissing scene, then I doubt it," I said, spinning around to lock up the shop. The superstitious man would have to return his videos in the drop-box. I had a character to sketch—or rather, a victim to research.

The sooner I determined the truth behind Cliff's demise, the less Mockbuster and Everland Theater would suffer. And I had the perfect excuse to chat with the people in Cliff's life.

"K—kissing?" Sett cleared his throat and furrowed his brow.

"Time for me to gather information," I said. I tucked my keys into my pocket and turned around.

He cocked his head. The hardened line of his lips told me he didn't like my plan. "Investigating is my job—"

I swatted at his shoulder, playing it off as all part of the plan. "Did I say information? I meant *inspiration*. I have a play to finish, and auditions start next week."

Sett's gaze fell to where I'd brushed my fingers over his arm. "All right, then. I look forward to seeing your new work on the stage."

I beamed, without the need to force it this time.

Auditions and character research: two perfect excuses to search for answers...or suspects. Whatever happened to Cliff, I'd find out and prove to Bewitcher's Beach that Mockbuster wasn't cursed.

Haunted by an angry actress-turned-ghostly-director, yes. But not cursed.

CHAPTER 5
FEATURE AT THE FARMER'S MARKET

AFTER LAST NIGHT'S events left me drained, I skipped the visit to Roller Shakes. So I resolved to pop by Cordelia's work tonight and draw inspiration from her real-life romance. *If* I could focus on the script after a person had been found dead in front of my shop and home.

Please let the gossip be over. I said a silent prayer as I ran a brush through my daughter's tangled hair. They'd returned from the sleepover messy but happy.

After securing a butterfly clip to hold Stevie's bangs in place, I tiptoed around a landmine of Hot Wheels cars and shouted for the boys to get their jackets on. Today, the Bewitcher's Beach town square transformed into a Farmer's Market with handmade clothing, homemade soaps, and plenty of vegetables. The gathering drew out all manner of people, and since this was the last market of the season, it was sure to be packed.

Hopefully, nobody would mention last night's terrible occurrence. Unless I discreetly asked them about it to determine who might have been involved.

We trailed down the stairs where a luminescent ghost waited for us. The kids greeted Hattie before heading to the snack wall to raid for after-breakfast treats. Growth spurts had them hungry for more, although they'd already downed a dozen Eggo waffles and an entire package of bacon.

Hattie folded her arms across her chest and pursed her cherry-red lips. The same glittery flapper dress that she'd died in never caught the light quite the right way, sometimes blinding me, other times looking dull. Today, it didn't shine, and the look on her face matched.

"And where are you going so early?" Hattie asked.

I tried to smile. "I'm going to get answers."

"Where's my script?" She ignored my plan.

"Hattie." I paused at the bottom of the staircase, leaning on the banister with both elbows. Squeaks skittered toward my feet and circled like a dog before settling on the top of my toes. "I have an idea. But I can't just sit down and write when Cliff's attacker might be out there and while people gossip about my shop."

The curtain of blonde hair swept across her face as she shook her head. "I understand that, and I don't doubt you'll be helpful with that nose of yours." Like everyone else in town, Hattie had already heard about last night's death. Or so I suspected, based on how quickly scandals spread through Bewitcher's Beach. She continued talking, pulling me from my thoughts. "But, don't you think Bewitcher's Beach deserves a happy romance to watch after all this talk of curses and killing? I went out for a walk this morning and everybody asked me about it."

All this talk? Only one night had passed since Cliff's demise, and the gossip already spread through the streets.

"There's good news," I promised. "I'll drum up interest in the play by letting people have a say in the new characters."

Hattie's thin lips curved down, but it wasn't a frown. Though she had plenty of emotions, I couldn't smell a ghost. With her, I relied on facial expressions only. Finally, she nodded, impressed. "That's not a bad idea. I'll join you later. Maybe I can get them involved in other ways too. Hollywood knows we need help building sets and props." Hattie used the human phrase, twisting it into her version of heaven. Though Hollywood wouldn't cast her again soon unless they needed a not-so-friendly ghost for a new blockbuster hit.

"And once they're involved," I said, "they'll want to brag about their work to friends and family. This'll bring in more visitors and help sell tickets."

Hattie beamed as she nodded. "Sounds fine," she spoke harshly, but her manifestation betrayed her, brightening with her mood. She hurried to vanish through the connecting wall between Mockbuster and Everland.

I crouched and unzipped the fanny pack at my waist. Squeaks knew the routine and crawled into the pack, curling up next to my wallet and a packet of to-go Kleenex.

We piled out the back door to avoid the roped-off crime scene in front of Mockbuster. I slipped my notebook into the large pocket of my jacket, complete with a list of character names from the still-unnamed play. Though the script remained unfinished, and I'd need to squeeze in plenty of writing time, the events around Cliff's death took precedence.

Four pups bounded ahead of me, shoving one another as they paused at the edge of the sidewalk. I glanced at the yellow tape still surrounding a small square of cement by the shop's front door.

"Look both ways!" I called from a few steps behind. Halen's arm shot out and blocked Stevie from wandering into the street while she chased a dragonfly. Dio whacked his brother for accidentally bumping him while protecting his sister. Jovi slowed to walk with me and chat.

"Did somebody hurt the man who fell in front of the shop?" he asked, pushing his thick-framed glasses up his nose.

A quiet growl slipped out of me. The only person who could have told the pups the upsetting news was Hattie's teenage daughter. Bette haunted the jeweled bracelet that matched her mother's necklace. The quiet and mousey girl mostly kept to herself, but she'd occasionally grow bored and tell spooky stories to the pups if they wandered into the theater.

I pulled Jovi in for a hug and scruffed his wavy hair. "We don't know, but it's not for you to worry about."

With that, he nodded and skipped ahead to join his brothers and sister. The mama-wolf in me flared. If getting justice for Cliff and protecting Mockbuster's reputation weren't enough fuel for the investigative fire within me, then reassuring my pups of their safety made up the rest.

Halen gave Stevie a piggyback ride across the street. I smiled, but thoughts of danger in Bewitcher's Beach tugged at me. A strange energy buzzed in the air, like imaginary eyes watched me from the bushes.

Was it the supposed spell? Or something more sinister? I shivered and resisted the urge to drop into my wolf form where I'd be faster and more powerful in case of danger.

Exposure wasn't a feeling I'd experienced since moving to Bewitcher's Beach. While I didn't necessarily believe in the legendary protection spell, I took comfort in its possible existence. Could a curse really undo it?

I shook the superstition away and scanned the view of town from the edge of the square. In the center, vendors with brightly colored tents and big hand-drawn signs covered the grass. Shop lights blinked on, and the soft glow in the windows looked like jack-o-lanterns with a candle brightening their jagged smiles. Crisp leaves and browned trees beckoned autumn.

This close to the sea, seasons weren't supposed to change with much fanfare. But Bewitcher's Beach had her secrets, and it was these secrets that drew visitors from all over the world. Where else offered a vacation with both the sand and snow, the bloom of wildflowers and rolling waves, the fall foliage and saltwater?

I picked up a crunchy leaf and twirled it between my thumb and forefinger. The scent of kettle corn and the white noise of overlapping conversations made me crinkle my nose and fold back my ears. The feeling of exposure still nagged at me, though nothing smelled suspicious.

The kids stopped at Triton's table and sampled odd flavors of taffy. I turned down Stevie's offer to try the black licorice. She shrugged and popped another piece in her cheeks as if she were a chipmunk storing them for the winter.

"Don't eat the chocolate taffies," I said, reminding them of their allergy. A familiar spiky tail caught my eye near the siren's clothing booth. Scaly half-dragon skin contrasted the muted colors of lacy handmade shawls and loose low-cut blouses. Mae's typical style of high-buttoned shirts and thick sweaters didn't match that of the booth she browsed.

The half-dragon was only there for one reason: gossip. She'd dropped a bomb on my shop at the crime scene, but she wasn't the first—or the only one—to mention a curse. And if nothing else, I could count on Mae to know the details I needed. She liked to chat and dig into everyone's lives, but it mostly came from a place of love with a side of boredom. I snorted and patted Halen's head.

He looked up at me, and his smooth, bowl-cut hair fell away from his face. "I know, I know. Chocolate makes us barf."

"Gross." I wrinkled my nose again. Halen only laughed as

if bodily fluids were the funniest joke. *Kids...* "I'll be at Chanel's booth. Find me if you spot something you want to spend your allowance on." I patted the glow-in-the-dark fanny pack secured around my waist. The coins from his savings jingled.

I shuffled through the crowd of supernaturals, humans, and vendors. Everyone attended, except vampires, who were busy sleeping the day away.

The siren's ringing laugh echoed across the grass. She waved flirtatiously at a man acting interested in a lacy shawl, and then she turned to Mae. I picked up the pace before the half-dragon spilled the magic beans and the rumor grew into a giant beanstalk.

My ears lifted and turned forward to catch their conversation as I loped toward them.

"When you live a thousand years, you'll stop wearing revealing clothes." The half-dragon arched a judgemental eyebrow at the siren who didn't so much as flinch. Nothing except trash in the ocean got under Chanel's skin.

"I thought you were only a hundred and ninety, which is young for a half-dragon," Chanel said. "A *thousand*, psh. Thank the good goddesses I'll never live that long. Lop off a zero and I'll be ready to move on from this boring town." She mimicked a yawn.

Mae slapped her claws to her chest in true Mae fashion. "Boring? Didn't you hear that Bewitcher's Beach might have a murderer?"

I shoved through two teenage gargoyles and made it to the booth, panting. If I was lucky, I'd stop the spread of rumors while simultaneously gathering what information the half-dragon had on Cliff.

"Tragic isn't it?" I said between gulps of air. "But we don't know that it's a murder."

"I do," Mae said, her red eyes unblinking as she scanned me up and down.

Well, that certainly felt ominous. I shook it off like drops of water on my fur.

"Who died?" Chanel asked. Before we could respond, she waved her manicured fingers in the half-dragon's face, demanding her attention.

Mae licked her lips and finally broke her gaze on me. Was that why I felt so exposed? A prickly sensation trailed up behind my ears and left me with goosebumps. Why did Mae insist it was murder? What wasn't she sharing?

Half-dragons weren't known for any special observational powers, nor did I ever suspect the elderly woman capable of hurting anyone. She'd been like a mother to me and a pseudo-grandma to the pups since we'd arrived in Bewitcher's Beach. Every weekend, she brought the kids homemade scones in the shape of dog bones. And, every weekend, she talked about upcoming holidays, the houses she owned, or indulged in gossip. But the sharing stopped there.

It'd never occurred to me that she rarely spoke of her past. Mae knew everyone's business but didn't often share hers, only telling stories as far back as the day she'd met her husband.

"Who? Who?" The siren continued. Minty aroma burned in my nose from Chanel's overwhelming curiosity.

"Goodness, Chanel, you sound like an owl," Mae said, *tsk*ing at the siren.

"How well did you know Cliff?" I asked.

"Better than most." Mae smiled, showing a pair of sharp teeth. Despite her soft, grandmotherly presence, I saw Mae in a new light. Behind her knitted handbag and the print-screen image of kittens on her pastel sweater, she was a woman with secrets. Or at least a woman who aired her neighbor's dirty laundry and never said a word about herself.

"Perfect," I said, pulling out my notebook. "What can you tell me about Cliff? He was a plastic surgeon from what I'd heard, right? I have a character with the same occupation but never had time to ask him questions." Squeaks squirmed inside the fanny pack, and then poked out with my pen in his mouth. I rubbed the tip of my finger against his tiny head then pried the pen from his teeth. "Maybe you can help me fill in those blanks. First, how did you know him?"

"He was looking at buying one of my houses," she said. "So, of course, I spoke with him many times. Vera and I have an agreement. Whenever she sells property in a neighborhood where I own a house, she introduces me to her serious clients. And Cliff was serious; she spent a great deal of time with him."

Bewitcher's Beach's best and only realtor, Vera Fang, was the sweetest woman I'd ever met. Though she wasn't supernatural, her name had me tricked. Last year, I'd approached her, hoping for another werewolf friend nearby. As a pack lover, I couldn't help but seek other werewolves. When Vera assured me she was human and admitted she'd changed her name to fit in with the supernaturals, she'd let me down easy. She was careful to take my disappointment into consideration and I never forgot it.

"Fascinating," Chanel said in a deadpan voice. The iridescent blue in her eyes seemed to fade with her disinterest. "Somehow, even murder in this town is a snooze-fest. And y'all wonder why I'll never settle down anywhere."

Mae raised her brows and gave the siren a knowing look. "I'd dare to consider ten years in one place putting down roots."

Chanel ignored her, sweeping to the other side of the booth with a seductress's sway of her hips. She greeted a male customer who thumbed the fabric of a sweater but didn't so much as look at it, instead staring at the siren's impossible beauty.

"Did Vera know Cliff well?" I asked, sidestepping to allow two women to get a better look at Chanel's products. They admired the intricate lace as they held shirts up against their torsos.

Mae cocked her head to the side, her lizard-like tongue flicking out to lick her lips. "Are you taking an interest in solving crimes?"

I noted the sparkle in her eyes—the same look she got when I first moved to Bewitcher's Beach and she'd hoped to hook me up with a single werebear. Mae didn't admit to being a gossip, but she wore the matchmaker title proudly.

I shrugged. "People might avoid Mockbuster until this investigation is over. I just want to help." I spoke around the issue. The faint smell of fear tickled my nose, but I couldn't identify the source with the dozens of people around me. Could Mae be worried about me digging for answers? Still, calling Cliff's death a murder raised flags the color of her eyes, in my opinion.

I gave myself a little shake, the way I did when I rid my fur of water. Mae was secretive and a gossip, but I could never picture her doing anything sinister. I was reaching for answers in my time of desperate need, and I needed to nip my overly suspicious attitude in the bud.

"Does the sheriff have any leads?" Mae nodded at something behind me. "You'd be the person to ask, right?" I turned my ear and pulled out Sett's voice from among the crowd. An upward curve tugged at the corner of her mouth.

Heat tingled in my arms and legs at the sight of her suggestive smile. I liked Sett, but we butted heads too much.

"Mae." I folded my arms, ready to squash any more rumors. "Just because I want to help get answers doesn't mean I'm working with Sett."

"Mm-hmm," she hummed as she bounced her spiky

eyebrows up and down. "I know my Wallace and I aren't the only ones taking romantic walks through town at night."

Had she seen Sett and me talking last night? It lasted no more than a minute. How did Mae see everything?

"That wasn't a romantic walk."

"Ah yes." She clucked her tongue. "I remember when Wallace and I were dating, we'd go on lots of platonic walks side by side. I daresay, Sett doesn't come to your shop just for the candy."

"It wasn't like that—"

The rumbling sound of her humming laughter cut me off. "Where did my Wallace get off to, anyway?" Mae spun around, nearly knocking me over with her widespread arms. I jumped back, crashing into what felt like a brick wall.

"Curses," I groaned under my breath, knowing exactly who I'd bumped into. I turned to meet his stony face while Mae meandered toward her husband at the beef jerky booth, effectively ending our conversation.

Sett folded his giant arms, and the scrape of rock against rock grated in my ears. "I'd hoped you wouldn't get involved."

"It was Fitz's idea," I suggested and then casually feigned interest in the booth beside Chanel's, though the scented soaps were far too strong for my nose.

As if summoned by his name, the mayor appeared. The short, shiny bald-headed man grinned up at us as he materialized from the crowd.

"I heard my name," he said. His beaming smile slipped into a serious expression and he leaned closer to me, dropping his voice low. "Have you thought about helping us solve this murder? As I always say, a community that works together is a community that *works*."

My heart skipped a beat. "So it's a murder? For sure?" I glanced at Sett, who grumbled something under his breath.

Finally, the sheriff spoke up just loud enough to keep the information inside our little triangle. "Unfortunately, yes, it appears to be a murder. And frankly, I just don't feel it's safe for you to be asking around about the situation."

Murder. The spooky word gave me the shivers as I let it sink in. I wrote it into plays plenty of times but had never dealt with a real-life case involving violence.

"How do you know?" I asked, thinking back to Mae's unsettling confidence on the subject.

"Oh!" Fitz raised a stubby finger in the air. "I just heard my name. That's my cue to skedaddle. I'll let my guy Sett explain the rest." He slapped the sheriff's back with his meaty hand and disappeared into the crowd. As the mayor and volunteer police officer, he was always pulled in a thousand different directions. It made sense why he wanted me to offer the station a little extra help. This case, on top of all the vendor contracts and legalities around the fall festival, was sure to overwhelm Bewitcher's Beach's tiny police department.

"So, was it poison like the coroner thought?" I asked.

Sett frowned but nodded, reluctant to involve me despite the mayor's request.

"How do we find out who did it?"

"*We?*" Sett scraped his palm over his face and sighed. I cringed at the sound but kept my face neutral. He'd only share information if he didn't catch on that I was putting my nose where it didn't belong—according to him anyway. Fitz wanted me to help, and once I decided on something, I threw my all into it. "That's all you need to know, Noema. I'm not in agreement with the mayor over this."

"That's too bad," I said, looking at my notebook and scraping the pen across it to create a dark scribble. "I wanted to understand a little more about how investigations work so I could include one in the script. Maybe even base a character on someone like—" I glanced up, meeting his gaze. "You."

The sneaky suggestion didn't work on someone as smart as Sett. "I think you still want to get involved."

I shrugged. "Is that so bad? Like Fitz said, I helped catch the thief in the bicycle case last year."

"That was stealing. This is murder. I'd never forgive myself if you got hurt trying to help."

For that, I couldn't blame him. As a mother of four, it was foolish to put myself in harm's way. But with Sett nearby, the biggest, most intimidating cop with stone for skin, I'd never get hurt. Except for the bruises I got when I tripped and crashed into him.

"Anyway, best of luck on your script. I know it'll be a block-buster hit." Despite his disagreement with my less-than-legal approach to things, he was always kind. He turned to leave, and his wings brushed against a lacy shawl, snagging it and dragging it off the hanger.

I stooped to pick it up and fix Chanel's display. "Wait."

Sett's heavy footsteps stopped, and he lowered a wing to see over his shoulder.

I continued. "The faster Cliff's murderer is arrested, the sooner it stops superstitions. This case could drive business away from the town and the fall festival. Business we all rely on. Not to mention, families deserve to feel safe." I nodded at Stevie who was yanking the butterfly clip from her hair and trading it for a little girl's jelly bracelet.

Sett followed my line of sight and then released another sigh about as dramatic as Mae's behavior. "What are you proposing?"

"Well, a few details for story inspiration wouldn't hurt. Right? I could ask around about crime or murder under the guise of research for my play and sniff out people's guilt. Besides, it'd make Fitz happy."

He shook his head. "Nobody can ever tell you that you're not determined."

I ignored the deflection. "So, can I help?"

Sett's slate eyes narrowed and he pursed his lips, refusing to answer. The more he pushed back, the more I saw the need to help. If the case was left up to him, it'd be next year before we got answers, and Mockbuster's busiest season, the fall festival, the play—all of it was just around the corner. The case needed to be cleared ASAP.

"If you'll let me on the case, just blink," I whispered conspiratorially. His stubbornness was already going to be the death of me, and we hadn't even begun to work together. Still, something about Sett Lawrence comforted me. His protectiveness felt like coming home to shelter in the warmth during a storm.

We stayed like that, staring at one another in front of Chanel's booth until the siren clucked her tongue and leaned over her table.

"Well, well, well, are y'all going to kiss or what?" she asked. "Because you're blocking my display."

Sett caved first, rapidly blinking his watery eyes.

"Detective Noema at your service, Sir," I said, victorious and with a little salute. Then, before he could argue, I spun around and hurried toward the sweet scent of the kettle corn to collect the boys.

"Darn it, Noema, that doesn't mean anything." He followed me, heavy steps squashing into the damp grass.

I shot him a look over my shoulder. "Don't worry, I'll keep to asking questions for plot inspiration only." I lied, but not entirely. Next year, if Hattie let me, I'd be back to writing a murder mystery for Everland Theater to perform.

"You promise?"

I paused but only smiled in response, and it earned a long sigh from him. He pounded the base of his closed fist against his open palm, a gesture of frustration. Or so I guessed; I couldn't smell his emotions.

"Noema…"

I crossed my heart. "I promise I'll be doing character research on Cliff's occupation."

"Fine. But don't go bothering Cliff's family. His ex-wife was on the other side of the world for a trip. Plus, she's a pixie, so when I asked her if she was involved, I knew she couldn't lie —fairy rules, or whatever."

Cliff was married? I squinted as if that'd help me recall what his hands had looked like. Had he worn a wedding ring?

"Only character research." Sett interrupted my thoughts.

I nodded. "And maybe a little about investigations," I added before turning and ducking behind a couple walking hand-in-hand. The quick escape didn't give him a chance to argue, and it'd take him twice the time to fit through the crowd to follow me. As much as I enjoyed being around Sett, working together certainly wasn't going to be easy.

But I could at least start a list of suspects and hand it over to Sett. Maybe that'd be enough to get the ball rolling and push him to solve the case quicker than he normally would.

What had inspired Cliff to move to Bewitcher's Beach in the first place? Did he have friends nearby? Family? And if so, were their behaviors suspect? The first person I thought to ask was his real estate agent since she'd spent the most time with him.

After shouldering through the packed square, I made it to the other side of the Farmer's Market in front of Vera's office and apartment. Like me, she lived above her place of business.

As a realtor, she wasn't often home, but I could at least leave a note for her through the mail dropbox.

Today, I'd learned two very important pieces of information: Cliff died by poison, and Sett would let me ask questions... maybe...hopefully.

I raised my fist to knock on Vera's door.

CHAPTER 6
WHAT SCARES A VAMPIRE

FOOTSTEPS THUMPED across the hardwood floor on the other side of the door. Vera cracked the door just enough to peek one dark eye through the opening. Thick eyelashes coated in makeup fluttered at me.

"Noema?" her voice came out scratchy until she cleared her throat. The door shut again and chains rattled as she undid a little lock at the top. She opened it again and smiled. "Come in."

Her long chocolate hair swayed against her back as she marched toward the desk in the middle of the office. The space was filled with file cabinets, fake foliage, and a modest desk with her name plate on the front: *Vera Fang.*

"I was just about to leave for the day," she said as she dropped her purse and giant keyring with dozens of keys on the desk. The keys landed with a clink. "But I was expecting you to show up."

I tilted my head, and the pineapple pizza scent of confusion emanated from me. "You were?"

"Yes." She took a seat and I mirrored her, slowly easing into the cushioned office chair on the opposite side of the desk. "I knew you and that little rambunctious family of yours would outgrow Mockbuster's loft soon. What kind of house are you in the market for? Beachfront? School adjacent?"

"Oh." I shook my head. "No."

The earthy scent of disappointment must have come from her because I didn't feel down. The slight drop of her shoulders matched the smell. I needed to get on with the questions and not waste her time.

"I'm just gathering a bit of information on the man who died yesterday," I explained. I thought of Sett's warning and my promise. This was just supposed to be character research, so I opted not to mention my agreement to help with the case. "I wanted to base a character in the play off of him, but now I can't interview him. I thought maybe you knew him well enough to fill in for me."

"Me?" She reached for the keyring and absentmindedly fiddled with the keys, spinning them around and around the thick ring. Several keychains decorated the ring, from a mono-grammed lock pick knife to a fluffy rabbit's foot, both in matching pastel pink.

"Because he was your client," I said.

"Of course, ask away." Vera leaned back, settling in the high-backed office chair with fancy swiveling options. She gently turned the chair side to side and thumbed the carved name *Vera C.* in the monogrammed keychain as she listened to my list of questions. Unfortunately, she didn't offer many answers, having only been around Cliff sporadically to show houses.

"Mr. Conflick had expensive taste. I don't know what else to tell you," she said. "Sorry I can't be of more help."

I thanked her and saw myself out. Disappointed and surrounded by the emotion's wet soil smell, I dragged myself across the street to the bustling market. The kettle corn tent was already sold out. I'd missed out on my favorite treat and didn't get a single name for a potential suspect. Maybe I wouldn't be as much help as Fitz had hoped.

To give myself a break, I gathered the kids for a game of tag on the beach. After two hours of running in the fresh air, I found myself at Roller Shakes, huddled over my notebook. I took the kids skating so I could turn my focus to the script and add in the romantic subplot.

I dug my fingernails into my unruly waves and scratched at my skull. My head didn't itch, and the movement didn't jog a single idea. I sighed and dropped my face into my palms, letting my elbows rest against the Notebook of Doom where ideas— and even murder investigations—went to die a boring, yawn-inducing end. Chanel was right; Bewitcher's Beach could put a person to sleep, *if* they ignored the secrets.

Like why did Mae insist she knew Cliff was murdered? And why didn't she ever talk about the hundred years of life she lived before she'd met Wallace ninety years ago? Who else was a suspect in Cliff's demise?

I rubbed my eyes and raked my fingers through my hair. Cliff was from out of town, which meant his killer probably was too. Memory of a Valen Halen T-shirt and swollen lips popped into my mind's eye. What had the woman said that struck me as odd?

"I never lose!" I slapped my hands against the table as I remembered her words. My fingers splayed over the vinyl top decorated with turquoise, pink, and purple stars.

A woman who wore a faded polo that matched the design on the tables gasped. Her hand shot to her mouth where her fangs protruded.

"Oh, Cordelia! Hi," I said, offering her an apologetic expression for my outburst. "I didn't mean to startle you."

The vampire leaned on the high-backed booth, where her leather belt squeaked against the vinyl.

She wiped the back of her wrist against her face. "I'm just jumpy."

"What's wrong?"

"You're the one who just screamed about losing something," she said. Her mahogany hair was secured into a high bun with two long strands pulled out to frame her face. Though she had technically lived longer than me, Cordelia had been turned into a vampire at twenty. She was always on-trend with others her undead age in both appearance and behavior. With a puff of air, she blew away a strand that had slipped between her eyes.

"I didn't scream," I muttered and straightened my back to see over the railing that separated the booth and the edge of the roller rink. Halen zipped around, racing Dio, who crashed into the walls for the fun of it. Stevie twirled in an impressive spin while Jovi sat on the black carpet with multicolored spots. He'd abandoned his roller skates beside him and rested an open book in his lap, totally engrossed by R. L. Stine's spooky *Goosebumps* tales.

"Are you sure you're okay?" I asked, turning my attention to Cordelia. While always pale, tonight she looked especially devoid of life.

Her shoulders lifted in a limp shrug. "Whatever." She repeated slang she'd heard from modern women. Based on the light scent of something bitter mixed with burnt toast, I knew her nonchalant attitude was a cover. The smell of regret wafted from her.

"You can talk to me," I offered. Cordelia and I had become recent friends. With her up during the night and me always home early to put the pups to bed, we hadn't had a chance until Hattie's daughter started babysitting. I'd spent plenty of hours writing away in this very booth in the past few months, and, during that time, I enjoyed dozens of delightful conversations with the vampire.

A sudden sob escaped her. "No, I can't." She sniffed and quickly straightened, wiping away tears before I could offer comfort.

"What do you mean? Why not?"

"You're helping Sett with that investigation, aren't you?" she asked, eyeing me.

Mae was nothing if not efficient. How else did Cordelia already know the rumor? And more importantly, why did it bother her?

"Is that a problem?" I asked.

Tendrils of hair framed her face and brushed against the collar of her washed-out work shirt. The point of her fang dug into her chin as she gnawed her lower lip.

The look on my friend's face twisted my stomach. Regret mixed with something I couldn't pinpoint drowned out the whiff of fried foods from the kitchen. I pushed the plate of left-over fries away from me. I focused my nose on my friend's emotions, hoping to help her through whatever trouble she faced.

Cordelia lingered, though plenty of tables needed to be cleared of bright blue trays and abandoned soda cups. The odor of indecision overwhelmed me. If I didn't know better, I'd blame the smell of feet on the roller rink's collection of used skates.

"Cordelia, are you worried whoever attacked Cliff will hurt you?" Maybe *attacked* was the wrong word. If he died by poison, his was a slower, spookier death than an attack.

Shaking, her hand snatched a tendril of hair. She twisted it tightly around her fingers until I worried it'd sever them at the knuckle.

I quickly hopped from the booth, banging my knee against the table. Cordelia's black eyes glazed as she stared at nothing. With my hands cupping her elbows, I guided her to take a seat on the bench.

I sat across from her, and she finally blinked. Easily, I changed the subject, asking how she'd met her boyfriend. She stopped twisting her hair around her finger and melted with her weight against the table. A smile snuck onto her face, revealing the tips of her fangs as she spoke about her love story, but it didn't take long for her nervous behaviors to return. Her leg bounced underneath the table and she glanced around every so often.

"What are you afraid of?" I asked after I closed my notebook. "I might be able to help."

She glanced at me through spider-long lashes and then back at the half-empty tray of discarded food between us. The odor of feet faded, taken over by the sour smell of ammonia. The same scent always stung my nose when shadows scared Stevie at night or when Dio feared a broken leg meant he'd never get to run again.

"I started looking into this investigation because people deserve answers and it's causing a rumor about a curse on the rental shop," I said with a shrug. "But now all I care about is keeping my kids and everyone else here safe."

The sourness stinging my nose faded and Cordelia's shoulders relaxed. She sighed and grabbed Halen's half-full paper cup of Sprite, pried the plastic top off, and then downed it like a shot of tequila.

She tossed the straw on the tray between us and chomped a piece of ice. "It's like this," she said. "Dr. Conflick knew something about me—" Manicured black fingernails fanned out as she threw up her hands in mock surrender. "But I didn't kill him."

I slid the tray to the side and patted her forearm the way I did when I comforted Halen after his nightmares. "I'd never think that Cordelia."

Dr. Cliff Conflick. I filed the thought away. Though I knew he'd worked as a plastic surgeon, I'd never referred to him as anything other than Cliff.

She groaned and pitched forward, letting her forehead press against the vinyl tabletop. "I was his last patient the night he died."

"I thought he was just here to scope out real estate," I said.

The vampire straightened, flinging the tendrils of hair from her face. "I didn't know about all that. But he was buddies with Doctor Pitt, or whatever, so DP let him use his clinic." Her voice cracked. She fluttered her hand as if to cool her face, except her skin was always ice cold. If vampires didn't heal instantly, I'd worry she'd scratch herself with the pointed tips of her acrylic nails. "I begged him to do it." A whine escaped her.

"It's okay." I took her hands in mine before the tips stabbed her in the eyeball. The erratic behavior definitely came from regret, though a dash of ammonia lingered in the air. "Plastic surgery isn't a crime."

"But I was the last person to see him alive!"

Cooking bacon sizzled in the kitchen, and the sound added drama to her statement. The effect made our lives feel like a movie.

"Not quite," I said, recalling Mae's explanation that she ran into Cliff when he was dying.

"I guess Doctor Pitt saw Cliff," she said. "He locked up the clinic after Doctor Conflick and I left."

I asked for details on the time of the procedure and if Doctor Pitt had acted strangely. *Pitt was normal, even joking with his buddy.* I recorded Cordelia's comments. *The procedure ended around 6:00 pm. Cliff left at 6:30.*

"Wait, what did you have done?" The question slipped out. My sharp vision didn't detect any changes in Cordelia's perfectly beautiful face.

She waved her hand again, sweeping the question away. "It doesn't matter; I healed back to my original face almost immediately." Her body slumped against the edge of the table. "But I had to try, you know? I had to try, for Henry. I told him Mommy had surgery, and that it was just another science experiment. It was just like the ant farms and sunflower seeds."

"What about Henry?" I asked, but clarity on her son and science experiments didn't matter right now. I was losing sight of what I needed to help my friend and get answers about Cliff. "Cordelia, are you sure Dr. Conflick didn't act weird? Was he scared of anything?"

"No, no." She shook her head, letting it hang, defeated, until she popped up and met my gaze. "Wait, except for when he was on the phone with someone. He said a few words I wouldn't repeat, you know..." Cordelia's dark eyes glanced around the roller rink, where a few kids held onto the wall on the other side of our booth. "Something about a homeowner's contract and a *darn* dragon. If you get my drift."

Mae? I wrote the name of the half-dragon who owned half the town's houses in the notebook's corner. Did Cliff's distaste for her make her a suspect? Who else did he interact with before he fell victim to poison?

"Anything else?" The information sent my heart beating faster. I'd chalked tonight up to a wash. Vera didn't have any information, and I never took the pups around the owner of The Oyster Inn. Barney was the only other contact I could ask about Cliff's whereabouts the night of the murder. As a fairy, he always spoke the truth—to a fault. He called my kids too loud, messy, obnoxious, and even smelly right in front of them. After that, we never went into The Oyster Inn again.

Several moments of consideration passed before Cordelia nodded. "Yeah, I couldn't hear the entire conversation. But he said she was hoarding the best houses like treasures."

"She?"

"I think he was referring to the half-dragon. I'm not sure."

After crossing out the question mark by Mae's name, I scribbled the information in the top margin of the notebook. I quickly slapped it shut again before Cordelia saw my awful handwriting. "Thank you. That'll help get answers."

The cook in the kitchen, a half-wizard who only worked magic with the fryer, shouted for Cordelia.

"Duty calls," she said.

"Yes, it does," I mumbled, thinking of the investigation.

When Cordelia slid to the side of the booth and stood, she paused. "Hey, uh, will you do me a huge favor?"

I followed, ready to gather the pups and head home for the evening. "Anything."

Her thin, dark eyebrows pressed together without a single wrinkle. How could her perfect, never-aging vampire face benefit from Cliff's work?

"Can you tell me when you find out if Dr. Conflick spoke to anyone else before he...you know..." She leaned in and whispered conspiratorially. "Died?"

I cocked my head to the side, ready to ask why. But the sudden, intense smell of ammonia and feet told me Cordelia exuded anxiety. Before I could speak, she hurried into the kitchen to retrieve two orders of waffles. I needed to let her do her job before she got into trouble. But I couldn't imagine what Cliff, as her one-time plastic surgeon, would know that Cordelia wanted to hide.

The sooner I got answers, the sooner I'd be able to help her.

Unfortunately, that meant I'd need to talk to Barney. Tonight. The grumpy fairy had likely seen who visited Cliff at the inn. Though he was my best option, Barney wasn't my biggest fan.

After we returned four pairs of stinky roller skates, we piled out of the rink. As we walked past the barbershop and its twin grooming company, Stevie ran to me. She nuzzled Squeaks's nose, who peeked out of the unzipped fanny pack. Puppies, mice, kitties—any animals really—were her best friends since she could communicate with them on a level nobody else understood.

Across the street, I noticed the yellow tape had been removed and Mockbuster no longer bore the evidence of a nearby murder. I dropped the keys to the front door in Stevie's palm.

Outside The Oyster Inn, I paused and enjoyed the fragrance from the flower boxes. On the inside, shamrock colored curtains framed each window. The same shade adorned the trim around the windows and doors, which contrasted the rest of the building's cream colors. The inn's outward idyllic look didn't match the grumpy fairy who stood inside.

"Kiddos!" I barked. "Wash up and find jammies, I'll be home in a few minutes."

Halen and Dio shoved each other to be the first inside while Jovi paused long enough to snag the keys from his sister and unlock the door. Stevie slipped through all three and made it into the shop before her brothers, giggling as she won whatever race they'd challenged one another to.

I waited, making sure Jovi locked it again. When the last furry foot disappeared inside, I shifted my gaze to the theater's window and gave the ghost a wave. The window in Everland Theater's attic often had a transparent face looking through.

Bette, Hattie's daughter, smiled and energetically returned the greeting. I pulled out my wallet and tapped it to indicate I'd owe her. Her bright manifestation faded from the window as she disappeared, eager to babysit and earn another chunk of change that she used to develop the film in her camera.

I turned and stepped under the green and white-striped awning. Though this conversation would be as unpleasant as getting matted fur or the stench of wet dog, it had to be done.

No doubt the owner would share a few choice words about my rambunctious kids, or how mothers were always so tired they looked half-dead. He might even dare to tell me the truth about the size of my ears.

Despite the fresh air, a lump gathered in my throat as I anticipated the conversation. The breeze carried a hint of coming rain which invigorated me. I took a deep breath before stepping up to the door marked *The Oyster Inn, call to book with Barney.*

CHAPTER 7
FACTS FROM A FOUL FAIRY

THE DOOR JINGLED with the same tune as Mockbuster's bell.

At the front desk, the fairy stood nearly as tall as me despite his poor posture. He scolded one of his employees with a wagging finger. The maid looked used to lectures, nodding along with mild disinterest.

"She's checking out tomorrow morning, so come in early for your shift to get the room cleaned."

The maid nodded before leaving and passing me on her way out. I approached the desk with my ears folded back as a sign of politeness.

Unlike Sett, Barney could fold his flexible fairy wings and tuck them inside his endless wardrobe of thick, beige cardigans. He preferred to downplay his fairy characteristics. The thin wrinkles that ran across his forehead and framed his eyes marked his age. His eternal frown created jowls that rivaled Doctor Pitt's werebulldog features.

"Noema," Barney grunted as he leaned both elbows on the desk. After removing his glasses, he rubbed his eyes with clenched fists. "Are you here about the noise complaints I've made against you? I've said it before and I'll say it again, this town needs a council. I'm tired of filing complaints to a sheriff who looks the other way. And just because he fancies you."

My ears flicked up, and I shook my head. "What? That's crazy. Sett is the letter of the law. I'm surprised it's not carved in the stone of his forehead."

The fairy rolled his eyes and ignored my statement. "We need a town council." Spit sprayed from between his tongue and teeth as he enunciated the words. "It isn't right that you're living in that building. You and the realtor both. And I suspect Miss Raven over at the dance studio lives in the attic above, too. It's all wrong! This area of town is zoned for business only. As soon as Sheriff Sett finishes investigating this murder, I'll insist he kick you out of that building."

"Don't you technically sleep on site now that Cordelia quit working the night shift here?" I asked, tapping my finger on the desk.

"Bah!" He straightened and swiped his hand in the air between us. "It doesn't count if I don't hang my clothes here."

Well, I'll have you know, I never hang my clothes. They're on the floor, or in a laundry basket... I kept the comment to myself, knowing an argument with the fairy would only lead to my own manipulation. He could talk circles around me despite my best efforts to defend our little loft home above Mockbuster. Nobody else cared that we broke the zoning laws, so his complaints never came to fruition. Yet.

"So, I was thinking," I started, hoping for a little innocent manipulation of my own. "Your work as the owner here is really fascinating. I'd love to write a character like you into the town's next play. What do you say?"

I caught the quick shine in Barney's tired blue eyes before he looked away. He busied himself by organizing already-organized room keys on a pegboard behind the desk. If nothing else,

I knew the pull of attention would intrigue him. Not all fairies wanted to be in the spotlight, but, like most people, he enjoyed at least a little recognition.

"Sounds like a waste of my time." Curiosity's scent of mint betrayed his words. He wanted to know more.

"It's just a few questions." I started with the basics, a few comments about his daily schedule at The Oyster Inn, and then sprinkled plenty of compliments throughout.

He eased into the conversation. "Did—" he paused and rubbed a finger under his nose, scratching dry skin against his mustache. With a sniff, he glanced at the window to his right where the pleated curtains were open for a view of Everland Theater. "Did Miss Hattie ask you to add a character like me?"

My ears turned forward, pricked with curiosity. Barney fiddled with the string that attached a key to its label.

"Uh." I couldn't lie to a fairy. Well, I *could*, but it'd be all kinds of bad because he'd likely figure it out. "Hattie doesn't create the characters, she directs the actors who portray them."

"Hmm." he nodded.

"Are you thinking of auditioning?"

He pursed his lips and then hung the key in its place with a sigh. "Sounds like a waste of my time."

"Well, I *can* tell you that Hattie likes the scripts to be accurate. And next year, I'll be writing about doctors—" He scoffed, but I continued. "It'll be a good way to commemorate Dr. Conflick after the short time we had with him in Bewitcher's Beach."

Barney arched an eyebrow, an impressive feat with brows that thick and heavy.

"Did Cliff have any visitors with him at The Oyster Inn?"

"That's none of my business," he said.

"Please." I nodded in the general direction of the theater. "Hattie wants the details to be immaculate."

"As she should." He nodded. "Smart woman, that Miss Hattie."

Was his interest in Hattie a recent development, or did my distaste for Barney blind me to it? His admiration for my friend warmed my heart—a feeling I never expected from a grump like him.

"Did Cliff spend any time here the night he died?" I dived in head first now, hoping he'd be willing to answer.

He nodded. "From what I can recall, Dr. Conflick had a meeting with his realtor here that evening. I also had to break up an argument between him and another patron."

"And who was that?"

Barney folded his arms and frowned deeper, if that were possible.

"Hattie's a stickler for details." I shrugged and smiled apologetically.

"Name's Piper June," he said.

Piper? My interest was piqued. I knew that name.

"And when was Cliff here?" I asked. His scowl intensified, deepening the folds of his loose cheeks where the shadow of a beard grew. I raised my hands in surrender. "If you don't mind me asking."

He huffed and picked up the corded phone on the desk, a signal our conversation was about to end. "He arrived here half-past six if I remember right."

"Thank you," I said, offering my hand. "I'll be sure to tell Hattie—Miss Hattie—how kind and helpful you've been."

With that, Barney accepted my hand, giving it a good, firm shake to end the interaction. He jammed the buttons on the phone's base and dialed, ignoring me now.

I flipped the notebook open and marched for the exit. Squeaks poked his nose from the fanny pack. The twitch of his whiskers brushed over the pen he held perched between his big teeth. I plucked the pen from his jaws and patted his head in gratitude.

Squeaks stared at the small bar in the corner of the lobby. A container of pretzels sat on the counter with a row of liquor lined up on the shelves behind it. Drool dripped from the mouse's gaping mouth to the laces of my Reeboks.

"You can snack when we get home," I said, scratching under his chin.

The bell chimed cheerfully as I pushed through. I paused on the sidewalk between the two pumpkins that framed the welcome mat. The awning protected me from the rain that filled the potholes between damaged cobblestones.

Maybe Barney was right to insist on a town council. A council might solve problems like the puddles in the uneven sidewalk.

After cross-referencing Cordelia's comments with Barney's facts, I confirmed Cliff's timing. He'd gone directly from the clinic to the inn, which meant he interacted with only half a dozen people on the night he died.

I listed the suspects in my notebook. Cordelia, Vera, Piper, Doctor Pitt, and Mae.

A prickly feeling crawled up my spine, making the fur on my ears raise like hackles. Did Sett let me off easy even though Cliff died on my doorstep? Would the investigation come back to me when the police found out I'd accidentally embarrassed the victim with the same movie that was in his lifeless hands?

I swallowed a lump, and Squeaks looked up at me with enormous eyes. A slight whimpering squeak escaped him.

The video tapes connected my shop to the murder, making the sixth suspect...me.

And only I knew I didn't have a motive.

CHAPTER 8
RUNNING INTO TROUBLE

AT HOME, I dumped my notebook and pen on the kitchen table among a mess of kid's crafts, Surge sodas, and half-eaten Hot Pockets. I thanked Bette and paid her before dropping into a kitchen chair.

I thumbed through the notebook and wielded the pen in my other hand. If a clue jumped out at me, I'd be ready. Not two minutes after Bette vanished, her mother appeared.

Hattie poked her head through the door at the top of the stairs, and the glow from her spirit brightened the combined living room and kitchen.

"Come in," I said with a wave. Hattie obliged, phasing through the wall and floating into the kitchen. The warm light above the oven caught the shine of her gold dress. The effect transformed my messy kitchen into a disco ball, with glittering dots projected over every surface.

At the opposite end of the table, she spun around. "Your idea worked."

I perked up. Which idea? Did my involvement in the investigation prove my innocence with the so-called curse? Had Hattie seen customers waiting outside Mockbuster? My overactive imagination carried me away to the image of a packed shop. I pictured crowds of movie buffs—maybe a producer or director —shopping among my aisles.

"What is this for?" Hattie's brassy voice cut through my heavenly daydream. I went from my happy place to squinting at a confused ghost. She peered inside Stevie's Easy Bake Oven. "Does it make miniature food?" Before I could answer, she turned and shook her head. "Are you hearing a word I'm saying?"

"Sorry." I dropped the pen and rubbed each eye with the heel of my palm.

She continued. "The people who plan to audition are already talking about inviting cousins and coworkers. Now, I want you to clear your head and focus on finishing ASAP. Capiche?"

I opened my mouth, but she waved it off and launched into a list of demands. *Take a break. Get enough sleep. Eat a well-balanced breakfast tomorrow and come back refreshed. Be careful with your character inspiration. Definitely do not copy a real person's story or we can get sued for defamation of character. Oh, and write fast.*

Sued? I seethed. I'd need to be more clever about my character inspiration. Maybe if I combined enough different stories, nobody would ever know.

Hattie's demands continued. Apparently, I looked so pale and frazzled that I "needed some beach therapy," according to her. Since a run in the sand sounded amazing, I didn't argue.

While the ghost settled in front of the loft's TV, I pulled on my Reeboks and popped a mixed CD into my Walkman. I said goodbye and told her I would spend the run brainstorming.

Of course, I couldn't promise that my mind wouldn't wander to the plotting related to Cliff's murder. Would I end up accused? I couldn't deny how suspicious I looked. He'd called me a witch in front of a full store of Bewitcher's Beach locals, and then ended up dead with his arms full of my VHS tapes.

I sighed and decided it was a good time to turn up the music. The lyrics to my favorite metal songs blasted into my ears, and I was taken right back to the eighties. While I walked across town, Guns N' Roses welcomed me to the jungle. The closer I got to the beach, the stronger the wind whipped my hair. Thankfully, once I shifted into my wolf form, my curly locks wouldn't be there to tangle in my eyelashes and stick to my lips.

The tide welcomed me, rolling in and out with a comforting rhythm. I kicked off my shoes, peeled my socks away from my feet, and let my clothes fall into a pile behind a bush as I dropped to all four paws. I shifted so quickly that I slipped from my sweater and jeans into fur and claws faster than the blink of an eye.

Thick clouds rolled in, erasing the moonlight's glint off the glittering water. I threw my head back and howled while the waves drowned my expression of joy and frustration. A murder investigation, a dwindling business, and a deadline waited for my help, my energy, my creativity.

But for now, I'd simply run.

The salty air tousled my thick fur as my paws sank into the damp sand. Occasionally, the scent of pumpkin spice wafted from the candle shop and Triton's Taffy and mingled with the salty air.

Waves crashed against the shore, sending mist to cling to my face and fur. Larger droplets splattered the top of my head. The drizzle built to a steady fall that soaked me faster than the ocean's spray. I gave my entire body a good shake before bounding away from the water toward the dozens of little lights in the town's windows.

If I didn't return soon, I'd reek of wet dog. I padded through the sand, heading for town.

Movement blocked my view of the shops, and a little gasp escaped me. I shook fur from my face and bared my teeth at an approaching person. Lights from town shone at their back, obscuring their face. The dark made identification impossible.

They walked with inhuman speed, barrelling toward me. Hundreds of hours spent watching, reading, and writing murder mysteries sent my mind spiraling. The terrifying possibilities ranged from those that hunted supernatural creatures to the murderer. Maybe the person who'd killed Cliff didn't appreciate my involvement.

The beat of my heart crashed against my ribcage, and a low growl hummed from within my chest.

The figure broke from my path. He didn't head for me or the ocean, instead stalking toward the lighthouse. His long black duster brushed against the sand on his way to the stone tower.

I released a bark when I recognized Cordelia's boyfriend, the young vampire who worked night shifts at the lighthouse. He returned my greeting with a nod before unlocking the oak door. As fast as he'd appeared, he disappeared inside and left me alone on the beach.

Rain pelted my head and back, dampening my fur and reminding me to hurry inside before the wet dog smell became unbearable, even to myself. Once sand met cobblestone, I dodged behind a bush and shifted back to my human self. The sweater and high-waisted mom jeans proved difficult to pull on as the wet fabric clung to my skin.

"Son of a hot dog," I muttered.

I couldn't waltz through town naked. But the dank, musty odor of soaked wolf's fur turned me off from shifting back.

All the tugging in the world didn't drag the jeans higher

than mid-thigh. It didn't help that the pants were from my pre-mother days. Even in dry and normal conditions, the jeans barely fit over my hips. I groaned and kicked them off again.

"I'll sneak," I said. "That'll work."

I tied the legs of my pants around my waist and tugged the sweater to cover my butt, though it was no use. The sweater's thin fabric glued to my skin, showing every curve as if the clothing didn't exist at all.

My muscles tensed and readied to shift into my werewolf figure. But my claws didn't grow, and no fur sprouted. My shoulders slumped, and I released a faint growl. I'd exhausted my ability to transform, something which took exorbitant amounts of energy. Motherhood, murder, and the run had stolen every ounce of strength.

I'd need to find another answer to make it across town unseen.

If I stayed in the shadows of the buildings, nobody would notice me unless they looked out their window.

Lights shone from the center of town, where all the shops faced the park. Each black iron lamp post cast odd, elongated shapes over the cobblestone.

Mockbuster mirrored Triton's Taffy, directly on the other side of town. I glimpsed the yellow in the apartment window above the video rental shop, a sign that my pups had left the bathroom light on.

I considered the slower, safer idea to duck from alley to alley. But the tempting option, a mad dash across the town square, would end my suffering sooner. With the chill of autumn and the growing downpour, I wanted nothing more than a toasty towel and a mug of Sleepytime tea, all of which were across the giant, glaring obstacle. As a human, running just wasn't an option. My legs were long, but also lanky and clumsy.

I sidled my way along the front of the closed taffy shop. Building after building, I quickly slipped into the shadows and breathed easier with every step closer. I dodged across the brighter sections of the sidewalk and into the large alley between Roller Shakes and Doctor Pitt's clinic. Voices echoed from between the clinic and the next shop.

"Curses and spells," I swore.

I crept to the edge of the clinic, keeping my back against the brick. I didn't dare peek until I gauged the distance between myself and the voices' source. From here, the only information I had was a hulking shadow stretching from the alley onto the sidewalk. The shadow's arms flailed, and I choked on my spit. I stifled my cough and pricked my ears.

"No thank you, Miss June." The deep voice matched the size of the figure but vibrated with nerves. I recognized the anxious tone that belonged to Doctor Pitt.

I observed the movement of the shadows and the distance of the sound, deciding he was far enough away that I could sneak a peek. I peered around the side of the clinic. The alley led to a parking lot, empty now, though the diner was open around the clock.

Doctor Pitt stood nearly twice the size of the woman in front of him, so much so that I could see nothing but the woman's outstretched arms. While the size of Pitt's body and eternally furrowed brow reflected his weredog characteristics, his behavior never matched. Instead, he was a soft-spoken man on the brink of a nervous breakdown. And I couldn't blame him, being a doctor to an array of supernaturals. Our odd ailments proved challenging and were likely the cause of his hair loss.

"Oh come on, I told you to call me Piper again," the woman said. "Please, you cared for me once. Just help me hide this."

Perfect, he's blocking her view. I can make a break for it.

Wait... What had Piper asked of him? So far, I'd only heard this visitor talk of Van Halen, settling a score, and hiding something. A shiver stole down my back and goosebumps pricked my bare legs.

I stepped one foot into the light at the same moment the woman circled the doctor. Familiar brunette ringlets caught my eye. The sight of the Van Halen fan meant she could see my half-naked body, if only she turned her head.

A gasp slipped from me, and I doubled back, plastering my spine between the clinic's bricks.

"I'm sorry." Doctor Pitt cleared his throat. "It's just...not exactly in my skill set. I wouldn't want to risk it. "

Goosebumps tightened at the back of my neck and behind my ears. The fear in the doctor's voice triggered my mama's instinct, though the giant weredog could take care of himself against the short woman... unless she was a hunter. Some people who didn't accept supernaturals had taken it upon themselves to track and capture us with powerful weapons uniquely designed for each type. But Bewitcher's Beach had never encountered a supernatural hunter before—one of its many delightful mysteries, like why the tide here didn't follow the natural flow of the ocean. Some believed the legendary spell caused these unusual quirks.

I peeked into the alley, hoping they both faced away from the street now. Piper circled Doctor Pitt like a hawk, walking close enough to him to benefit from his small umbrella. With focused vision, I scanned for weapons tucked inside her coat but found nothing threatening. Of course, Piper was a shapeshifter, not a hunter. I breathed easier with that memory.

"Fine," Piper snapped, venom dripping in her voice. "But this won't be the last you hear from me."

Was that a threat? I couldn't resist a little eavesdropping, especially if it helped keep the town safe and furthered the investigation.

Either way, I had to act fast. The conversation was over, and they were headed right for me and my half-naked body. I backed away, ready to dodge into the next alley.

When I spun around, I collided with what felt like a brick wall if it wasn't warm and breathing. Though nobody had ever used warm to describe the town's sheriff before. My heart jumped into my throat.

If I wasn't in a pickle before, I'd definitely found trouble now.

CHAPTER 9
PROBLEMATIC PANTS

A YELP ESCAPED ME, and I doubled back. My heel bumped into a bulbous stone and threw me off balance—an impossible occurrence if only I'd stood on four paws. The uneven surface of a cobblestone sidewalk would be the death of me and my clumsy gait.

Before I crashed to the ground, the sheriff looped his arm around my waist and broke my fall. The sturdy, corded muscles of his forearm pressed against my spine as he pulled me upright.

Heat prickled the back of my neck and snaked up to my ears, where black and gray fur lingered on their pointed tips. Even in human form, the stubborn cartilage refused to transform, though my thick hair kept the wolf ears mostly hidden. Except for when the humidity of rain twisted my waves into curls and exposed the leftover fur.

Sett's slate eyes didn't narrow in on my ears, instead dipping to the other body part left exposed.

The burn in my cheeks surely turned my face an embarrassing shade of ruby. The color red suited sirens and looked good on a vampire's lips, but it didn't match werewolves. I cleared my throat and straightened to stand as dignified as possible, then I tugged the sweater as far over my butt as it would stretch without exposing my cleavage too.

"What are you doing?" Sett's expression never broke. He was a statue of stoicism. The leathery tips of his wings flinched. The gargoyle looked me up and down, appropriately averting his eyes when he noticed my bare thighs. For some reason, I caught no specific scents when around Sett and had assumed he must not have feelings—or maybe it was the stony skin that blocked his smell.

"I'm..." I paused. The truth? I eavesdropped, which I'd been caught doing by Sett before, many times. Plus, I'd promised him my only involvement with the investigation would center around character research and sniffing out guilt.

"I had writer's block," I said, finally. Thankfully, I had this truth to fall back on before enduring a third lecture from the sheriff about respecting others' privacy.

I shook the wavy locks from my face and tried not to shiver from the gust of wind sweeping under the overhang. Rain splashed off his boots and soaked my feet, still bare after leaving my shoes at the theater.

"And that requires you to remove your pants?" The flat line of his lips flickered with a smirk.

I'd slap him for enjoying this if his hardened skin wouldn't break the bones in my hand. With my hands on my hips, I frowned. My stern mom expression could make even a gargoyle, a cop two heads taller than me with stone-like skin, cower.

Sett took a step back, giving me space. His gaze flicked to something behind us, and I heard footsteps leaving in the other direction. Doctor Pitt and Piper must have left because nobody besides the gargoyle commented on my naked legs.

"It requires I go for a run to clear my head, and I'm willing to bet you've never run and then tried to pull on jeans right after."

"Actually, I did a 5k race—"

My hand shot up to interrupt him. "*After* birthing four children changed the shape of your hips?"

He bared his gargoyle fangs in a cringe before his lips returned to a flat line. The teasing stopped immediately. Sett had gotten in my way more than once with his protective behavior of Bewitcher's Beach, but I knew how to handle him. Mentioning kids or parenthood was a direct route to the stony sheriff's soft spot. My keen observations had quickly pinned Sett as a man who saw himself as the guardian, a pseudo-parent to the entire town, since he didn't have a chance at being a real father yet. And that very reason was why I couldn't get him out of my head at times...

"Now." I smiled, showing my own fangs. "Would you mind escorting me back to Mockbuster?"

My slight shiver suddenly sparked his attention.

"Oh! Right, of course." Sett pulled off his coat and offered it to me. The giant duster swallowed me, easily covering my bare legs. "After you." He held out his hand.

The gesture was almost romantic. Like how Wallace always opened doors for Mae or offered his arm to escort her.

"That's it!" Thoughts of romance flooded me, washing away the worry of my half-naked body. I never got a chance to ask about how Mae and Wallace met. If I melded their story with Cordelia's, I'd stay within Hattie's demands. I squealed and grabbed Sett's arm without thinking. "You just saved me."

Sett glanced at my hand on his forearm and his leathery wings expanded ever-so-slightly. "It's just a coat."

"No." I shook my head, grinning. "You gave me an idea. I'll call Mae. She's the perfect person to talk about love with!"

"Love?" A faint squeak broke Sett's voice. He coughed and cleared it away.

"What?" I asked as we stopped in front of Mockbuster's clear glass door that matched the giant windowed walls. The wind died down, joined by the slowing rain. Droplets rolled to the tip of the white gutters and dripped in heavy splashes.

Sett shook his head. "I didn't know you were dating."

My whirling brain came to a halt back in reality. "Who's nosy now?" I folded my arms and smirked.

He raised his stony fingers in surrender. "It's none of my business."

"Mm-hmm." I arched an eyebrow. Sett wouldn't know love if it bit him in the rocky butt. As far as I knew, the cop's relationships only lasted a month, two tops. Who would want to live a life with that many rules? He took life too seriously.

I shrugged off the giant coat and returned it to him before spinning around to unlock Mockbuster and slip inside. The bell chimed, and the door swung shut behind me. I glanced back to see Sett still standing under the overhang before hurrying upstairs where I could get myself dry.

Now in clean clothes—with pants that fit—I'd give Mae a ring and ask her to tell me the story of how she'd met her husband.

Romantic subplot, solved.

If only I could say the same about Cliff's murder and the mystery of the curse.

CHAPTER 10
SUBPLOTTING A MURDER

IF DRINKING Diet Pepsi with my breakfast was wrong, I didn't want to be right. The fizz of bubbles combined with caffeine kept my mind awake enough to buzz over Mae's story in relation to my script.

Four superhero backpacks lined the oak table, fresh and ready for a new year at Bewitcher Elementary. I stuffed identical peanut butter and jelly sandwiches into each lunchbox.

I refused to let my mind mull over the investigation early on a Monday morning. Back-to-school season with quadruplets was hectic enough without trying to puzzle out the pieces of a local murder. That'd have to wait until after another Diet Pepsi and opening duties at Mockbuster. If customers dared risk the curse.

I packed lunches and filled water bottles while turning my attention to my unfinished script.

A squeal interrupted my train of thought, and all subplot ideas vanished in a puff of imaginary smoke. Stevie bounded into the small kitchen, followed by Halen sliding in on his socks. Dio crashed into his brother, and a fight quickly ensued.

"I love school," Stevie sang, repeating the phrase to the tune of the alphabet song.

"Dweeb," Dio said.

Halen snapped back. "I know you are but what am I?"

"I know you are but what am I?" Echoed Stevie, spinning around in a ballerina pose and talking to nobody in particular.

"Everybody grab a backpack and pile into the van!" I called. Two at a time, I hopped down the steps and into the shop.

The clock on the wall said we ran five minutes late, and on the first day. I hurried the kiddos out the door.

"Aww, I wanted to walk to school," Dio whined, letting the backpack sag off of his shoulders. "We can run faster than the stupid van."

"Don't say stupid. And no transforming in the rain; I'm not sending you to school with a wet-fur smell." They climbed inside, and I slid the Astro van's door shut.

Kid's voices overlapped as they discussed soccer and school and if snot counted as a booger. Fighting ensued when Dio begged to get out of the car because he wanted to wolf out and sprint to the campus. Jovi argued the inaccuracy of Dio's statement. Werewolves could not, in fact, run faster than a minivan. The other two boys shouted over one another and Stevie stared out the window, still singing familiar tunes with her own made-up lyrics.

At each red light, my mind wandered.

The fall festival always carried the shop and theater through the winter. During the stormy months, visitors dwindled, and rentals from those staying at the Oyster Inn went from dozens a day to one or two. And now with the curse rumor...

I needed to figure a way to both investigate the crime while keeping Mockbuster's doors open. Closing the shop would only perpetuate the rumor.

"If only I could get the suspects to come rent a movie," I said to myself, despite the fact that I couldn't so much as hear my own voice over the chaos.

I hit the brakes in front of the red brick school.

The pups hopped out, backpacks dangling from their shoulders and jackets half on. I watched until they shoved through the white iron gate and disappeared into the little red schoolhouse, then flipped a U-turn and drove back.

The van's wheels squealed as I slowed near the alley between Mockbuster and the neighboring grocery shop.

A gaggle of customers milled about outside Mockbuster, bumping umbrellas. I squinted at the unusual sight. Who wanted to rent a movie on a Monday morning? Did my popcorn trick work that well? Did they want to make the start of their workweek feel like a Friday movie night?

I pulled the van into the alley beside Mockbuster and parked behind the tall building that looked more like a 1950's movie theater than a small-stage auditorium and video shop.

After hurrying through the back door, I unlocked the shop and invited everyone inside. The bell chimed as a dozen people filed in.

"Good morning. What type of movie are you in the mood for?" I asked the gangly human who ran Triton's Taffy. I rounded the front desk and turned to face him from behind the computer.

Triton shrugged his bony shoulders then leaned in. "I'm just here because Chanel said she planned to audition for the lead female role," he whispered. "I heard it's a romance this year."

I winced. Hattie had promised Bewitcher's Beach a play with romance. Could I deliver?

"Triton, Honey." I patted his arm. "You know Chanel is in a relationship, right?"

The scrawny human shrugged again. "Nobody has ever seen him. I'm beginning to think he's a rumor."

"Then where did those two come from?" I pointed at the twin towhead boys beside the siren. Chanel swung her hips with every step, nearly knocking her sons over as she marched through the crowd.

Triton wasn't wrong. Chanel spoke of her boyfriend, but he never made an appearance. Besides, the poor guy couldn't help it. When the siren worked her charms on others, as she often did to get her way, they fell head-over-heels for her. Today it was Triton, tomorrow the sheriff would likely have eyes for her.

The reminder of Sett left me wondering why he'd lingered outside the shop the other night. The gargoyle only gave his attention to those who needed protection. Was he worried the murderer would come for me? Or did he suspect me? I shook off the thought, giving my shoulders a little wiggle.

"Wait, did you say auditions?" I asked, focusing on Triton's skinny face and shaggy hair. He looked like Scooby-Doo's human counterpart come to life.

Triton nodded with a sparkle in his eye. "I've never acted before but—"

"Excuse me." Chanel shoved her way through the line of people, none of whom held a video in their hands. The siren's long sun-kissed hair brushed against her behind. The silky locks swayed from side to side with every step. She reached the front and leaned on the desk, pushing her cleavage out farther. "Noema, Darling, I'd just die for a chance to sing on stage. Hattie told me y'all aren't doing a mystery this year. Plus, I heard you're basing characters on people in town." She batted her eyelashes at me.

"Yes, but it's not a musical," I said, trying to catch up with the situation. Mockbuster wasn't packed with customers. The crowd of humans, two half-fairies, a siren, and one shifter in the shape of an octopus had arrived not to watch actors in films, but to become actors in Everland Theater's next play.

"Well." Chanel whipped a section of thick hair over her shoulder and straightened. "We can certainly change that with a song or two, can't we?"

"Yes..." Triton said, his voice trailing as he nearly drooled on the siren's feet.

I rolled my eyes. "No, Chanel, I'm not—" I stopped myself. Half the town didn't need to know how behind I'd fallen on the deadline. If they couldn't trust me to create good scripts, why would they take my recommendations when it came to movies? I had to keep my reputation for spotting a compelling story. I cleared my throat. "Auditions aren't until this weekend."

"Mmm," Chanel hummed. "The starlet says otherwise." She referred to Hattie's former life as a Hollywood actress. The poor ghost, though she loved the control of directing, ached to act again.

"It's just scouting," Hattie said. Her whisper tickled the back of my neck. I spun around to see her glowing manifestation. She passed right through the desk to stand next to me and face the crowd. "We have the characters; you just need a subplot, correct?"

My shoulders slumped from the weight of the pressure. Everland Theater needed the money from this play. Mockbuster needed the business. And I needed to finish writing it, but that wouldn't happen with a shop full of actors—or rather, people hoping to get their fifteen minutes of small-town fame.

"Actually, I have a subplot," I growled defensively. *And a way to bring suspects into my shop.* If the opportunity to star on stage drew this many people here on a Monday morning, could I entice the suspects here for an audition?

"I knew you would." Hattie beamed, her ruby lips expanding into a picture-perfect smile. Her confidence in me never wavered, which meant I needed to live up to the expectation.

The ghost's manifestation blinked from behind the desk to the middle of the crowd. She beckoned everyone to draw closer to her with the wave of a princess. Once they leaned in and listened to her harsh but slight voice, she gave them instructions on accents, personalities, and mannerisms to practice for the official audition.

Like a school of fish, the crowd collectively turned to leave. The door chimed again as most filed out. Only Chanel and her boys, the shapeshifter kid, and a man remained. Even Hattie disappeared, passing through the wall between the shop and the theater to retrieve the necklace that her spirit haunted.

"I'm going to pay Mae a visit to go over costuming," she said. With some effort, the ghost solidified enough to carry the object she was bound to.

"Can I run the idea by you first?" I said.

"Do you need to?" Hattie paused by the front window. "I trust your writing skills, Noema."

Noodle, the little shapeshifter boy, still stuck in the shape of an octopus, peered over the edge of the desk and licked a giant rainbow lollipop. The others browsed the aisles of videos.

"I wanna hear it," he said. He gripped the stick in one tentacle while the other seven balanced him. For as long as he and his parents had been in Bewitcher's Beach, the ten-year-old shifter had stayed as an octopus. Since he homeschooled, he'd show up anywhere at any time, and always with a snack in hand.

Hattie pursed her lips. After a moment, she gave me a brief nod to signal that she'd stick around to hear me out.

"Okay," I started. "So, the heroine and the hero run into

each other at the bank, and they both get so engrossed in an argument that they don't realize the building is closing."

"Oh!" Noodle interrupted with his lollipop extended into the air. "Do they get trapped inside?"

I opened my mouth but nothing came out. The kid had just ruined my plot twist.

I turned to Hattie. "So, what do you think?"

"I like it. It's not your best. But I like it."

"Me too!" Noodle chimed in, taking another lick of his lollipop. He'd wandered away to survey the shelf of candy against the wall.

I folded my arms across my chest. "I warned you of this when you insisted on adding romance."

"It'll do just fine," she said. "We'll talk more later." Hattie blinked through the wall, appearing on the other side of the door. Raindrops passed through her, only catching on her vague form now and then. Occasionally, they dripped down the shape of her head and shoulders.

All that was left was to write the darn thing. I plopped my rear-end on the stool and pulled a notebook from the shelf under the desk.

While Chanel let her boys open every single empty box of VHS tapes and Noodle stared at the wall of candy, I wrote, furiously scribbling the scene down from start to finish. The words flew out of me now, and the feeling of total immersion consumed my attention as my favorite movies always did. Writing and movies were the same to me: entertaining safe places to explore anything from murder investigations to space travel. Something about their endless possibilities made me feel right at home as both a human and werewolf, mother and manager, movie buff and playwright.

I sighed, folding the notebook shut with a satisfying slap of my palm against the cover. The play was finished, for now.

Once Hattie and I hashed over how it'd transfer to the stage, considering I often wrote with film in mind, there'd be plenty of revising to do. Despite all the practice I had writing for Everland Theater, I couldn't help it. Movies were my passion.

And mysteries. Where could I get details on Piper?

I grabbed the phone and dialed the number for Mae's house. It wasn't until I twisted the phone's cord around my wrist and fingers tight enough to cut off circulation that I realized how anxious I was for the plan to work.

When she answered, I skipped the pleasantries. "I'm wondering if you'll do me a favor."

"I already spoke with Hattie about backup costumes—"

"It's not about that." I stopped her before we dove into an hour-long conversation about fabrics and colors and budget. "Remember how I told you I'm basing characters off of people right here in Bewitcher's Beach?"

Mae hummed the affirmative, which was my cue to complete the plan.

"Perfect," I said. "I'm offering VIP auditions this afternoon at the rental shop."

Mae gasped. "Where the gentleman was murdered?"

"I can't shut down my entire business." I continued twirling and untwisting the cord around my hand. "Besides, the crime scene is cleared." Squeaks skittered to the top of the desk, pausing to sniff my white-knuckled hand. He knew when I needed a little calming therapy. Without hesitating, he crawled up my arm and curled into the nape of my neck. His warm fuzz nuzzled me, effectively lowering my blood pressure. "Here's the deal, I'm looking to audition people with the following knowledge: a real estate agent, a doctor, and a shapeshifter—oh, but not Noodle's family. I thought, who better to gather them than the lady who's friends with everyone?" With a few suspects—or at least people who knew Cliff—in my shop, I could sniff out information and stay within Sett's expectation of legal investigating. No eavesdropping or sneaking around required.

In the moment of silence, I snuggled closer to Squeaks with my chin.

"You want me to gather them for auditions..."

"Oh! I forgot the most important character: a landlord. Are you willing?"

A delighted giggle came from the other line followed by something muffling the phone. Mae's distant voice echoed as she shouted to her husband about heading out for the afternoon.

The crackling noise quieted and her voice came through clearly. "I'll see you in half an hour."

With that, the line went dead, and I hoped I could nail whoever had done the same to Cliff.

CHAPTER 11
JUDGE, JURY, AND ACTOR

THE NEON *open* sign went dark, and I let go of the chain. I peeled a piece of tape off of my thumb, plucked the paper from between my lips, and stuck it to the door with the message side facing out.

The bell chimed its cheerful jingle as I opened the door and leaned halfway out to double-check the readability of my handwriting.

Auditions in progress looked more like *Animals in problem.* I squinted, deciding the alternative message wasn't wrong. Mockbuster transformed into a play yard for four rowdy pups, though they weren't currently in wolf form.

Dio and Halen raced remote-controlled monster trucks down the action movie aisle. The crashing sounds and shouting matched the video's genre, tempting me to zone out and imagine what this moment would be if it were a scene on the screen.

Stevie and Jovi joined the races except with Jovi carrying his sister like a backpack and dodging the RC trucks. The drama sent the other two in an uproar. Accusations flung at Jovi, claiming an unfair race since he ran faster than a toy.

I rounded the desk and plopped on the stool, dialing the number for Sett's personal line. If the sheriff had learned new info on Cliff's case, I hoped to pry it out of him. The faux auditions would be more helpful if I went into them armed with clues.

"Hello?" His deep voice rang through the other line.

"Hi Sett, it's Noema. Any news on the murder?"

"Noema—"

"Oh." I interrupted before he listed a dozen dangers that I doubted I'd face. If you asked me, Sett was overprotective of this town. One murder near my shop didn't mean I had a target on my head. "I'm just hoping to combat some of the rumors about the curse with facts. Did you find out if Cliff was here for more than buying a house?"

The gritty sound of his grinding teeth came through the other line.

"What is it?" I straightened, scooting to the edge of the stool. I pinched my other ear to block out the sound of the kids' cheering. Apparently they'd all tied at the finish line.

"It's nothing for you to worry about. It looks like Cliff ingested paraquat."

My eyebrows shot up. "Paraquat?"

"A weed killer," he said.

"What? How would someone end up eating gardening chemicals?" I spied my pen and notebook leaning against the computer tower on the floor. With a tug of the phone cord, I leaned sideways to grab my notation supplies. This explained why the odd scent reminded me of plants.

I happened to know Mae did the yard work for the rentals she owned. When she decided to put the house on the market, did she clear the weeds to raise the price? I moved Mae to the top of my suspect list.

"That's a good question," he answered. "And one an officer of the law should be asking, not an innocent citizen."

"Could this have to do with yard work on that house he bought from Mae?"

"All I know is that Cliff wanted to pull out of the contract because he claimed Mae fudged the square footage. But it was already a done deal. How he got into paraquat, I don't know, but I'll be the one to find that answer."

If Sett thought the conversation ended there, he had another thing coming. Not when Mockbuster was accused of a curse.

What'd he call me? *Determined. Oh, boy, you better believe it.*

"I'll let you go," he said, after I didn't respond.

"Did that upset Mae? Is she a suspect?" I twisted the phone's cord around my finger like a teenager talking with her crush.

"No, no, Mae didn't fudge anything, according to Vera. Her sales are always on the up and up," he insisted. "But that information wasn't confirmed until after Cliff passed."

I cared for Mae. But did anyone really know her? And what about the past she never spoke about other than referring to it as shameful? Cliff had insulted her, and Sett failed to see that this discovery put a giant blinking *open* sign above Mae's head —*open for murder,* that is. Why had Cliff wanted out? Did Dr. Pitt kick him out of using the clinic?

"So who are the suspects? Do you think Cliff wanted to steal some of Pitt's business?" I asked.

"Pitt is a general practitioner and Cliff was a plastic surgeon. The two specialties don't overlap. I'm sorry, Noema. I'd love to keep chatting with you. Really, I would, but I have a million permits to verify for the fall festival. I'm drowning in paperwork over here." He paused for a second, letting silence fill the line between us. "In fact, I wouldn't mind some company while I go through them. I'll be at Roller Shakes—"

Dio screamed at his brother, and I didn't catch the rest of the sheriff's statement. He hopped on Halen's back, and both brothers crashed into a spinning display of candy. The fight sent a rainbow of Skittles packets to the floor.

"I have to go," I said, slamming the phone on the receiver. "That's enough wrestling!" As I approached, I smelled the citrusy scent of happiness and realized the boys were laughing, not fighting. Still, their roughhousing might wreck the shop if I didn't nip it in the bud.

I crouched and let Squeaks skitter down the crook of my arm like a ladder. He hopped to the carpet and zoomed for the end of the action aisle. At the finish line, marked with empty movie cases, Squeaks stood on his hind legs and curled his front paws under. He gave the air a victory sniff as if he understood my thoughts.

"Okay." I clapped my hands. "I declare this race officially forfeited because you've all been outrun by Squeaks."

"What?" Halen whined. "I didn't see him on the race-track." He pointed to the scuffed carpet along the aisle.

I folded my arms. "That's because he's so fast you can't see him."

"Actually," Jovi started.

"Forfeited!" Before he ruined the distraction with facts and statistics, I overruled them with my goddess-given mom author-ity. "Time for all werewolf pups to run upstairs. If you check the freezer, you'll see a surprise for dinner."

Frizzy pigtails flapped up and down like wings as Stevie bounded in place. She reminded me of a living pogo stick. "Ooh, is it pizza bagels?"

I winked, and with that, she scrambled for the stairs, jumping two at a time despite her small stature. Stevie wasn't technically the runt of the litter, but strangers often mistook her for being younger than her brothers because of her compact size.

"Pizza!" Dio's scream turned into a howl. "I love pizza!"

Both boys with RC controllers shoved one another. They fought to be second up the stairs, all thoughts of winning a monster truck race abandoned for the cheesy goodness of frozen TV dinners.

Another one of my sneaky secrets was keeping a box of Pizza Bagels hidden in the freezer at all times. For occasions when I needed them to entertain themselves, I wielded the lava-hot treats like a weapon against chaos. I hid the little pizzas inside a recycled Healthy Choice box of sweet and sour chicken and steamed vegetables. It kept the treat reserved for days I needed it. Today, I'd revealed the box and placed it on the shelf in the door.

"Thanks, Mom," Jovi said, pausing to give me a quick hug.

I settled into my stool and inputted the returned titles in the computer log. Outside, the endless gentle breeze swirled in its predictable, curious way. Brown, yellow, and red leaves danced along the cobblestone. With each passerby, my heart lifted. Was my customer base returning? I hoped, holding my breath, hinging on the direction of their feet. But each one took a wide berth around Mockbuster and the spot of the crime scene. Like an anchor, my heart fell again, solid and angular in my stomach.

This curse would be the death of me and my movie sanctuary.

The stomping upstairs confirmed four happy kids had found their dinner. Their energy boosted my courage and determination. If Sett wanted to keep secrets and twiddle his thumbs, I needed to take matters into my own hands.

I snagged the phone, dialed the coroner's office, and chatted cheerfully with him about character research. As with Barney, I prodded for details on Cliff, suggesting he'd receive a tribute in my next script.

In my notebook, I recorded the times. *Paraquat can take days to weeks to kill. But Cliff's dose nabbed him within forty-five minutes.*

Once I thanked the coroner and hung up, and I mused over the timeline. Cliff had to have ingested the poison no earlier than six fifteen.

I returned the movie cases to their correct places when the bell chimed again.

Only an hour after I'd given Mae the request, she arrived with a real estate agent at her side. Vera walked in behind her, dodging the sway of the half-dragon's hips.

Mae waved her claws as she sauntered inside and stopped to lean her elbow on the display shelf. A dozen videotape copies of *Twister* rattled under the weight of her movement, almost toppling to the floor.

"My, my, it sure is tricky trying to find a shapeshifter outside of Noodle's family," she said. "I called over at The Oyster Inn to snag that new gal, but Barney said she checked out Saturday morning."

I furrowed my brow. Piper was just here.

This piece of the puzzle didn't fit. One piece was two-pronged and the other, well, missing. Piper rented a video from me the day before and was seen arguing with Cliff at the Oyster Inn that same night. Did they share a movie night? A *deadly* movie night? And how did the poison factor into that? Poisoned popcorn or a soda?

I hurried to the computer to see if Piper had returned her rental. If not, it'd give me an excuse to have her come back into town to pay the late fee.

"So, does your play have a real estate agent in it?" Vera

asked. Her long, smooth dark hair was coiled in a side braid over her shoulder, and she wore a tie-dye sweatshirt and jeans—something I'd never seen among her always prim and professional wardrobe.

"Yeah," I lied. "I'm thinking of making the heroine an agent." At least that part was halfway true. If Hattie approved it, I'd add to the drama of the script and give the character the exciting job of a special agent hunting for criminals. Besides, that'd give me more excuses to research crime.

Vera held up a packet of papers. "I brought my study notes from the real estate license exam."

"Oh, Vera, Honey," Mae said as she straightened. The movement shook the wire shelf and sent the cassettes trembling. "We aren't just here for research. We're auditioning for important roles." A sparkle shone in her red eyes.

When the computer finally loaded, the bright screen pulled my attention from Mae. What had Piper rented? I squinted as if that'd help me recall the first and only day she came into the shop. It worked, and I tapped *Scream* into the keyboard.

"Believe me, I know." Vera smiled. "I've always wanted to be an actress, and I'm curious who else would be here trying out."

When she glanced around, I caught her drift. The quiet shop didn't look like a bustling audition for the town's biggest play of the year. I needed to cover my butt.

"These are VIP auditions, only for people with..." My voice faded as the screen in front of me showed a zero next to copies of *Scream*. The missing movie gave me the perfect opportunity to call Piper. I blinked and gave the two backseat suspects my attention again. They'd fallen from the top of my list and in line with the other names on my quest to find Cliff's killer.

"Only for people with what, Dear?" Mae asked.

"Motive—" I clamped my jaw shut hard enough that my

fangs dug into my gums. I flinched. "Motivation. People with motivation." I laughed and tried to smile. "You know? Those really willing to memorize lines and put all their effort into making this the best play Bewitcher's Beach has ever seen." The statement slipped out so easily it was as though my subconscious had been carrying that idea around for a long time.

We needed the play to do well to refurbish Everland Theater and make our dreams come alive. But the rumor of the curse on Mockbuster only furthered my desire to do something right and prove to the whole town that I ran both a safe rental shop and wrote successful stories. Not to mention, I needed to pay next month's rent...somehow.

Mae nodded, and Vera wrung her hands. I took a sniff, catching a whiff of ammonia, gasoline, and banana cream pie. The scents overlapped, which meant I couldn't identify one obvious emotion from the mixture. Both suspects gave an array of feelings, from nerves, to impatience, to excitement—all emotions anyone would feel at an audition.

"Here are the lines." I handed them a page with dialogue I'd torn out of the notebook. "Take a look, maybe practice a bit while I make a quick call, and then we'll get started."

The phone rang and rang until a bright voice finally answered. "This is Piper."

"Hello, I'm calling regarding a late return for the movie *Scream*?"

"Oh, shoot!" Piper said.

Shoot huh? Was a gun your backup plan of action if the poison didn't take? Of course, that was unlikely, and the thought was sparked by the prop gun we still needed to purchase for the play.

"The tape must have made it into my suitcase," she said. "I

live one town over, but I'm leaving the area tonight. Can I just mail it to you?"

"It's stolen material if you keep it any longer than tonight," I said, lying again. Sett would back me up when I exposed Piper's murderous past, right?

"No kidding?" she asked. "Wow. Okay, um, I guess I'll drive it back now." A nervous laugh escaped her.

Yeah, you don't want to return to the scene of the crime, huh? I've got you now — my ears straightened as soon as I realized I sounded like the witch in *The Wizard of Oz*. Maybe I was a little too eager to pin the murder on her when I didn't have the facts. But it was easier to call this stranger a killer rather than Mae or Cordelia.

"Thank you!" I said, then returned the phone to the receiver, satisfied that I'd get answers. Tonight.

Vera and Mae repeated the lines several times, acting out the dialogue with different accents and a variety of gestures.

When they finished a third round, I clapped. "Wonderful. Now I need to make sure I've got the details right. Vera, when you're working with a client, how important is it to you that the client doesn't change their mind at the last minute? Is that a lot of paperwork?" I avoided glancing at Mae. Though the question was for the real estate agent, Mae was the one who almost lost the most money when Cliff accused her of dishonesty.

Vera fingered her braid, plucking sections out to loosen it. Once the hair fell loose, she methodically tugged each section to tighten the style again. "It takes some work, but that's all part of the job."

I nodded and added that to my notebook. "What about the loss of money?" *Money you almost lost when Cliff tried to turn the sale upside down.* "Does that throw you for a loop? How should my real estate agent character act if she's about to make a lot of cash and then it's all torn away?"

Vera shrugged, dropping her thick braid against her shoulder. "I guess how anyone would act. Disappointed? It's frustrating but not uncommon."

"Oh, that's right, didn't that doctor just do that?" I asked. I cringed at the rising smell of gasoline and the following scent of smoke. Impatience and anger seeped from one or both of them.

"Yes, but he's not the first, and he certainly won't be the last," Vera said. "But it's tough, especially when business is struggling. Nobody wants to move out of Bewitcher's Beach, so they rarely need a real estate agent." A sigh escaped her and she placed her hands on her hips. "But such is life, I guess.

Mae stepped up with arms crossed, looking like the bouncer at a club. If she wasn't wearing a kitty sweater and knitted handbag. "Are we talking about how Mr. Conflick backed out of the sale at the last minute?" Mae huffed with a tiny puff of smoke from her nose. "*Supposedly*, he thought he was coming into a lot of money but was about to lose it and claimed he couldn't afford the house anymore. You know what? His lie just gets my goat and I don't want to talk about it. Besides, Wallace is waiting for his dinner." Mae took a step closer. "Can you just tell me if I got the part, Noema?"

I pointed my nose at her, but the intensity of the scents didn't change.

"Sorry, Mae. I'll get to you in just a moment—"

Mae tossed her handbag on the desk, not caring that lipstick rolled out and fell into my lap. I picked it up and set it on the table while she swiped the script from Vera's hand.

"Let me show you that last line again, but with more enunciation." She rolled her shoulders back and stretched her neck before clearing her throat. With a quick glance at Vera, then me, she began, bellowing the line with a lower pitch.

I nodded along and offered her an encouraging smile. If it

was she who carried the scent of anger and impatience, I didn't want to get on her bad side.

When Mae broke for a quick breath, Vera stepped up, tapped the desk with one manicured fingernail, and pointed at the door.

"I've got another house to get ready for a showing," she said. "Will you call me if I got the part? It's paying right? I hate to ask, but I really need the money."

"Actually—"

Mae cut me off with the start of the next character's dialogue. She shared my determination and apparently wanted a bigger role than backstage seamstress.

Vera mouthed a *never mind* and *thank you*. I tapped the notebook to confirm that I'd gotten what I needed from her.

I returned my attention to Mae and clicked my pen, ready to seriously consider her acting skills. I gently pushed items that had fallen from her purse off of the open notebook, including the lipstick, a credit card, a tin of mints, and loose pieces of wrapped Werther's caramels.

I opened her purse to return the items when a familiar name caught my eye. A lump gathered in my throat as I read the name on the credit card.

Cliff Conflick.

Why did Mae have his personal credit card in her handbag?

I hurried to slip it back into the purse before she finished the monologue, but it didn't matter. A distraction shoved through Mockbuster's door and allowed me to return all the items to Mae's bag without notice.

The woman with the swollen lips and most perfect perm burst inside. Piper looked better now: less reddening on her skin, and with impossibly smooth curls as if she wore a wig. The shapeshifter skills mildly masked her slow healing. She hiked her bookbag higher on her shoulder and produced a videotape from inside.

"Here's the return," she said between gasping breaths and a lingering look at Mae that flickered into a frown. I glanced between them and felt the crackle of tension. "Now it's not considered stolen, right?"

Mae folded her arms, clearly ticked off about the interruption from this young woman.

"Please." Piper slammed her palms on the desk.

I flinched. She was in my face now, almost nose-to-nose. Breath left my lungs and I couldn't blink, too stunned to move.

I expected the fragrant scent of shampoo, but I smelled nothing beyond the pure, nose-stinging and ammonia-soaked whiff of fear. Was it mine, or Piper's?

"I returned it," Piper said, stabbing the VHS tape with her finger. "So you can't call the cops on me. I can't get in trouble with the law again."

I swallowed the lump in my throat and glanced at Mae. Maybe her initial didn't belong at the top of my suspect list.

"Thank you?" I squeaked as I slid the tape from beneath her finger and held it up.

"Good. I can't spend another second around here!" Piper spun around, but not before I saw the nametag pinned to her orange polo.

Right beside her name was a matching orange square that read *The Home Cheapo* in blocky white letters. The outfit announced Piper worked at the discount copy-cat of The Home Depot department store.

My ears folded back. Mae might have had Cliff's credit card, but it was Piper who worked at a home improvement store that carried buckets and buckets of weed killer.

As fast as she'd burst inside, Piper left in a blur of orange fabric and brown curls. The door swung shut, and she nearly dove into the car she'd left at the curb.

I glanced at the last one left in the shop to see Mae staring out the window after Piper. Did they know each other? Had Mae dragged her into helping her end the man who messed up the sale on Mae's house? If Mae felt she'd lost money on a canceled contract, was the credit card how she'd intended to make it back before Cliff died? Or had she killed him to hide her theft?

I tried not to frown and expose my thoughts to her. Dead men didn't report stolen property. It all made sense, like a puzzle, except with money and murder rather than cardboard and cat pictures.

Mae had a motive, Piper had the paraquat.

CHAPTER 12
THE WHOLE CRIME YARDS

MINTY CURIOSITY BURNED in my nose.

My ears flicked forward, listening for the sound of Mae's heartbeat. It thumped twice as fast as a normal heart rate, even for a curious half-dragon.

"Foolish," she mumbled. When she noticed me staring, she marched toward the desk. Did she call me foolish or Piper? Had she seen me spy the credit card? My pulse matched hers, too erratic and in a never-ending race.

If this were a movie, she'd whip a knife out of her jean skirt's pocket and then threaten to kill me for what I knew. But it wasn't, and I considered Mae a friend—a friend with plenty of secrets, anyway.

"I'll admit," she started, arching an eyebrow, "I'm not as agreeable as Vera."

I didn't like the sound of that. Her red gaze shifted from the script in her hand to me. A slight shiver stole down my back. What didn't I know about the woman in front of me? Why did she hide her past, and how did she come to own so many of the houses in Bewitcher's Beach? But the smell of mint didn't denote aggression or lies or anything remotely threatening.

"I refuse to wait." She folded her arms.

Hints of frustration echoed in her voice. Enough to tighten my muscles and sniff for the guilty smell of fish.

"Will I be cast in the play, or not?" she asked.

All at once, my limbs melted into the chair and I breathed easier. What did I think would happen? That she'd whop me upside the head with her handbag? I'd never seen Mae so much as swat a fly buzzing by. Of course, a fly didn't accuse her of dishonesty and try to pull out of a contract with her, either.

"I have to discuss roles with Hattie before I make any final decisions," I said, choosing to twist the truth so I could use the excuse of auditions again.

A long sigh sent tiny puffs of smoke from her nostrils. "What if I refuse to sew the costumes unless I get a chance to perform this year?"

The heavy weight of my heart slammed into my stomach. "You'd do that?" My voice cracked.

"Of course not." She swatted the air with her claws. "But is it so wrong that I'm tired of being backstage?"

No, but stealing a credit card is wrong. Murder is wrong. If Mae killed Cliff, my conscience couldn't take casting a murderer. Besides, Mockbuster and Everland Theater wouldn't survive that scandal on top of the rumored curse. I was stuck. What if I gave a guilty woman small-stage fame? What if I didn't, and she decided to make good on her threat? Without Mae's costuming expertise, Hattie would go poltergeist on me.

Sweat moistened the fur on my ears. I needed to confirm Mae's innocence. Or guilt. Either way, it'd help me make a decision.

To cast or not to cast her? That wasn't the question that slipped out.

"Did you poison Dr. Conflick?"

Mae's jaw dropped. After a moment of shock, she snatched her handbag from the desk and hugged it to her chest. *Yikes, even with the serial bicycle thief, I wasn't* this *impulsive.* The stress of losing business and the looming rental bill left me on edge.

"Well, I never—" she scoffed. "How could you? Why?" Unlike her boisterous delivery of the script's dialogue, Mae couldn't finish a sentence.

I sniffed the air for the putrid smell of guilt, like rotten milk that'd been left out to spoil in the heat. Instead, I couldn't pinpoint one particular emotion between the scent of coffee, orange, gasoline, and a dozen other aromas. Shock often shuffled through a myriad of smells, like a broken video tape skipping from scene to scene, as the person attempted to understand the situation.

"I'm sorry, Mae. We can't cast anyone involved in the investigation," I scrambled to explain, worried I was way off base.

"What would ever make you ask such a thing?"

I chewed the inside of my cheek before answering. Biting my lips shut was the only way I stopped myself from slipping more impulsive accusations after finding the credit card.

"Well." I stood so she wasn't towering over me. "It felt like you wanted the whole town to blame a curse on my videos."

"Cliff is the one who said it." Steam still emitted from her nose.

Skipping around the subject only dragged out her shock and stress. I'd talked myself into confronting her. No more Ms. Nice Noema.

"Mae." I pointed to the flimsy knitted bag still clutched in her claws. "I saw the credit card with Cliff Conflick's name on it."

The puffs of smoke disappeared as she sucked in a sharp

breath through her nose. Her throat rippled with a hard swallow.

"Holy cannoli, Noema. You don't think..." Her voice trailed. Her fingers expanded as she pressed her open palm to her bosom and then leaned into the desk. "I need to sit down." The desk creaked and swayed with her.

The shifting smells still overlapped, making it impossible for me to identify her feelings. The stench of spoiled milk hung in the air, but it wasn't alone. Mae felt guilt, sure, but it was joined with embarrassment, regret, sadness, and even...nostalgia?

She clutched tighter to her chest. Instinct overwhelmed me, and I jumped to her aid.

I quickly carried the stool to the other side of the desk and helped her climb onto the tall seat. The point of her claws snagged on the handbag's stitches as she set it in her lap.

"Are you okay? Should I call a doctor?" My mind rippled as fast as her spread of emotions. Thoughts of poison and Cliff's lifeless body cropped up like kernels popping in the microwave.

"I'm okay," she said. "I'm embarrassed is all."

"What happened? Why do you have his..." I pointed to the purse in her lap. "You know?"

"Well, it's been a long time since I've considered myself a liar, so I suppose I should tell you the truth." A little huff escaped her as she forced herself to meet my gaze. "I stole it."

The fur on my ears raised.

"I know, I know," she said, with a wave of her hand. "It's humiliating just saying it out loud."

"I think I should call Sett now." I circled the desk and reached for the phone, but before I could grab it, she shot to her feet and put her hand on mine.

"No! Please, don't get the nice Sheriff involved."

I straightened but stayed close to the phone. "It's a murder investigation, Mae." My ears folded back. As much as I hated to admit it, I needed Sett's help, in an official capacity. Though it wasn't the one I'd expected, I'd uncovered a crime.

"Oh, Honey, I didn't hurt Cliff. I may have caused him quite the scare when he noticed his credit card was missing, but I wasn't in town until you saw me on our nightly walk. I held an open house until six-thirty at a cottage for sale on Cauldron's Court."

Six-thirty? With Cliff poisoned no later than 6:15, the open house provided Mae's alibi. No way did Mae have time to make it from Cauldron's Court and into town to slip weed killer into Cliff's dinner.

"But why did you go to an open house without your husband?" I asked, recalling our conversation during the walk.

The twist of Mae's mouth lifted. "Because I sold that house as a surprise to cover the cost of his birthday trip."

I couldn't help but smile. Theirs was a love like the one I had shared with Christopher. If only I hadn't turned him into a werewolf, he'd still be with me. I shoved the thought away and focused on the clues.

"Still, if you stole it, I need to let Sett know," I said.

Her hand shot out again, like a scaly stop sign. "I'll return it to his family. He said he had a relative that lived nearby, so I'll find them and get it to them. I didn't take a dime from the man, I promise."

Mae looked like a candle after its flame extinguished. Regret's smell of burnt toast filled the air. This wasn't the feisty, gossiping woman I'd considered the grandmother of Bewitcher's Beach.

"Then why'd you steal it?"

"Oh, he just made me so mad. He toured one of my houses

four times. Twice with Vera and twice without. Every tour, he made rude comments about the paint colors we'd chosen, calling them tacky. He even said my handmade curtains were cheap and outdated. Outdated, Noema! So he'd bought the house and then tried to back out at the last minute. He even had the audacity to move his crap in before the contract closed. Out of the goodness of my heart, I always hand out the keys early for families to prepare for the moving process, but I should have known with that chump." She flipped the handbag open and plucked the credit card. "So, I slipped his wallet and took the card. He was so busy judging my homemade welcome rug that he didn't notice when I put his wallet back."

I'd never pinpointed Mae as a thief, much less a successful one. A gossip? Yes. Dramatic and a little desperate for attention? Definitely, but weren't we all?

"You don't need to share more if it embarrasses you," I said. "I'm sorry I suspected you. I just didn't want whoever did this to him to get away with it and make our town feel unsafe."

The swirl of smells calmed to a comforting lavender. We'd both found peace, her with a confession and me with an apology. With our emotions calmed, I caught the scent of burnt pizza bagels drifting down from upstairs. I glanced to the left to see Squeaks climbing the steps one at a time, pausing to wiggle his butt then launch himself to the edge of the next one. He knew he'd get plenty of crumbs from the burnt pieces Stevie scraped off.

Mae sighed and met my gaze. "Actually, it feels right as rain to say it out loud. I've hidden it for too long, and I swear it's aging me. I'm only a hundred and fifty, and I look as though I'm a thousand years old!"

I cocked my head and gave her my full attention, ignoring the stomping upstairs and the millions of questions running through my head.

"Say what out loud?"

Mae licked her lips and shrugged. "Darling, I pray this doesn't ruin your opinion of me. I'm not that person anymore."

The anticipation was killing me. I'd never been considered patient.

"Out with it!"

"I told you Wallace and I met at a bank some hundred years ago, right? Well, it wasn't at a bank. It was at a bank *heist*."

Now, *I* needed to sit down. I knew everyone had their little secrets, but Mae's was twice the size I expected.

"It's true." She straightened, regaining her dignity in the face of truth. "I robbed a lot of banks, and Wallace was my accomplice. Only the corrupt banks, mind you. Still, it was wrong, and I stopped many, many years ago. Wallace says I've since swapped that adrenaline rush with hoarding houses. He might be right, but I've come to love fixing up old buildings around Bewitcher's Beach and selling or renting them to nice families."

"Wow, Mae." I folded my ears back. "I had no idea."

"I couldn't help myself after his atrocious behavior. Dr. Conflick was too easy to steal from."

I nodded, remembering the rude comments Cliff had said to me. If I had skill with stealing or something similar, would I have attempted an act of revenge too? With Mae out of the picture, the suspect list narrowed to four.

Cordelia saw him, but she wasn't a suspect; the girl was too busy following fashion trends and fawning over her boyfriend. That narrowed the suspect pool to Vera, Doctor Pitt, and Piper.

"So did I get it?" Mae asked, shattering the puzzle I pictured with my mind's eye.

"Get what?"

"A spot in the performance!"

My ears shot up, and I shook my head. "I really have to discuss it with Hattie first. I'm sorry."

"In that case, don't call me. I'll call you if I'm still interested." Mae slid off the stool and sauntered to the door. She paused with her claws around the door's handle. "If you're hoping to find out who hurt Dr. Conflick, I'd start with that girl who came in here tonight."

I blinked away my thoughts of timelines and access to poison, and *what motive would Doctor Pitt have for attacking his own friend?* Didn't he and Cliff go way back? Doctor buddies, or whatever? Of course, I'd yet to pin a specific reason why Vera or Piper might have attacked him.

"Piper?" I asked.

Mae pointed at me, wagging her finger. "That's the one. She has the look of guilt all over her. As soon as I saw her at that first open house, I told Wallace 'That girl's a gold digger.' And I have the right to say that, because I've stolen gold. Although I'd never have stooped to her method of hanging on doctors' arms for it." She gave her body a little shake. "From what I understand, she's a struggling actress, probably mooching off the older men she attaches herself to. Anyway, good luck."

The door chimed as she exited, and with that, tonight's investigation had ended—the interview part of it, anyway.

I grabbed my pen and crossed out Mae's initial. I circled the P on the list several times and drew an arrow all the way to the next page where I added a question. *Why did Piper go with Cliff to an open house?* Was she more than a client? Cliff's unknown sibling? A girlfriend, perhaps?

Thankfully, I had the perfect excuse to call her, considering how fast she rushed out earlier and I didn't get to process her late fee. I pushed the case that read *Scream* to the side and tapped Piper's name into the keyboard. The computer popped up with a screen that showed what she owed.

"Bingo," I said to nobody. Not even the mouse was around.

Stevie's voice echoed from the top of the stairs. "Mommy, I can't find any PJs to wear."

I shut down the computer, tossed the video's case into the return bin to check tomorrow, and made a quick note on the page to call Piper first thing in the morning.

Tonight, I had a script to polish.

CHAPTER 13
YOUR GOSSIP IS AS GOOD AS MINE

AS I STOOD at the shop's register, the satisfying crack of a fresh can of Diet Pepsi filled my soul with hope for the new day. And finishing the play filled me with an unmatched sense of satisfaction—another reason I loved writing stories that came to life on the stage and, hopefully, on the big screen someday.

I pressed the aluminum opening down and poured the fizzing drink into a plastic cup. The syrupy bubbles tasted like heaven, and for a minute, I smelled nothing but the soda.

Even the slight ammonia coming from the early morning customer didn't seep through my moment of relaxation. After another sip, the slow computer still hadn't finished loading the customer's file. I really needed to update the system, still using the same computers the original Mockbuster owner left behind.

I blinked at the werefox woman in front of me, waiting to process her late fee payment. We shared a similar issue: one piece of her other self remained in her human form. Her bushy tail flicked back and forth through the custom spandex outfit, in an orange that matched her fur.

"It's what I wear for Zumba," she said, as if reading my mind. But my ears were where her gaze lingered. "It gets my animal energy out and I get better sleep. At least on the nights my little foxies don't wake up."

"Is the class at Miss Raven's studio?" I pointed out the window. Across the street and out of sight was an exercise studio that shifted with the current workout craze. Miss Raven, the reaper who ran it, scared all the moms into becoming healthier.

The werefox woman nodded, eyes narrowed and keys jingling in her hand. Her tail still twitched nervously and the ammonia smell grew stronger.

"Is it almost ready?" she asked.

The two family films she'd dropped on the desk and backed away from—*Honey I Shrunk the Kids* and *Anastasia*—ran three days behind the return schedule. Each time she glanced at the door and flicked her tail, I grew more impatient with the loading screen.

"If you're in a hurry, we don't have to do this now," I offered. "You don't need to pay the late fee until you rent again."

"No, no," she said with a slight shiver. "I want to clear my account, because of...well, the curse." She whispered the last word.

"That's just a silly rumor," I said, forcing a lighthearted laugh. The smell of fear suddenly made sense. I wanted to get this woman's nervous energy out before she snagged her tail on a wire display stand and blamed the so-called curse.

Finally, the computer blinked and listed the woman's account. It showed she owed three dollars, which she quickly paid by sliding three bills across the desk. Her tail nearly caught in the door as she hurried out.

I sighed and threw back the red cup, downing the rest of the Diet Pepsi. A flat, unopened bag of popcorn floated across the floor. Dragging it along was a tiny mouse who matched the color of the carpet. I shook my head at Squeaks' attempt to get a snack and reached for the phone.

The mouse dropped the bag by my foot and crawled up the outside of my pant leg. To my surprise, the call didn't go to Piper's answering machine. After we exchanged greetings, I cut to the chase.

"Unfortunately, you slipped out of here so fast that I wasn't able to grab the late fee from you yesterday."

"Late fee?" she echoed. "Uh, sure, no problem. Can I send you a check?"

"I don't take checks," I lied. "Any chance you have a friend or family member—maybe a boyfriend—nearby who can pay the fee for you?"

I couldn't smell her emotion through the phone, but I caught the faint sound of sniffling. "No," she said through a cracked voice. "It's no trouble. I'll be in town on Monday after work for an appointment."

An appointment? But Dr. Conflick was dead, and her swollen lips surely came from plastic surgery—not Dr. Pitt's department. My mind buzzed with possibilities. Why would she come all the way into Bewitcher's Beach when the next town over offered more options? And based on their spooky conversation in the alley, Piper had a bone to pick with Pitt.

"How about I make it easier on you? I'll be running errands in the afternoon. Tell me where your appointment is and I'll come grab the cash from you."

"Perfect!" she said. "I'll be at Dr. Pitt's clinic."

If Mae spoke the truth, which might have been embellished, Piper could have her sights set on the next richest man in town. Would she kill Dr. Pitt too? And for what? She wasn't married to these men, so it didn't award her the money of an insurance scam.

Now it was time for the clincher—using Mae's other nugget of information.

I took a deep breath and dove in. "I'm also working with the director of Bewitcher's Beach's next play and offering VIP auditions. I've heard you're a talented actress." Compliments always got people to relax. I'd learned this trick long ago when I wanted to mask stinky emotions with happiness' orange scent.

"Oh goodness, you've heard of me?" Her flat business voice shifted to bright and cheerful.

"Should we schedule an audition?" I prodded.

"I don't know," she said with a sigh. "It sounds like fun, but I'm going through a lot."

Guilt does that...

"Let me just get your answers for a quick questionnaire and I'll keep your name on my list in case you change your mind. We still haven't cast the starring role." Or any role other than wherever Hattie put Vera. At least the mock audition gave us one skilled performer so far.

When Piper agreed, I dove into the faux survey, humming along to her answers as though I took notes.

"Our cast is primarily residents; are you related to anyone in Bewitcher's Beach?" I asked.

"Nope."

"Friends?"

"Nope."

"Enemies?"

She paused. I pressed the phone closer to my ear to make sure I didn't miss her response.

"That's a little personal, isn't it?" she asked.

I shrugged, though she couldn't see me. "We need our cast to work as a team. But don't worry, you're the real talent. If there's any trouble between you and another cast member, we'd choose you."

"That's awesome," she said. "Hmm. Well, I'm not a fan of being around doctors after I had a botched surgery. It's such a drag that I have to go see Dr. Pitt for the swelling, but he's the only one who agreed to take muffins as payment. And, you know, struggling actress, and all that. Anyway, I wouldn't love it if he were part of the cast."

Dislikes doctors. I scribbled notes. Annoyed by the movement of my arm, Squeaks jumped off of me and skittered down the computer's power cord.

"Noted, and I'm so sorry to hear that. If you're suffering any injuries, we'd be happy to accommodate you on stage."

"That's so sweet!" she said. "I'm okay now, it was plastic surgery."

"Seriously?" I said, with the same pitch and intensity as Mae does when steeped in gossip. Squeaks stopped hopping across the carpet to stand on his hind legs and twitch his whiskers at me. "I've been looking into that. Who was your surgeon?"

"Dr. Conflick," she said. "He's not, uh, practicing anymore."

"No way, are you the actress he's dating?" I dove in headfirst, tempted by the conspiracy of gossip. If this wasn't for an investigation, would I still indulge in rumors? Maybe I'd imagined it, but I swore I caught Squeaks shaking his head at me before he lowered to all fours and continued hopping toward the stairs.

"I, well, yes, but we broke up before he—" She paused, and only the waves of her breath came through the other line. "Anyway, you asked about enemies. I think the owner of the inn counts; he always scowled at me."

Barney scowls at everyone except for Hattie. I didn't add him to the notes until a thought popped into my head. Did he simply scowl at her, or did he scold her and Cliff for arguing in the lobby?

"Also, there's a lady who yelled at me for walking on grass. It's silly, but she was always so rude after that. I mean, I swear she wanted to hate me for no reason. She'd tell me I wore too much perfume and didn't allow me to go into an open house once because, and I quote, 'people would sneeze.'" Piper scoffed. "Ridiculous, considering she wears more perfume than I do."

An open house? Did Mae lead me to Piper and Piper attempt to lead me back to Mae? No, Mae never wore perfume, one of the many reasons I'd enjoyed our friendship. Strong, artificial smells didn't mix with werewolf noses.

"Do you know her name?" I asked.

"Nope, but I think she was a realtor."

It has to be Vera.

"Crazy," I said, so she'd know I was invested in her drama. "Does Vera Fang ring a bell?"

"Who knows?" She laughed. "I never caught her name. After she was so rude, I stopped going to the open house tours. Anyway, I've got to jet. Keep me in mind. I'll consider auditioning."

Before I could get more information about her whereabouts the night Cliff died, much less say goodbye, the dial tone beeped. Her dislike for the other two suspects left my stomach sour. Or maybe that was my soda pop breakfast. I stood and grabbed the bag of popcorn, disappearing upstairs for a quick buttery snack—one I'd eat at any time of day with my partner in crime.

I returned to the desk with a full bag and a mouse on my shoulder. Squeaks nibbled a piece while I polished the script's dialogue.

In three hours of writing, Mockbuster's door didn't chime once.

THE NEXT DAY passed the same as yesterday with a quiet morning and a boring afternoon. Only three visitors stopped by the shop—dismal, even for a Wednesday. Clearly, the shop *was* cursed, by the rumor, anyway.

Noodle's dad arrived to borrow a copy of *Men in Black* and buy a pile of candy for his kid. Then Triton braved the curse to rent *Never Been Kissed*. I resisted the urge to ask if the title of the movie reflected his personal life. My gut twisted. Two rentals wouldn't cover the coming bill headed my way. I needed to solve this darn curse drama ASAP.

Hattie upped the count to four visitors, though she'd only passed through to grab the script and print copies. After reviewing the play, an idea sparked. I'd call Mae and Vera and schedule a costume fitting for the main character's best friend. It'd give me another opportunity to question Vera about where she was the night of Cliff's murder—discreetly, of course—and ask what she knew about Piper.

I paced the aisles, speaking my thoughts into the silent shop. If this moment existed inside a movie, I'd be the conspirator who turned the back wall of *new releases* into an investigation board. I pictured the board complete with dozens of photographs, notes, and overlapping red string.

Finally, the clock struck three, and the door's bell rang with a cheerful ding. The half-dragon arrived, having only agreed to continue the costumes when Hattie called and offered her a role as the main character's mother—a part I'd had to add just to appease her.

When Vera followed a moment later, I led them from Mockbuster to the theater where Hattie's manifestation stood at the center of the stage.

Pleasantries quickly turned to gossip. Mae measured Vera while Hattie discussed rehearsal expectations.

The ghost clapped her hands, but it made no sound. "I'll give you both the official information once we've secured the entire cast. Now, Noema fell behind with the script, which means we only have three weeks before the fall festival and our first performance. That's the fastest we've ever put a show together, so I expect you to practice lines and placements now. We will do the rest of the auditions this Saturday, and you'll meet the cast then."

Once Hattie finished, the gossip resumed. Mae discussed how worn the seats in the theater had become, blaming it on a few careless people in Bewitcher's Beach. Vera and Hattie nodded along.

"So many slobs in this town," Vera said. "You wouldn't believe the state some people try to sell their house in. I've resorted to sprucing them up myself to make the sales go faster."

Mae huffed as she plopped into a seat in the front row. "Darling, it doesn't matter if you spruce it up. Grumpy people still find a way to snub it."

Poor Mae. Though I didn't condone her theft, I didn't blame her for hating Cliff's insults.

"Or they'll ruin your hard work," I said, thinking of what Piper said about the grass. "I can't tell you how many times people return videos in damaged cases."

Hattie vanished through the stage's floorboards, leaving the three of us to chat while she retrieved fliers. We meandered off the stage to join Mae in the front row.

"It's how careless people can be," Mae said, shaking her head.

"Right?" I folded my arms and jutted my hip out. I'd seen the soccer moms stand the same way when exchanging bits of drama about the coach or another parent. "Vera, didn't you say Piper trampled your lawn?" She didn't, but Mae talked enough about others that I took a gamble Vera wouldn't remember who said what.

"The shapeshifter from the town over?" Vera asked.

Bingo. She took the bait. Now it was time to reel her in and smell the fishy guilt. Did the real estate agent have a motive to hurt Cliff? And what did Vera know about Piper?

"That's the one," I said, glancing at Mae. She'd scooted to the edge of the seat to stare up at both of us.

Vera put her hands on her hips. "Ah. My little nickname for her is 'Viper.' She traipsed into Bewitcher's Beach and Cliff's life like she owned them. Literally. She even stomped all over a garden at an open house and only offered to fix the flowers after I called her out on it. She doesn't care about anyone but herself." Silky dark locks swayed back and forth at her shoulders as she shook her head.

"Is it true that she dated..." I nodded to the right where the theater's wall connected to Mockbuster. "The victim?"

Mae clucked her tongue. "Absolutely. Right, Vera? You knew Cliff pretty well, with him being your client and all."

"It's true," she said. "And she was half his age."

"Hmm, young and clueless." Mae shook her head. Her half-dragon horns glinted off the stage lights from under her wavy wig. "But if I'm not mistaken, it sounds like *somebody* is jealous."

Mae side-eyed Vera, who blinked at her in confusion.

The half-dragon smiled mischievously. "Tell me if I'm

wrong, but now I'm wondering if you had a tryst-and-kiss with a certain rich and handsome client of yours?"

My mouth gaped as I turned to stare at Vera.

Her sudden retching caught us both off guard. Mae and I leaned away from Vera, who gagged and coughed to contain herself.

"Sorry." She patted her chest. "The thought of kissing Cliff is the most disgusting thing I've ever heard."

I didn't disagree with her. Cliff, while conventionally handsome and stylish with his frosted tips and tall stature, didn't attract me either. Overall, he wasn't the friendliest guy and dripped with arrogance to boot.

"I was wrong to suggest it," Mae said before diving back into the gossip about Piper.

I soaked in the information. Both women exuded the minty smell of curiosity.

Vera tucked her hair behind her ears. "Piper was just clueless. Really, you can't blame the girl. Cliff's the one who should have known better."

I tossed in a gasp, playing as if clueless myself. "Do you think Piper's the one who attacked him?" Hopefully, the bold question would get the ball rolling and shift this clique into a conversation full of clues.

"I wouldn't put it past her," Vera said, nodding along. I found my foot tapping to the rhythm of her head. I froze it and squeezed my legs together as if that'd keep my impatience in check.

"It's not the first time she's dated a rich man around here. Remember Taylor? The lawyer?" Mae added.

We both hummed in agreement. Then we fell silent, recalling the crazy lawsuit. Taylor had won an enormous case for a client accused of using a telepathy spell to win a poker game. He'd cited the long-believed legend that Bewitcher's

Beach protected all supernaturals from being tricked, attacked, or discovered by hunters. In fifty years, not a single supernatural had suffered those fates, and that sealed the deal for the jury to accept the legend as truth.

"Poor Cliff," I said. "It's chilling how sudden his death was.

"I heard the rumor of the videotape curse. Any truth behind it?" Vera arched her eyebrow. The scent of mint still filled my nose, as strongly as if I were brushing my teeth. Another, more muted smell mingled with it, but I couldn't identify the aroma beneath all the curiosity in our conspiratorial circle.

Questions bubbled up inside me like a shaken can of soda. If I opened my mouth, I might pop and spill thoughts and theories all over a suspect. I held my breath, suppressing the urge to ask everything. *Where were you when Cliff died? Is your dislike for Piper deeper than a few smashed flowers?* If I didn't respond to Vera's loaded question, the rumors would only grow.

"Definitely not," I said, breathless. "Others would be hurt too. Cliff was attacked, and my instinct tells me it was personal. Do you know if he had any enemies? Was that why he wanted to move here? Maybe he heard about the legend?" I clamped my jaw shut after the third question. If only I could learn to wait, these casual interviews would stay casual.

Vera raised her eyebrows, wrinkling her forehead at the widow's peak of her chocolate hair.

A resounding gasp echoed from Mae's throat. The theater's acoustics caught the sound and carried it to the far corners. If I'd succeeded at nothing else, at least casting Mae was a win. She suited the role of the dramatic mother perfectly.

"If Cliff was supernatural, and murdered, that means our half-century of safety is over," she said.

"That's just a legend, Mae," I said. Our circle of gossip and judgment expanded with Hattie approaching. The effort to solidify enough and carry the fliers left her slumped and breathless. I quickly took them off her hands.

Mae stood and put a fist on her hips, mirroring Vera as they both stared at me. "For a werewolf who moved here *because* of the legend's protection, you're sure skeptical now."

"I didn't move here for that. I simply heard Bewitcher's Beach was a good place to raise kids," I said as I distributed a handful of fliers to the two cast members.

Mae hummed her disbelief and turned her attention to Vera. "I, for one, certainly want to know if Cliff was supernatural and if the protection is broken. Dr. Pitt will need to prepare if supernaturals start getting hurt."

Vera shrugged, attempting nonchalance, but I caught the sudden aversion of her gaze. Instead of looking at us and indulging in gossip, she kept her eyes on the stage's floorboards.

"I'd ask Dr. Pitt," she said, still looking down. "Cliff worked out of his clinic a few times, and they were best friends once. From what I've heard, anyway." She held up the fliers that announced the date the tickets went on sale. "Time to spread these around. I'll see you ladies later."

Her silky hair swayed like a waterfall as she hurried up the aisle to the double doors. The smell of cinnamon lingered in her wake. It wasn't quite the spice of a liar's aroma, but Vera definitely didn't share everything she knew. The troubled feeling of carrying a secret came with the scent of fish. Why did the mention of Dr. Pitt unsettle her so quickly?

Don't say it, don't say it, don't say it.

"Do you know if Dr. Pitt had a motive to hurt Cliff?" *Son of a witch! Ever heard of subtlety, Noema?* I silently scolded myself while jogging after her.

She flicked her hair over her shoulder and glanced at me. "I know they were super competitive. I don't know much about motives, but I think when a guy dates his friend's ex, it gets dicey. Even when he's the one who dumped her."

"Wait... Piper and Pitt?" My ears turned forward.

Vera's pale lips spread into the same smile I'd seen on Mae just before she shared a juicy bit of gossip. "That, too. Really, I guess it was Viper who drew the short straw both times. Honestly, I can't believe Cliff didn't make better romantic choices given the example of marriage he grew up with."

This confirmed everything I'd heard about Piper June, the young shapeshifter who went after older men with big...wallets.

"Did you know his parents?" Mae asked as she bustled up to us. "Will they be moving here too? I trust you'll let me assess them before they buy a house near one of my rentals?"

"Oh, I think they passed away," Vera said, her voice cracking slightly. How well had she known her client?

Before I could ask, the double doors shut behind Vera, and all the smells of her various emotions vanished with the sudden rush of salty sea air.

The gossip left me drained and needing a night off. I took a deep breath, enjoying the theater's familiar old smells, from the stained oak stage to the lingering scent of popcorn. I promised myself I'd take a break this weekend—just me and the kids.

CHAPTER 14
BE KIND, REWIND

THE SCENT of freshly-cut grass refreshed me like a glass of ice-cold water. Even with my involvement in an ongoing murder investigation, my concern for the shop's dwindling business, and the upcoming play, I refused to miss my children's soccer game. Plus, the scent of the soccer field gave me the break I needed from the minty, spicy, and sour smells of negative emotions.

All four pups pulled on their cleats while I popped open a lawn chair. Squeaks poked his head out of the neon fanny pack attached to my waist. Twitching whiskers and a tiny nose were all I could see through the open zipper. Carefully, I scooped him from the pack and placed him on my shoulder where he could watch the game.

I took another long whiff of fresh air from the breeze that swirled in the town square. The earthy scent of the damp grass filled me with anticipation for the game. As a werewolf full of energy, I loved anything that involved running. Physical activity was how we werewolves stayed sane. If only I could run and write at the same time, I'd be unstoppable.

That idea sent me my imagination into overdrive. If my life

were a science fiction movie, I'd invent a machine I could use to write and run at the same time. But I supposed my reality more closely matched a comedy. I imagined myself as a wolf running on my hind legs while balancing a notebook and pen in my paws. The ridiculous image sparked a laugh until a shout pulled me from the daydream.

The kids' coach called for the players to gather. He waved a crooked arm toward the left end of the field.

"Good luck and break a leg!" I called after them. I cringed and wanted to rescind the latter suggestion. With the way Jovi ran, slightly sideways, I worried he *would* break a leg. And considering how aggressively Halen and Dio played the game, they could break someone else's leg with one kick of their heavy paws. Stupid superstition nagged at me like an itch behind the ear. "Scratch that last part. Absolutely no leg breaking!" I added, covering my superstitious butt.

Three mothers standing beside me turned and gave me quizzical looks. I forced a cringey smile and casually waved as if fanning the awkwardness away. They went back to their conversation.

More parents arrived with their players. Pretty soon, the smell of the fresh grass was drowned by banana cream pie, or rather, the scent of delighted excitement.

Parents set up lawn chairs and umbrellas and dragged coolers onto the field. Finally, the game began. Players of all sorts ran up and down the field. The pups kicked harder and ran faster than some of the other children. The fairy players matched their speed with the help of buzzing wings, while twin gargoyle girls, both thick, stony, and tough, blocked the goals as they played on opposing teams. The human and shapeshifter players used their deft, agile limbs to their advantage. Easily, they tricked their opponents by slipping the ball side to side or with other impressive footwork. Each person, no matter their fur or wings or lack thereof, had particular skills that only improved with plenty of practice.

My eyes locked onto the black and white ball, and I enjoyed every minute of the fast-paced game. When Dio passed to Stevie, I cheered for her to get it. Instead of the ball, she went after a bumblebee that buzzed by. If Stevie wasn't the fastest runner on the team, the coach might have benched her for getting too easily distracted. Thankfully, a human boy on their team swooped in and snagged the ball. With his dancing feet, he passed it to Halen, who kicked it into the goal.

I nearly fell out of my chair as I howled and cheered at the impressive score. I'd scooted to the edge of the seat and leaned forward to get the best view. When I stood, the chair fell over and folded shut.

The whooping and hollering of supportive spectators and proud parents died down. Every so often, one of the three women peeked at me with cautious curiosity.

Squeaks grunted. I tilted my head to meet his beady gaze.

"Are you thinking what I'm thinking?" I whispered. I'd spent enough time with Squeaks that I noticed when his reactions matched my emotions. If I was scared, he'd run and hide. When I got angry, he'd grunt or rattle his tail. And in my moments of happiness, the little mouse always chirped or pointed his ears to the sky.

Squeaks carefully lifted himself to his hind legs, using my shoulder bone as a place to balance. He tucked his nose under his forepaws as if hiding. But I didn't want to hide. The ladies' conversation seemed directed at me, and that got under my fur.

Of course, if I believed the VHS tapes from Mockbuster were a threat to my family, I'd sure as heck return them and refuse to rent more.

"There's only one thing to do," I told Squeaks. "We need to reassure them there's no curse." When I met his gaze again, I caught the slight dip of his chin. The tiny mouse seemed to nod in agreement, but the little hiccup that followed said he'd snuck a sip of my Diet Pepsi.

I drew in another whiff of grass and banana cream pie before lifting my chin and marching the few steps over to the group of women.

"Hi Delia, Celeste, Missy," I said, nodding to each of them as I stood just outside their triangle.

Delia's single, half-fairy wing flattened against her back to make room for me. Warmth filled my heart as a sudden but fleeting feeling of home came and went. For a moment, I felt like part of a pack. Bewitcher's Beach gave us a place to live, but an empty space in my heart still longed for a home with a family I couldn't remember—if I ever had one.

Celeste smiled at me. As a half-vampire, her single fang poked out of her lip. She managed to exist in the sunlight as long as a giant hat covered her face and plenty of fabric protected her skin. Like the other partial-supernatural women, Missy's impossible beauty revealed the siren in her mostly-human bloodline.

Despite their friendly expressions, the smell of ammonia stung my nostrils. I wrinkled my nose and tried to ignore their fear of me—or rather, their fear of the rumor surrounding me and my shop.

"I've missed discussing rom coms with you, Delia," I said and then nodded at Celeste and Missy. "And predicting which Disney movie would be our kids' newest obsession."

Delia's wing fluttered. "It's just—" She glanced at the others before meeting my gaze. "We're a little nervous..." She tilted forward, leaning closer to the center of the circle until her can of Arizona tea almost spilled in the grass. Her voice dropped to a conspiratorial whisper. "That is, we don't want to risk..." Her words trailed off again.

Celeste cleared her throat and spoke up. "You understand what it takes to keep our babies safe."

"Oh, of course!" I said. I met their hoarse whispers with a cheerful voice. "But I can assure you, there's no—"

Missy's hand shot to her mouth, where her fingertips hovered over her lips in silent shock.

"There's no risk," I finished, careful not to use the "C" word that started the rumor.

"How can you be sure?" Celeste asked, the most level-headed of the group. Missy's brow twisted in concern while Delia's wing fanned me with its buzzing flickers.

I nodded across the field and at the shop. "Well, my pups and I watch the tapes all the time, and we're as healthy as a centaur. Also, Cliff rented a lot of movies from me, but we don't even know if he watched them."

Missy and Delia seemed to relax. Celeste gnawed on her lower lip with her fang.

"So the tapes weren't played?" she asked.

For a moment, I thought I saw Mockbuster's neon *open* sign turn on. While it remained dark, I realized it was my mood that had brightened. Why hadn't I thought to check if the tapes were played? Based on his past behavior, I knew Cliff was not the type of customer who chose kindness and rewound the VHS tapes before returning them. In fact, I had a record of no-rewind fees all over his account. Not once had he taken the choice to be kind and prepare the tape for the next renter.

If none of the films he'd rented needed rewinding, it proved he didn't watch the videos. Giddy excitement bubbled up inside of me, and the delicious sweetness of banana cream pie filled my nose.

I could spread that important piece of information all around town. Pretty soon, Bewitcher's Beach would know my video tapes were safe and curse-free!

The coach's whistle screeched, and Delia nearly jumped into my arms with the help of her buzzing wing.

"Noema?" Celeste said with a tilt of her head.

"Um," I stuttered. I didn't want to lie, so I did the next best thing—offer a promise. "I don't think they were played. But I'll find out and let you know ASAP."

With that, Celeste straightened and took a sip of her cold tea. She seemed satisfied and my excitement returned. If I could convince moms, I could convince anyone.

The women turned their attention to the field, and I returned to my seat, unfolding it before I sat down in a daze.

"How did I forget to check that?" I asked. I'd said it to myself, but it was Squeaks who had the answer.

He chirped until I tilted my head to see him. Once he had my attention, he raised on his hind legs and crossed his forepaws over his furry chest. His beady eyes narrowed and he released a series of grunts, mimicking a grumpy person. After that, he crawled closer to my face and then pushed his little snout against my cheek like a kiss. He repeated the entire process until a lightbulb went on in my head.

"The sheriff!" I said, pointing to him with my other arm like this was a game of Charades. "Hey, wait a minute. He's never kissed me." I shot the mouse a sharp look.

Again, Squeaks lived up to his name with several victorious squeaks.

"You're right, though. I didn't forget to check the tapes because I don't have them. Sett took them for evidence." I said aloud what the mouse couldn't. I leaned back in the creaking lawn chair and peered past a group of parents hovering over a cooler. Though I couldn't see the police station from here, I looked to that side of town while I formed a plan.

"How can I get the evidence?" I asked. "Sett won't let me march into the station and demand access to it. He seems to think I'll spontaneously combust if I help with the investigation."

Squeaks chirped at that, and I took it as a laugh, though I didn't find Sett's overprotective behavior very funny. I appreciated his eyes on the community, but I believed Bewitcher's Beach would be a lot safer if he accepted help.

"Wait," I said as I scooped Squeaks from my shoulder and cupped him in my palms. "I can't march in there, but *you* can."

The mouse tilted his tiny head and his whiskers tickled the heel of my palm.

"Don't worry, I'll show you what a tape looks like when it's rewound."

With that, we turned our attention to the game until the final goal was scored. The afternoon was a whirlwind of shared pizza parties with both teams. Though our team had lost by one goal, both sides celebrated together at Roller Shakes with plenty of pepperoni slices, half-drunk milkshakes, and arcade games.

When the coaches offered to buy skating tickets for the players, the teams cheered louder than when they'd scored goals. The pups exchanged their cleats for roller skates and took a spin around the rink. While they skated, I slipped out and hurried to Mockbuster.

Quickly, I showed Squeaks that a rewound VHS tape shows all of the white film on the left side of the tape's two windows. He chirped once when I held up a rewound tape and twice for one that wasn't rewound. Since he passed the test, I grabbed a bag of Orange Creme Savers and headed for the police station.

Once inside, I saw Sett at his desk with the phone pressed to his ear. He sighed and repeatedly told the person on the other line, "No, I can't arrest someone just because they didn't want to pet your dog, Miss." With him distracted,

I unzipped the fanny pack and let Squeaks crawl down my pant leg.

Sett finally acknowledged me with a curt smile and a finger in the air.

"No rush," I mouthed. I pointed to the bag of candy and approached the desk. From there, I could see Squeaks slip into the closet by the bathroom. To avoid suspicion, I fixed my gaze on Sett.

I pricked my ears and carefully listened for any sounds from Squeaks. With my ears turned forward, I caught the faint skitter of his tiny paws on the linoleum. The sound came to a halt. I assumed he'd crawled onto a table, or inside a box, or wherever Sett kept evidence from an ongoing investigation. After a moment of silence from the mouse, I heard chewing sounds.

In a box it is.

Sett finally stood and hung up the phone on the wall. He eased into the chair and rolled it back to his desk.

"It's nice to see you, Noema," he said. His slate eyes brightened as he reached for the bag of candy.

Squeaks chirped, and the sheriff froze. My heart skipped a beat. If Sett found out I'd sent my animal friend to tamper with evidence, he might toss me into the tiny holding cell in the back of the station.

"Did you hear that?" Sett asked. Like cracks in concrete, his stony brow wrinkled.

I held my breath. *Please be rewound, please be rewound...*

"Hmm." Sett shrugged and picked up the bag.

The crinkle of plastic almost drowned out the sound of Squeaks' second chirp. Cliff had watched the movies, or at least one of them. Thankfully, the rustle of the candy bag made Squeaks's chirp impossible to hear if you weren't listening for it.

"This is so kind of you, Noema," Sett said, opening the bag. "I was just going to come by the shop to see if you'd gotten another shipment of these."

"Well, there it is," I said as I rocked back and forth from my heels to the balls of my feet. Innocently, I clasped my hands behind my back until I realized I looked like a guilty child trying to hide cookies. I forced myself to relax.

"Thank you!" Sett's genuine appreciation temporarily melted my frustration.

I couldn't use an unwatched tape to prove to the town that Cliff hadn't died from cursed movies.

But thanks to Sett's gratitude, for the second time today, the hole in my heart filled. In fact, the warm feeling was twice as strong as it had been earlier.

The police station wasn't my home, and Sett wasn't family. But the joy in his eyes at the sight of me was exactly how a pack member looks at another pack member. I couldn't break my gaze from him, even when a movement caught the corner of my eye.

I assumed Squeaks slipped out from underneath the crack at the bottom of the closet door. Moments later, tiny paws tugged the back of my pant leg.

My heart jumped when I realized Squeaks would expose himself if he tried to crawl for the fanny pack.

"You're welcome," I blurted before I spun around and scooped up the mouse.

I slipped him into the fanny pack and shoved through the door, hoping the sheriff didn't see my tiny partner in crime.

Though I hadn't given Sett time to respond, I glanced back, catching his gaze before the door swung shut.

The joy was still there, in the faint curl of his lips and the light in his eyes.

Like a movie, maybe even a rom com, I strolled and relished

the feeling of Sett's gratitude with heat on my cheeks. Crisp leaves swirled about my feet as I carefully avoided the protruding cobblestones and pumpkins along the sidewalk. Black lanterns hanging outside each shop swayed in the gentle wind. Bewitcher's Beach was decorated for Halloween as soon as the first leaf hit the ground, and I soaked in every minute of it.

The warmth lingered in my chest until I returned to the roller rink, where the air conditioner blasted too heavily.

I found a booth at the edge of the rink and watched my pups skate in circles. Stevie zipped faster than everyone else while Jovi held onto the wall with both hands. Squeaks popped out from the pack and scratched at the zipper to get my attention. When I looked, he made the 'half-time' motion the coaches at the kids' soccer games did and squeaked twice to tell me only half of the movie was watched. It made sense. Piper was seen arguing with Cliff in the lobby, which meant they probably started fighting before the movie ended. Half was still enough to trigger townspeople's superstitions.

I sighed and tried to focus on my plans for Monday, when I'd get a chance to talk with Piper. My mind kept wandering back to the sound of Sett's voice when he'd thanked me for the candy... and that unique smell of citrus mixed with vanilla.

CHAPTER 15
THROWN TO THE WOLVES

ON MONDAY, I killed time by refreshing myself on the clues I'd gathered.

While I waited for Piper's appointment, I sat at Mockbuster's front desk and mused over the clues. After hours of writing with a numb butt, I'd become accustomed to the stool and deemed it my brainstorming spot.

Squeaks curled in my lap, snoring softly to the sound of my voice as I mulled over the information aloud.

"Mae is out. Vera doesn't have a motive. Dr. Pitt dated the same woman as Cliff."

Though I'd closed the shop early, it didn't matter; nobody came to the door. Passersby didn't so much as walk by the windows, choosing instead to give the curse a wide berth. In the last half hour alone, I'd witnessed three people step into the gutter rather than risk walking too close to Mockbuster.

I sighed. Sett had said investigations move slowly, but I'd hoped to have clearer answers by now. At least clear enough to prove poison wasn't because of a cursed video.

"Speaking of which," I mumbled and leaned over to scoop a handful of VHS tapes from the return bin. I fell into the rhythm of opening each case and checking that the correct video was inside.

"Motives are the key," I said, circling Dr. Pitt's motive. *Jealousy?* I dragged the crayon to Piper's motive and underlined it several times until the crayon snapped. Broken flecks of red wax rolled off the paper as I huffed and puffed them away. I wiped the page of the remaining pieces and stared.

Was Piper and Cliff's breakup related to Dr. Pitt? If so, it seemed odd she'd return to his clinic for care. Unless it wasn't for his care but to...

"Settle a score," I breathed. The first time I'd met Piper, she overshared with that one phrase. Did she hate Cliff for ending their relationship? And was it somehow Dr. Pitt's fault? Or did she have a vendetta against all her ex-boyfriends?

I reached for *Scream*'s case and popped it open. Sweeping blue font labeled the VHS tape inside.

"The Swan Princess?" I shrieked, reading the title aloud. Squeaks awoke with a start and dove off of my lap. He landed on the desk with a thud and scrambled for protection from the shock. His little body squeezed beneath the keyboard where the small hinges propped it up.

How did the movie Cliff had rented end up in the case Piper returned? It was proof enough for me. Piper had watched half a movie with Cliff that night, and then he'd ended up dead with the tapes in his hands.

A lump gathered in my throat, and I squinted at the clock on the back wall. I'd lost track of time, too invested in the mess of theories in my notebook. The afternoon was almost over, which meant Piper had already arrived and Dr. Pitt was in danger. If, in fact, he was next on her ex-boyfriends murder rampage. And with the muffins she'd pay him with, she had somewhere to stash the poison.

I grabbed the phone and jammed the buttons.

"Pick up, pick up."

The professional recording on his answering machine blared. I dialed again but he didn't pick up.

"Son of a witch." I squeezed the phone so hard my fingers ached. I tried Sett's line, hoping the sheriff was in his office.

A deep voice answered. "Bewitcher's Beach police—"

"Sett, it's Noema," I interrupted as words stumbled over one another. "Piper is going to murder Dr. Pitt at the clinic right now." It sounded silly as the suspicions slipped from me. "Okay, that might be dramatic. But I've heard she dated both him and Cliff and now that Cliff was offed...I'm worried for Pitt's safety"

Maybe Mae's drama had rubbed off on me, but if I didn't pressure Sett, he'd drag his feet. He relied too heavily on the rules to "keep people safe" when, in this situation, it'd only result in a second dead doctor.

"Whoa, whoa, whoa. Back up. What makes you say this?"

"Dr. Pitt could be next on her list because he dumped her. Cliff died after Piper and he had a fight, maybe a break up. It all made sense after I heard them talking in the alley, and she told me she'd come here to settle a score. Also, she works at The Home Cheapo, which probably gave her the idea to use weed killer to spice up her muffins. Got it?" I gasped for breath.

"I'm lost..."

"Just meet me at the clinic so we can stop her. It could be all speculation, or we could save another one of Piper's ex-boyfriends from danger!" My gaze locked on the clock. Another minute ticked, signaling Piper's appointment had begun.

Before Sett disagreed with my plan of ambush, I hung up. I hopped to my feet, gave Squeaks a quick scratch under the chin to apologize for startling him, and then ran out the door.

People milled about Bewitcher's Beach. The one-way

breeze gently tugged brittle leaves from the branches and swirled them in a sky dance.

The calm environment only set me more on edge. Piper said she'd come to town after work—a place that stocked plenty of paraquat for all people's weedy and murder-y needs. I felt silly running across town, but it was better to be safe—and silly —than sorry.

I narrowed my eyes and focused on the clinic. The rough-hewn brick building didn't match the colorful shops and Roller Shakes' neon sign next door.

Silhouettes moved in the front window, and my heart leaped. I recognized the hulking shape of Dr. Pitt's figure and Piper's curls. He held something in his hand that could be a medicine bottle...or a muffin. Could it be poisoned? Or was I getting in my head?

Thoughts of my late husband came back and how he'd fallen ill from the very thing that was supposed to save him. As a werewolf, he had been poisoned by antibiotics with traces of silver. And now, maybe I was too sensitive to the thought of anything relating to poison.

My human feet didn't move fast enough. I dropped to all fours, shifting with the energy of adrenaline. In my wolf body, the clothes slipped right off. I left them behind in the gutter at the edge of the park, and my paws hit the cobblestone.

I bounded across the street, twice as fast now on four legs. When I jumped, the door handle gave under the weight of my paws, and it flew open.

The two-room clinic left little space for privacy. The moment I pushed through the door, I twisted to the right and faced the little examination room past the front desk. Both Piper's and Dr. Pitt's heads snapped to me.

A paper plate piled high with muffins balanced precariously in his hand. The sight of the poisonous pastries kicked my instincts into high gear.

I bounded into the exam room and used the force of my hind legs to launch myself forward. Paws connected to the plate, and the muffins went flying. Blueberry pastries rained down, each tumbling to the floor with a dozen thuds.

The sound of Piper's shriek sent my stomach into my throat. I whipped around, bared my teeth, and released a low growl at the lady with the laced muffins.

Dr. Pitt stepped back with eyes bulged and spine pressed against the little counter. Of course, it was me he stared at, not knowing I'd just rescued him from certain death...maybe. The nervous doctor's chest heaved with every breath.

A shadow darkened the exam room. A tall, thick figure appeared in the doorway, suddenly making the space look like a doll's house. Dr. Pitt already took up half the room, but Sett barely fit through the doorway.

A smell I could only describe as pineapple pizza filled the room. I recognized it as confusion. The scent overpowered the shock and fear that'd stung my nose.

"What the haunt is going on?" Sett asked. Despite the gravity of the situation, he only blinked at us. I barked, but he made no move to apprehend the killer.

I showed my canines again, nodding my head toward Piper. *What are you waiting for? Get her!* Piper mirrored the doctor, frozen.

Sett's eyes shifted from me to the murderer, and then his gaze finally fell to the muffins scattered across the linoleum.

"First, is everyone okay?" he asked.

They exchanged glances and cautiously nodded. If I knew Sett, I knew what came next. Instead of taking the quickest route by having Piper try one of her own muffins, he'd kindly ask her to come to the station. There, questioning could take hours. Hours of opportunity for her to think up clever excuses and threaded lies.

I didn't know if Piper was capable of such manipulation, but it had worked with the bicycle thief. Sett had followed the slow-moving rules, which meant three more bikes had disappeared before he confirmed and arrested the perpetrator.

I whined and scratched at the floor by a muffin.

Because of his sigh, I knew he understood. He ducked into the room, and stone scraped against stone as he crouched and scooped a pastry into his hand.

"Is-is s-something wrong?" Dr. Pitt asked, wiping his brow with an old-fashioned and too-small handkerchief. Like his umbrella, it didn't fit the size of his body and looked like a miniature tissue in his hand.

Sett cleared his throat, glancing at me before standing. With the muffin held out, he turned to Piper. "Is there any reason I shouldn't take a bite of this?"

"Um." She curled her still-swollen, but less painful-looking, lip under. "It fell on the floor?"

Sett inspected the smashed muffin with narrowed eyes. It reminded me of the poisoned apple in Snow White's palm. If he took a bite, I expected him to collapse like the princess. In a movie, the pastry would roll across the floor to Piper's Mary Jane shoes, and she'd smash it under her heel.

Life didn't play out like a movie. Instead, Sett apologized—he actually apologized—to a murderer!

"I'm sorry, but I'm going to ask again. Aside from a little dirt, are these muffins safe to eat?"

Piper nodded, her curls springing with the movement.

I barked and hopped with my front paws. Wolf nails clicked against the linoleum, but it wasn't enough to get Sett's attention. Before I could stop him, he bit into the muffin.

"Do I have to pay if he eats them all?" Piper pointed to the muffin in the sheriff's hand.

Dr. Pitt ran his palm over his bald head. "No, no. Though I'm not s-sure I understand what's happening."

Piper shrugged. "No idea. I'm going to head out, if that's okay. I have to run over to the rental shop."

Clearly, she didn't recognize me in my wolf form. Unlike shapeshifters, I didn't resemble my other face when I changed. While a werecreature fully transformed to another animal, shapeshifters shared similar features across all forms they took. I scoffed, but it came out more like a snuffle—a cross between a sneeze and sniff. *You can keep your two dollars.*

Both men nodded, and Piper slipped out the door behind Sett.

I whined, and my forepaws bounced up and down. A muffin smashed between my claws where it belonged. Not in Sett's mouth.

The sheriff popped the rest of the baked good into his mouth. He swallowed, and I didn't breathe. When nothing happened, his wings lifted with his shoulders in a shrug.

"Noema was concerned for your safety," he said to Dr. Pitt. "Since another doctor became a victim, it was right of her to worry about you. But it seems all is well."

The doctor only glanced between us, brow furrowed in thick, rolling wrinkles that reminded me of his bulldog form.

"So-so it's true? Cliff was killed?"

The weird, but not unpleasant, scent of pineapple pizza confusion gave way to the burn of ammonia. The smell swelled, and I couldn't stop the series of sneezes that ensued. My snout involuntarily flung about until I pawed at my nose to make it stop.

"Everything is under investigation," Sett said vaguely. "If

you have any information, be sure to stop by the station and let me know."

The stench grew stronger, and the doctor dabbed at his forehead again.

Why did Dr. Pitt expel the aroma of fear so suddenly at the mention of Cliff? Sure, the doctor was often nervous, but the rising stench far surpassed ordinary anxiety. I'd been so sure it was Piper. What if Piper was the plot twist? She could be the surprising but inevitable part of the film where her role shifts. She looked like the murderer because she dated the victim, but she also dated the victim's best friend, and he was alive and well.

I took a whiff of the doctor's scent. Only the icky smell of fear came from him. I wrinkled my nose. I struggled to picture the nervous, sweaty, stressed Dr. Pitt premeditating murder. But jealousy, or perhaps revenge, did strange things to a person.

"Can I talk to you, Noema? Outside?" Sett nodded at the front window.

I barked and pawed at the counter where fresh hospital gowns sat folded in a neat stack.

From one werecreature to the next, Dr. Pitt understood immediately. He shuffled from the room in a hurry to give me privacy. Sett watched him go then turned to me, blinking.

I barked again, hoping he'd get the point. *Unless you understand wolf speak, we're not talking.* And talking was what I planned to do with Dr. Pitt as soon as I got changed.

"Oh! Right. Right." Sett dipped out of the door and closed it behind him.

I dragged the curtain shut with my mouth. Once I transformed into my human self, I slipped the gown over my head and emerged from the exam room, eager to ask the doctor a few questions.

"Hey, Dr. Pitt." I approached the tall counter at the reception area. Dr. Pitt only employed a secretary in the mornings when appointments were in higher demand. "Have you ever treated a poisoned patient before?"

"Noema..." Sett started.

I ignored him, thinking of Fitz's request and the smell of the suspect. "I ask because I've got the four pups, you know, and they get into all kinds of junk. Stevie ate my lipstick once."

"Well, uh." He rubbed the back of his neck and took a seat behind the computer. The chair squeaked beneath his weight. "Lipstick won't hurt her in small quantities."

If he was guilty, his intense fear made sense. Dr. Pitt could have killed his friend in a fit of jealous rage for dating his ex-girlfriend. I tapped my fingers on the counter. I hated talking around the real question. Now, with fear overwhelming him, it was the perfect time for a confession to slip—or so I'd observed in movies.

"What about gardening supplies? You garden, right?" I pointed to the boxes of daisies that decorated the outside of the windows. "Have you ever known anyone to swallow, say, weed killer? Maybe a friend of yours?"

"Noema," Sett said. The tips of his rough fingers brushed over my arm. I slipped from his grip before he could pull me away.

"Or was Cliff not really your friend anymore? Not after you both fell for the same woman?"

Dr. Pitt's chest rose and fell rapidly. He scooted to the edge of the chair and dropped his head into his palms. The ammonia stench grew stronger and stronger and combined with the pungent stink of rotten milk. I almost dry heaved from the mixed smell of fear and guilt.

"Oh no, oh no," he repeated.

"Noema!" Sett was the one barking now. The odor of burnt wood and smoke suddenly overwhelmed the other smells.

Anger beat fear in the fight for my nose's attention. For once, I'd caught Sett's emotional scent.

A strong, stony hand grabbed my elbow. Before I could get Dr. Pitt's confession, Sett gently pulled me to the door.

He quickly pushed it open, let go of me, and held his hand out as if to say *ladies first*.

Though he'd already released his hold, I yanked my arm further away from him for good measure and marched through.

"What are you doing?" I spun around as soon as we stood on the sidewalk outside. "Didn't you smell his guilt? I mean, did you see it? He was sweating worse than a wolf on the beach!"

"This is not how investigations are conducted." He spoke in a stern voice as if scolding me. It enraged me, but I swallowed the urge to fight back. The focus needed to turn back to the doctor.

I'd come here to expose a suspect. And though it wasn't who I'd thought, Dr. Pitt might have revealed the truth right then and there. Thoughts of people avoiding Mockbuster may have pushed me to be too impulsive. But Fitz had wanted me to help sniff out the killer and close the case before the festival, after all.

Sett folded his arms and faced me, as solid and rough around the edges as the brick building itself. "Have a level of respect for people who've lost a loved one in this way. Murder is sudden and brutal, and the doctors had been friends for a long time."

I pointed to the glass door that read *Ralph Pitt, M.D.* "But he was acting so—"

"Sad? Scared? You were interrogating him after you interrupted his daily routine and left a mess in his office. If he's guilty, I will know. But as I said, these things take time. If I question suspects too early, they know I'm watching them, and it gives them an opportunity to think up lies and hide evidence."

"But they can do that if you don't question them too."

"I *did* question him. Dr. Pitt is acting guilty because he had an affair with Cliff's wife before they'd separated."

"Wait—what?" I recalled Vera's words. *That, too*, she'd said. "They both got with the same two women, twice in a row?"

Sett nodded. "It seems that way."

"Yikes." I eyed him. The faint oily smell of fish told me he wasn't sharing everything he knew. I hated that he thought he needed to protect me. Solving the murder was what protected me and the rest of the town. So why not let me help? "You know more about the case."

"Look, Noema, I know you want to help." He rubbed the back of his neck with his palm and sighed. The fur on my ears stood up, defensive. "But you're putting yourself in danger. What if Dr. Pitt or Piper was the killer? What if they both were?"

"But—"

He held up his hand to stop me. "Bewitcher's Beach has never seen a murder. They're scared, so they blame a curse. And let's not upset them any more, because spooked people do dangerous things."

I gnawed on my lip. The urge to argue bubbled in my chest like a shaken Pepsi bottle, ready to fizz out. But he was right.

The curse started *because* of fear. Bad things thrive on fear, and the people here didn't know how to deal with it. Not after fifty years of believing in the protection of a witch's spell.

The sheriff nodded at Mockbuster. "Walk with me," he said. "I'll tell you his alibi. It's about as good as something you'd see in a movie."

Frustration burned like flames caged by my ribs. Sett had interrupted my quest for a confession. As mad as I was, the twinkle in his slate eyes intrigued me. He knew I couldn't resist a good real-life moment that matched a movie scene.

For now, it squelched the urge to argue.

He slipped his hands into his coat's pockets and started walking. I groaned and hurried to cross the street in his wake.

A breeze blew up from the shore, snaking through the scattered shops behind us. It swept all lingering smell of emotions away. The sting of seawater brought with it the chill of the northern beach. The salty air mixed with the aroma of apple pie from every shop that burned seasonal candles and beckoned buyers inside.

The hospital gown billowed at my thighs, nearly exposing my backside to the entire town. I tugged the gown lower and hurried to grab my clothes on the edge of the grass.

For the second time that month, Sett escorted me across town while I wore no pants.

CHAPTER 16
HIDING IN PLAIN SIGHT

EXACTLY THREE DAYS LATER, I stood pantsless in front of the entire town again. Well, pantsless, but not naked. I stood still while Mae mused at the handsewn dress she'd created for Vera's role in the play. Curious eyes peered through Mockbuster's window as they waited for auditions to begin.

For the second time since the rumor of the curse began, a crowd gathered outside the shop. People lined the cobblestone, gabbing, laughing, and exchanging practice lines while they waited for the doors to open that evening. Many eyed the costume ideas Mae had hung along the wire movie racks.

"I, for one, agree with Sett," Hattie said. Since her short hair and flapper dress were forever frozen in the style from the moment she died, I got stuck testing the costumes. "We've got a performance to focus on, and your impulsiveness does nobody any favors."

Leave it to a ghost to deliver the blunt truth.

I snorted and tugged at the skirt's too-short hem. Mae designed it for Vera's character, but Vera didn't show up at the Saturday audition, having already secured a spot in the play.

"I don't do any favors? Ha! Tell that to the seven people

who got their bikes back after I sniffed out the thief." My gaze followed Hattie as she flitted about, organizing stacks of script copies on the front desk.

Mae nodded and instructed me to spin around. Her spiky tail flicked right through Hattie, who hurried to hang paper signs at the end of each aisle.

For the role of the male main character, line up here.

For the role of the villain, line up here.

For the role of the female main character's brother, line up here.

So on and so forth until she taped the last sign on the glass door. The final message asked those who weren't selected to work as an extra or volunteer for a backstage project. While in previous years the number of helpers had waned, the allure of a romance story gave Hattie the confidence that people wanted to be involved again.

I'd never understand how anyone grew tired of mysteries. But Hattie had hit a blockbuster idea when she'd suggested I write a romance. Even on the cusp of autumn, love was in the air, apparently.

"Do you feel that energy?" Hattie asked. She balled her hands into fists and shook them for a brief celebration. "What does excitement smell like, Noema?"

"That depends." I slipped my spandex capri pants under the short skirt for an extra layer of coverage. As a person whose natural state was covered in fur, the exposure of bare skin left me chilly and uncomfortable. "Is the excitement coming from the anticipation of something great? Or from the feeling of getting good news?"

Hattie squinted. "Hmm, the first one."

"Ah, then it's the scent of banana cream pie. Something plain that got a delightful makeover."

"I don't envy that nose of yours, Noema." Mae burst into a

raspy laugh. A hundred and fifty years of breathing fire did that to a half-dragon's throat. "My sense of smell is atrocious, and I still have to plug my nose every time I walk past Miss Raven's studio. Did you know she doesn't wear deodorant?"

Leave it to the gossip queen to share something uncomfortably personal about an innocent member of our town. I didn't indulge.

"Okay." Hattie slapped her hands in a silent clap. "We're ready to start the auditions." She marched to the back of the video shop, expecting me to follow her to the theater.

I wiggled the skirt off and handed it to Mae. After unlocking Mockbuster's door, I hurried to follow Hattie.

Inside the theater, four wolf pups and one teenage ghost played hide and seek. Bette covered her eyes and counted. What my kids didn't know was that a ghost could see right through her own hands.

They busied themselves while Hattie and I stood in front of the stage. Mae agreed to bring the hopeful actors in one-by-one.

The side door opened, and a swanky siren marched to the middle of the stage. Chanel belted the main character's lines, and then she mimicked a romantic kiss with an imaginary costar.

"I never thought I could love again." She quoted the script, pursing her pouty lips.

"Thank you, Chanel," Hattie said. "We'll let you know by the end of the day. Will you consider a role as an extra if you're not selected?"

Chanel's long, sparkling fingernails raked through her luscious hair. "I suppose."

The next hopeful shuffled to the center of the stage. The timid woman wrung her hands and delivered the lines with a shaky voice. She could have been a troll or a human, the only difference between the two being a slight hunch in the back.

But humans slouched too, like the way she stooped over the script in her hands. Though nerves made her difficult to hear, her accompanying facial expressions impressed Hattie and me.

If this was for a movie, she'd earn the role of the main character. Then, she'd train up her enunciation to become one of the best stage actresses of the year for a tear-jerking comeback story.

"Thank you for scheduling the auditions after dark, and for moving me up the line," Cordelia said. The vampire wiped her palms on her psychedelic blue and purple Roller Shakes polo.

"Of course. Now time to focus," Hattie said, pointing to the script in Cordelia's hand.

Though Cordelia kept wiping sweat on her shirt and pants, she delivered the lines from memory and with impressive facial expressions. We assigned her the role of the main character's twin sister. With another cast member chosen, my script came alive.

A giddy excitement thumped in my chest. In four short weeks, I'd see another one of my stories performed on the stage. Finally, people found excitement in the theater arts again, and it was all thanks to Hattie's persistence. I'd written too many mysteries that followed the same formula and didn't believe I could create a romance.

But Hattie believed.

"Mae, send us the next auditionee," she demanded.

Triton strolled in, arms swaying like broken branches.

"Hello." He gave us each an awkward bow and reached his bony arm to the ceiling. Once he turned his palm to his face, it looked as though he cupped someone else's imaginary head. With enough emotion to give me a sneeze, he delivered a line that didn't appear in my script. "A rose by any other name—"

"Triton, Darling," Mae shouted from the side of the stage. "Read off the script."

He ignored her and bellowed the rest of the famous quote.

Hattie shrugged and let him finish the scene from *Romeo and Juliet*. While he quoted Shakespeare, my mind wandered.

I pictured the alibi Dr. Pitt had given Sett. The doctor said he took private ballroom dancing lessons at Miss Raven's studio that night. Miss Raven confirmed this with a story about the doctor's two left feet. To my surprise, she claimed he took the classes because of Hattie's harsh rejection. He'd auditioned for one of our plays two years earlier, and Hattie swiftly listed his mistakes. According to her, he'd stomped onto the stage and hadn't moved with grace or poise.

Speaking of stomping, a teenage boy sauntered onto the stage.

"Men don't behave like that, Sis," he said, delivering the lines of the main character's younger brother.

His voice faded as my thoughts took over.

I appreciated Dr. Pitt's effort to better his stage presence with the dance lessons. The timeline proved he wasn't involved with Cliff's death, but it still bothered me that he knew the victim and didn't offer help with the investigation. If Dr. Pitt truly stood by the clinic's mission to give people aid, he'd tell us everything he knew about his late best friend's life. Even if it risked his reputation over an affair. Instead, he hid with his guilt and nerves.

What if the killer struck again? The curse wasn't from my videos, but an unsettling danger still existed in Bewitcher's Beach.

Was Dr. Pitt protecting his ex-girlfriend? Piper, Vera, and Cordelia were the only people left on the list without an alibi. As Cliff's realtor, Vera didn't have a strong enough motive. Sure, she'd lost money when he pulled out of a contract, but did that inspire a murder? It made little sense since he was still her client, and a rich one at that. With his next purchase, she'd gain plenty of money. Dead men didn't buy more houses. And if they died with unfinished business and became a ghost, they'd haunted objects of importance, with no need for a house.

"Noema?" Hattie's sharp voice broke through my thoughts. "What did you think of her?"

"Her?" I blinked and trailed my gaze to the double doors where she pointed. A skinny human woman pushed through the doors. A stream of bright light flooded in and blinded me.

"She's fine," I lied. I didn't have a clue whether the hopeful actress had the chops for our main character or not. The fishy smell of my own guilt almost made me gag. I pinched my nose and tried to focus on the stage.

Hattie huffed and shouted for Mae to hold the line.

When she turned to me with folded arms, I knew I was in trouble. "You're still thinking about the investigation, aren't you?"

"Hattie, a man died. He died right in front of my shop, and half the town thinks my videos cursed him. Not only do we deserve answers so we can be safe, but I'm going to lose a ton of business if this doesn't get solved!"

"Right." She nodded, her hair shifting in perfect shiny sheets along the sides of her face. "Solved by law enforcement who are equipped with protective gear and training, not an impatient werewolf."

"Hey! Fitz asked me to help, and there's a murderer on the loose in our town—"

"Right again. Do you think existence as a ghost is fun, Noema? I guarantee you have unfinished business. If this murderer found you, you'd be stuck in the eternal haunt with me. Try mothering four pups when you can barely lift their lunch."

My ears folded back. "I'll be fine."

"Sett just wants to protect you, you know? And I'm beginning to think you throw yourself into danger because the crush is mutual." She pursed her ruby lips, a look of confidence in her words. "And you don't have to impress the mayor to keep your shop open anymore. He knows it's a worthy business."

The smell of new shoes filled my nose—the scent of embarrassment. I turned my head to give my shoulder a sniff and confirm it came from me. Hattie's blunt words had revealed uncomfortable truths before, but they didn't usually embarrass me.

"I don't have crushes. You know what happened to Christopher." My voice cracked with palpable pain. The mention of my late husband silenced her, if only for a moment.

Hattie licked her lips and side-eyed me. "There are safer ways to get a man's attention, you know?"

Blunt as always. What did I expect from her? But this crossed the line. I'd vowed to never care for another man again, not after turning Christopher. He was a happy, healthy man when we met. I never meant to make him a werewolf.

"I'm just saying—"

"Don't." I interrupted, and she clamped her mouth shut. New shoes now smelled like burnt shoes. Anger's smoky scent caused me to cough. "Do *you* know supernaturals can't get attacked within the town's borders?"

Hattie turned her gaze to the stage again. "Ah, the witch legend. Nobody knows if it's true."

"Oh, but it is!" A half-pixie woman said. She stood at the back of the stage, where the acoustics caught every little sound and carried it throughout the theater. Her one wing flitted with nerves, and even that slight buzzing sound echoed around us. Unlike Barney, she didn't obscure her supernatural side, clearly feeling safe enough to be her true self. It was likely all thanks to the legend. "The people who don't believe it are the ones who never saw the spell book. But my mom did, before it vanished."

"Thank you, Dani," Hattie said. "Please, begin your audition."

The half-pixie giggled between lines but otherwise delivered an exemplary performance. It landed her a secure role as the main character's coworker. She half-flew, half-leaped off the stage and paused next to me on her way out.

"Keep looking into the murder," she whispered.

I glanced at Hattie, who was distracted by Mae disrupting the audition. I cocked my head and eyed the woman.

"When Dr. Conflick almost bought my house, he said he might live there with his *lady*," she said. "I assume that meant he planned to get back together with his ex-wife. It breaks my heart that a fellow pixie lost her husband just when they were ready to reunite."

A jolt of energy shot through me. With her support, I felt like the underdog called to solve this crime. If this were a movie, I'd shift into a wolf right now and track the murderer's scent. But I didn't have a trail to follow, and real life carried responsibilities.

"You don't believe the curse?" I asked.

The pixie shook her head. "I believe in the protection spell. If only the gentleman who died had been supernatural, it might have saved him."

Though I knew she couldn't lie, or at least not well because of her ties to her fairy side, I still sniffed for the smell of fish.

She smiled and marched off, leaving no scent in her wake—which meant she believed every word she'd said.

How could I follow up on an investigation when Sett hounded me to leave it alone? I had two suspects without motive and a third who'd skipped the perfect opportunity to strike another ex-boyfriend. But what if Piper only wanted to hurt Cliff? What if she didn't care for Dr. Pitt and truly loved his best friend?

The half-pixie's information shined a new light on the case. This put Piper June, the girl with the access to paraquat, back to the top of the suspect list.

My ears popped up at a familiar voice. I spun and the fur stood on end as Piper stepped into the stage light.

"I decided to try out after all."

Mae stood beside her, patting her shoulder. "Piper's the last one. She's auditioning for the role of the villain."

I coughed, nearly choking on my spit.

Piper's green eyes stared right through me, and the memory of our first encounter came rushing back. She'd said she came to Bewitcher's Beach to settle a score—surely regarding a boyfriend who'd decided to reunite with his ex-wife. Maybe I was wrong about her attack on Dr. Pitt, but that didn't clear her from killing Cliff.

I had to hand it to her, auditioning for the play to get on the town's good side was a genius plan.

"Hiding in plain sight," I mumbled. "Nice try."

I'd find proof. Before she won over the people with her acting skills and homemade muffins, I'd find proof.

You won't get past this nose.

CHAPTER 17
AN AUDITION A DAY
KEEPS THE DOCTOR AWAY

ONE WEEK into rehearsals and half the cast had already memorized their lines. The prognosis for this year's play looked better than Hattie had predicted. Thankfully, the actors and actresses picked up my slack for the late start.

I ran around backstage, discussing cues and character dialogue. Halen trailed me like a lost puppy with his video camera balanced on his shoulder.

"Let me get a close up, Mom!" he said. Squeaks obliged. The mouse poked his nose out of my fanny pack and leaped the few inches to Halen's open palm. Satisfied with that, Halen zoomed the lens close to Squeaks' whiskers. "Do you wish this play was about cheese? It'd be way better than kissing. Bleh."

I ignored them, busy smoothing out a mistake in the script. Just as I approached the star of the show to discuss a change to her penultimate scene, the theater's doors flung open.

A half-dragon-shaped figure filled the doorway. When they stepped into the light, everyone turned to see Mae. Her chest heaved as she fanned her face.

"There's a lurker," she said between breaths. "A stalker, outside Mockbuster!"

The cast buzzed with conversation about murders and curses and all manner of scary rumors and half-truths. I groaned. Why did Mae have to stir up drama? Or was I too casual? Was this lurker also the killer, returned for more violence in front of the rental shop?

If only Sett would let me help, maybe we wouldn't be in this situation. *Please, leave the investigation alone.* I recalled the sheriff's polite demand with a surge of frustration. Still, he'd never said I couldn't observe the suspects left on the list. Good thing the three women ended up with roles in the play and watching rehearsals was part of my job.

Hattie snapped at the cast, demanding they return their attention to the performance. "Noema, will you?" She gestured in the general direction of Mae and the doors. "Please?"

Curious, I obliged and quickly hopped off the stage and into the aisle. The acting resumed with an intense scene where Vera's character held a prop gun to Piper's character's face.

"First, are you okay?" I asked Mae when I reached the back row.

She nodded. "Yes, but I saw someone lurking around the shop at the last rehearsal, too. I'm just concerned."

Me too. But what murderer dared return to the scene of the crime? I folded my ears back, considering this.

Instructions from Hattie drifted to the back of the theater, only because the acoustics caught her quiet voice. She showed Triton how to bend and gracefully bring his pixie costar in for a stage kiss.

"And you didn't see the person's face?" I asked. I took a seat beside her and sank into the worn red cushion.

The half-dragon shivered. "No, I hurried to come in through the theater instead."

I stood and took a sharp breath for courage. "I'll take care of it."

I slipped out the double doors. A blast of chilly autumn air blew my hair from my face. I hugged my torso and stepped over a pumpkin with the performance information written in permanent marker across the orange skin.

The yellow bulbs in the ornate lamp posts didn't offer enough light to see the person's face, but it took only one look to see the stalker was Dr. Pitt. He wiped at his brow with a hand-stitched handkerchief—Mae's way of paying for her eye exams.

"Dr. Pitt?" I said as I loped to the other side of the enormous building. "What are you doing out here?"

"Oh!" He froze and slapped his hand to his chest. The coat he wore was two sizes too small with sleeves that only reached his forearms. "Noema, I was just. W-Well, that is, I am." He coughed to clear his throat. "I was building up the courage to go into Everland Theater."

I furrowed my brow. Chunks of wavy hair blew into my face until I tucked them over and behind my pricked ears.

"Is there something you want to tell me?" I asked. Thankfully, the seaside breeze blocked most of the stench from his nerves.

"I'd like to try out, but I know I missed the auditions." He shook his head and dabbed at his temples with the soaked square of fabric. "You see, I was worried my involvement with Cliff's wife might make you think poorly of me. But, but I've prepared for this all year. I graduated from Miss Raven's dance classes the night—" His voice suddenly dropped, and he cast his eyes at his feet. We stood where the victim's body had been found, and I understood.

The perfect trade popped into my mind. Sett had warned me off searching, but what if the answers came to me? The victim's best friend, and one of the last to see him alive, paced outside my shop and asked for a role in my play. What could one little question hurt?

"I'll give you an audition if you answer something for me."

He raised his eyebrows, the only hair left on his head besides the tufts in his nose.

"I'm sure you already know that people are afraid," I said. "And I'm worried we won't have an audience at the performance if the murderer isn't arrested before the fall festival."

Dr. Pitt nodded and scratched his jaw.

"So, who do you think killed Cliff?"

He rubbed his palm over his face. "Nobody."

My ears turned forward and stretched to their extent. "What?"

"I—well, after twenty-five years of working as this town's practitioner, I've come to believe the legend. Not once has a supernatural physically suffered at the hands of another. It's a wonderful blessing upon this town, and it means nobody could have hurt Cliff." Dr. Pitt hit his stride while talking medicine. The beads of sweat dripping down his temples stopped as fast as a faucet.

"But Cliff wasn't supernatural..." My voice died in my throat at the look on Dr. Pitt's face.

"I suppose he didn't make it obvious. I didn't know when we were in medical school together. Not until I'd met his parents at graduation. His father was a troll and his mother human."

"Cliff was a half-troll?" I whispered. My eyes scanned Mockbuster where the victim had fallen to his demise. For a moment, I allowed myself to get lost in thought like a flashback in a film. Now the murder weapon made sense. Nobody, not even a crazed murderer, could match a troll's strength. So, poison it was.

"Absolutely." Dr. Pitt nodded. "His father was a good man too, rest his soul. Cliff wanted to move here after his parents passed, and I believe the last remaining one just did."

If a half-troll died right in the middle of town, what did that mean for the safety of other supernaturals? What about the supposed protection granted by the witch's spell?

When I met the doctor's gaze again, the rainy smell of sadness filled my nose. "The legend," I said, shaking my head. "It's not real. Or it's been undone. The police confirmed Cliff was poisoned, right here in Bewitcher's Beach."

Dr. Pitt's dark, beady eyes nearly bugged out of his head. He looked like a cartoon character tossed into the set of a horror movie.

"It can't be..." He crumpled the handkerchief in his meaty fingers and brought it to his temples. Carefully, he dabbed the edge of his eyes. "I know it's real. I know it is. I've seen the spell book and witnessed the protection at work."

I gingerly touched his arm before he lifted it to wipe at his forehead again. The musty smell of sweat and the sting of ammonia lingered on him. He lived and breathed nervous energy, but the stench of fish didn't accompany it. Dr. Pitt had nothing to hide.

"I can't believe it." His voice cracked. "My friend was killed."

"Do you need to sit down?" I checked my jean skirt's pockets for my keys until I remembered I'd left Mockbuster unlocked. Nobody risked the curse to come inside, anyway. Only cast members used it to enter from the side of the stage at rehearsals.

I cupped the doctor's elbow and guided him inside. The stool creaked beneath his weight as he slouched into the seat.

"I know he wasn't a great man," he said, staring with glazed eyes. "But who would do this? Even his ex-wife didn't hate him that much. And she had more money than Cliff stood to gain from his inheritance, though it was a lot."

Big inheritance? That definitely had *motive* written all over it.

Squeaks must have sensed the need for therapy snuggles and snuck through the crack in the baseboard between Mock-buster and Everland. He skittered across the floor and climbed onto Dr. Pitt's shoe. The mouse spun around like a dog, a move he'd copied from the kids many times before, and then settled in a snug little circle.

"Maybe he wasn't murdered over hate," I said as I retrieved a soda from the snack wall. I offered it to him, and he took it without breaking his stare into the void. Instead of drinking it, he used the can as a cool compress against his temple. "Maybe he'd witnessed another crime." I recalled Piper's mention of trouble with the law. Though her name stuck to the top of the list, both Cordelia and Vera still lingered without alibis.

Dr. Pitt nodded, finally blinking his gaze into focus. He craned his neck and stared at me with wide eyes. "That's it."

Those were my two favorite words. I said them many times when an idea lit up my mind and broke a bout of writer's block. I said "that's it" when I solved crosswords and challenging Sudoku puzzles.

"What's *it?*" I asked. I wrinkled my nose as the stench of his nerves returned. Maybe I'd start carrying a box of matches or smelling salts to block out ammonia. If the town found out about the end of the legend—whether it was real or not—a lot more fear and nerves would permeate the air.

"Cliff treated a patient the night he died."

Cordelia... While, technically, I'd left her included on the list of suspects, I never considered her a possibility. All Cordelia cared about was her beloved boyfriend, their five-year-old son, and fashion trends. The plastic surgery she'd received likely came from a current magazine craze.

Dr. Pitt continued. "He confided in me. He told me a

young lady shared a sensitive piece of information with him while she was sedated."

What did Cordelia have to hide? I mulled it over as my gaze wandered to Squeaks. He comfortably snoozed on the doctor's loafer, and his tiny furry chest rose and fell in rhythmic breaths.

As my friend, I knew what made Cordelia tick. She obsessed over shoes, hairstyles, and dressing her son in the most fashionable clothes for kindergarteners—aka, whatever Macaulay Culkin wore. *No, it can't be her.* Of course, as a vampire, she'd lived almost half a century longer than me. I didn't know the details of her past.

Dr. Pitt took a long breath and shook his head. "He struggled with whether he needed to tell the police."

My head snapped up. "The police?"

The doctor shrugged and stood. Squeaks hopped off of his foot and skittered to latch onto my pant leg. He followed the seam until he reached my arm. I held it out for him to hop onto. He jumped, landed on my forearm, and trailed up my turtleneck's sleeve until he stopped to perch on my shoulder.

"I wish I could be of more help. I believe Cliff wrote an anonymous letter and planned to send it to the police, but I don't know if he ever did," Dr. Pitt said. "I hope the sheriff finds Cliff's killer and brings them to justice. B-but if I talk about this too much longer, I fear I may suffer a panic attack. May I watch the rehearsal, i-instead?" He pointed to the back wall. Sounds of enunciated voices buzzed on the other side of the door. "I'd like to take notes before my audition next year."

"Right, yeah. Sure." I nodded, though not sure of anything.

Cordelia? The vampire who glued rhinestones to her fake nails and tracked Jennifer Aniston's every hairstyle change wasn't capable of murder.

"Dr. Pitt." I spun around.

He paused before opening the door to the theater and shuffled to face me. His wrinkled brow told me he was still worried. Or perhaps the proximity of the stage sent his fried nervous system into overdrive.

"Do you know if Cliff ever accepted home-baked goods as payment for surgeries? Like you do?"

Dr. Pitt furrowed his bushy brows and then nodded. "It's possible. Cliff had a raging sweet tooth."

I frowned. The answer twisted my stomach worse than when I'd eaten a dozen Mentos after downing a Pepsi.

I circled the desk and plopped onto the stool. "I don't like this, Squeaks."

The brush of his whiskers against my cheek barely calmed me. If Cordelia's secret was worth killing over, and if she'd paid Dr. Conflick in treats, she had both motive and opportunity. Maybe he ate his home-baked payment when he got back to his hotel room.

I swallowed a lump in my throat and forced one foot in front of the other. It was easier to pin suspicion on the out-of-towner I didn't know very well, but my own friend? When I questioned Mae, my anger over her gossip had clouded my feelings. I didn't suffer this icky guilt that came with suspecting a friend.

My motherly instincts kicked in. I wanted to shield Cordelia from whatever trouble she'd gotten herself into. At tomorrow's rehearsal, I'd pull her aside and run lines, possibly slipping in a question or two about secrets.

And when I didn't smell a spot of fish, I'd cross her name out of my notebook. No fuss, no drama, and as easy as microwave popcorn. But I didn't have the energy to do it tonight.

Tonight, I'd focus on the play. I grabbed the doorknob and twisted it.

CHAPTER 18
SUSPECT ROULETTE

BRIGHT STAGE LIGHTS FLOODED IN,
momentarily blinding me. As soon as I opened the door, somebody burst through and slammed into my shoulder. I stepped
back and rubbed my eyes.

Shiny dark hair swayed as the woman marched down the
row of horror movies and turned to the door.

Vera shoved through Mockbuster's front door. The bell
dinged, announcing her quick exit. What had creamed her corn
enough to make her run out in a huff? The behavior was akin to
my pups' toddler tantrums.

I entered stage right and spotted Hattie with Cordelia on
the opposite side. Behind the curtain, they chatted and
observed the current scene. Triton rehearsed lines with another
actor playing the role of his character's friend. Piper stood at
the front, waiting for her cue to act as though her character ran
into Triton's character.

"What happened with Vera?" I asked as I reached the other
side of the stage.

Hattie nodded her chin at Piper. "No clue, but we've done

this scene three times now." Hair fell into her face as she pinched the bridge of her nose. "Each practice, Piper nails her lines, and Triton looks like a skeleton."

"Skeleton, huh? Funny thing for a ghost to say," I joked, trying to ease my nerves at the sight of Cordelia. Questioning her, no matter how necessary, didn't feel right.

If looks could kill, Hattie shot daggers through my soul.

"You know?" I shrugged. "Because you don't have one?"

The death glare didn't waver.

"Anyway," I said, sucking in a breath. "Vera just left in the middle of rehearsal."

"She did what?" Hattie rolled her eyes and marched across the stage. Though her stomping didn't make a sound, the silent rage of their director froze the entire cast.

"Continue," I said.

Piper dove in, sidling up to Triton. As the villain—or the antagonist who'd try to seduce Triton's character from dating the main love interest—Piper fit the role perfectly. She arched her eyebrow and faced the empty audience.

"You can't date her because you're mine!" She delivered the line and crossed her arms.

"Son of a witch," I mumbled. "She's made for that role."

"Yeah." Cordelia said between sips of a synthetic blood juice. The liquid in the clear straw matched her red lipstick. "That's what Hattie just told her in front of the entire cast. I don't know about everyone else, but it makes me motivated to get my lines down." She tapped her to-go cup with pointed black fingernails. The tips of her nails stabbed the words splashed on the side of the cup. It read *Roller Shakes* and the big, bold letters matched the rink's interior. "I mean, I know it makes some people jealous but, like, Piper even said she's had actual life experience being the other woman in a relationship.

That's cheating when it comes to being an actress, right? She even eloped with the guy, or tried to, or whatever."

Wait, eloped?

I scooped Squeaks off of my shoulder and let his nose nuzzle my cheek. The quick snuggle gave me the guts to ask. If Cliff married Piper, she may have had access to his inheritance. Still, I had no proof Piper hurt him, and Cordelia was the one with an obvious motive.

"Hey, Cordelia," I said, turning to her. I took a deep breath and prepared to slip a few discreet questions into rehearsal talk. Questions like *Do you have real-life experience telling lies?* came out all wrong. This required finesse and cleverness. I cleared my throat, but the words that spilled out were neither clever nor discreet. "Didn't you say you have a secret that Dr. Conflick knew about?"

Her thick bottom lip dropped. Large, doll-like eyes blinked at me in shock. Cordelia frowned and my least favorite smell overwhelmed my nose.

Oh, no.

"I didn't hurt Dr. Conflick," she said. Thankfully, the ammonia was masked by a distinct scent. The aroma of truth reminded me of lavender, with its gentle floral notes and calming aspects.

It wasn't foolproof. Technically, if Cordelia lied skillfully enough, remaining calm and relaxed the whole time, I'd smell lavender and consider it the truth. But she wasn't that good of an actress, was she? How much did Piper's performances inspire Cordelia to step up her game?

"Okay." I patted her arm the way I do after a heart-to-heart with one of my pups. "Thank you for telling me. I knew you were with him that night, so I had to double-check. Just to be fair. You understand, right?"

Cordelia fiddled with the straw, bending it side to side.

"Not really, but I know you're just stressed. The place we're raising our kids doesn't feel so safe anymore, does it?"

A lump gathered in my throat. The sudden rush of emotion swelled. Maybe Cordelia sensed feelings better than my nose smelled them. I hadn't realized how tense I'd felt since finding Cliff's body that night. And with Sett telling me to back off the investigation, I felt helpless to keep my kids safe in the town I'd chosen to raise them. What kind of mother would I be if I didn't insist on making our home safe?

I'd suppressed the thought and the emotions that came with it since the investigation began. It overwhelmed me now. Stinging tears flooded my eyes, but I blinked them away before anyone saw.

Cordelia can't be the murderer. Impossible.

But what proof did I really have other than a few smells and a mother's intuition from one mom to the next? None.

None, until Sett agreed to go along with me and get proof.

"Tell Hattie to finish rehearsals without me," I said. I slipped from behind the curtain, trailing the edge of the stage.

In the aisles, I found Halen with his camera pointed at the rehearsal. Stevie tried to jump in view of the lens to block his shot. Jovi and Dio sat with their legs criss crossed on the floor playing rock, paper, scissors.

I popped a kiss on each head and told them to get ready for bed. They whined and argued, acting like four lawyers on the case against bedtime.

"But I can't miss recording," Halen said with a scowl. "Auntie Hattie paid me five bucks to tape the whole thing so she can watch it again."

"I think she'll manage without the last five minutes," I said. "Time for bed. It's a school night."

And the night before mommy is going to sniff out a killer.

I followed four moping children into Mockbuster and up

the stairs. A plan formulated in my brain, puzzling the pieces of information I'd gathered.

One piece of the puzzle was shaped like a gargoyle. If I could connect Sett's piece to the section with the investigation, I'd get a finished puzzle with a picture of the killer's face. He had the resources, and I had the nose.

Sett worried my impulsive quest for answers put me in danger, so all I had to do was tap into a little patience and bring backup. I'd wait and watch Piper until she slipped up. Then I'd bring the sheriff himself to confront her.

While the kids crowded for room at the sink in the bathroom, I plopped into a chair at the kitchen table.

I snagged the phone from the wall and pulled the cord to reach the table.

"Bewitcher's Beach police department, this is Sett."

"Hi, it's me."

"Noema!" His voice shifted from monotone to bright, and I suddenly felt cozy, like a blanket wrapped around me. "I've been meaning to come by and rent that movie you recommended. Is *The Fifth Element* available?"

"I think so. Hey, Sett, did you know Cliff had a huge inheritance and Piper might have been married to him?"

"Oh." The monotone sound returned. "Right. Getting information is slow since he didn't live here and everything has to be faxed or mailed over. So, thank you. I didn't have the details on who he was seeing or if it was serious."

What did he have to be a grump about? I'd just given him important clues! If this were a movie, my help would have him falling head over heels for me. Or maybe I just had romance on the brain thanks to Hattie's insistence—or genius, if tickets sold out like she predicted.

"You're welcome," I said brightly.

"So, uh, would you like to watch it with me?" he asked. I

hadn't realized we'd both been silent for a whole minute until his voice crackled from the other line again.

"Watch the case? Absolutely! I thought you'd never ask." Butterflies took flight in my stomach. The giddy feeling reached my heart, sending it beating twice as fast. "Tonight?"

"No—" he cleared his throat.

"Are you busy tonight?"

"Uh, well, yes I have a stakeout planned."

A gasp escaped me but I resisted squealing. "A real, live stakeout?" *Like in the movies?* I kept that comment to myself, though it took every ounce of self control.

"Right. With Cliff's inheritance on the line, I'll be watching his new house to see if relatives show up for his stuff."

I tried to make sense of the sheriff's plan, but I didn't have the full picture. Wouldn't papers be with a personal accountant? Or at his house out of town? I'd get more answers tonight. Excited, I did a little dance while twisting the phone's spiral cord around my finger.

"I'll be there," I said.

"Noema..." His voice trailed.

"At sunset, sharp." I tried to sound official before he reminded me that I wasn't law enforcement or any official investigator. "Be there or be square. It's a date." As soon as the words left my mouth, my cheeks burned. I glanced at my reflection in the microwave's glass window, spotting the rosy shade that bloomed over my face.

"A date?" he said in a low voice.

It wasn't what I'd meant. Not like that. I'd vowed to live as a lone wolf, which meant I'd never date again. Before nerves got the best of me and I put my foot in my mouth again, I kicked my chair back and slammed the phone on the receiver.

I sucked in a breath, and my canine snagged on my lip. "I

can't wait," I whispered. The romantic notion of capturing a criminal filled my imagination.

If my life was a movie, tonight would be the climax, the stakeout, the chase that'd bring a murderer to justice. Tonight would provide proof that Cliff's death had nothing to do with my VHS tapes, or a curse.

CHAPTER 19
SNACKS AT THE STAKEOUT

IF SIDE-EYE COULD KILL, I'd be a ghost with Hattie. When I told her about the stakeout, her look said more than enough. She'd agreed to keep an eye on the pups while I met Sett.

It was what came after that haunted me. Her suspicious hum and raised eyebrows suggested the stakeout was more than a criminal investigation.

"It's not really a date," I announced as I slipped from the theater and into Mockbuster. The door swung shut behind me, but my voice still carried and bounced off the theater walls. I silently prayed that Hattie wouldn't follow and tease me. Between Cliff's hovering inheritance and tonight's plan, my mind was already packed, and my heart fluttered with excitement.

I picked up the pace and made for the door, covering the space of the small shop in only a few strides. The wall of snacks caught my eye, particularly a package of orange hard candies. I froze just past the register and walked two steps backward.

"Hmm." I stared at the bag of Creme Savers before snagging it off the metal peg. My stomach grumbled, announcing its complaint. Apparently, eating my kids' leftovers wasn't a well-rounded meal. If I was going to make it through an all-night stakeout, I needed sugar. I grabbed Halen's Ninja Turtle backpack from the bottom of the stairs and emptied the trash out before shoving Red Vines, a Big Hunk, two Ring Pops, and a half dozen packets of Dunkaroos inside.

It didn't take long to get to Cliff's house—or rather, his *almost* house. The two-story beachfront home had a white wraparound porch. Small seagull statues perched at the top of the staircase railing like guard dogs. The shapes of the decorative white awning reminded me of a candy shop, and the red striped curtains doubled-down on the image. If only yellow lamplight glowed from inside, the picture would be complete.

I sighed. The beautiful house deserved the warmth of life. Instead, darkness served as a reminder that nobody lived here and nobody had shown up.

At that thought, my ears twitched and my eyes sharpened in the dim glow of the moonlight. This close to the beach and outside of the neighborhood there were no street lamps. Instead, the beach house was only brightened by the rotating shine of the lighthouse's bulb.

The white glow flooded the sand-covered concrete, and it caught the glint of a vehicle's headlight. I hurried to Sett's car, discreetly parked in the cover offered by overgrown bushes along the street.

When I yanked the door open, Sett released a snort and blinked rapidly. He straightened until the top of his head bumped the car's ceiling.

"Were you asleep?" I asked.

He rubbed his eye with the heel of his palm, and the scratchy sound of stone scraping against stone made me cringe. "What? No. Anyway, I thought you'd be here at sunset. *Sharp.*"

"It's only eight," I said. I plopped into the passenger seat and swung the Ninja Turtle backpack to the meticulously clean floor. Not one crumb could be found in Sett's car, an impressive feat in my eyes.

"Don't you ever have to eat on the run?" I asked as I scanned the glistening dashboard and empty cup holders.

"What?" He cocked his head. "No. Never."

No sounded like his favorite word.

"It's so clean I'm worried you'll arrest me for contraband," I said and pointed at the turtle-shaped backpack.

His brow pinched, eyes shifting from the turtle to my cringey smile. The twangy pineapple-pizza-scent of confusion filled the air. Before he thought the worst of me, I unzipped the backpack and revealed the goods.

"Snacks," I whispered, as if Dunkaroos were illegal. "Lots and lots of snacks." I wiggled my eyebrows and slowly pulled the bag of Creme Savers from its burial place at the bottom of the pack. "Can we break your rule if I give you these? I'm starved."

His eyes narrowed to slits so small that I could no longer see the gray. "Are you bribing me, Noema Wolf?" He called me by the pseudo-last name since I didn't know my real one, the one I had before I became a werewolf.

Before I dove into the emotional waters of wondering about my long lost family, I shrugged and ripped a bite off the end of a Red Vine. "It's not like we're breaking the law."

"Rules are like laws," he said with a side-eye. Why did everyone keep giving me that look? It was as if my involvement in the case was more nuisance than helpful. I had a nose for guilt, and I wouldn't let it go to waste when a murder investigation was afoot and threatening my business. "Without rules," he continued, "we'd all descend into chaos."

I yanked another bite of the rope candy and chewed as I mulled this over. "Way ahead of you."

His wings twitched, though they were squished against the seat. "What does that mean?"

I shrugged. "Just that it sounds like a regular Tuesday in my life. When you have four pups the same age, chaos is all you know."

He raised his hand, waving the comment away. "No, no, that's not what I meant. When kids are playing, it is a happy sight. Rules and laws are for keeping civilians safe. You know, like civilians who invade an official police investigation."

I swallowed the bite of Redvine before it was fully chewed and coughed as the lump stuck in my throat. The hint-drop fell heavy on my shoulders. I slouched, and my own frustration emitted a slight smoky smell with a dash of black pepper.

"I'm here now, and I'm not leaving," I said. With that, I popped the last bit of the rope candy in my mouth.

"If you got hurt, I'd never forgive myself," he said. Sett's brow wrinkled in concern. How many times had he said that? At this point, I could turn his predictability into a game.

"I'm a werewolf, Sett." I bit my tongue before saying the rest. *People get hurt because of me, not the other way around. That's why this isn't a date and never will be.* "I can outrun most people and smell danger a mile away." The latter wasn't entirely true since smells often mixed and emotions were unpredictable, but it helped my case. Sett nodded, agreeing to let me stay. "Now, tell me why we're watching an empty house."

Sett pointed the unopened package of Creme Savers at the building across the street. "It won't be empty for long if the killer did it for money. I got in touch with Cliff's accountant, and he says Cliff was very old-fashioned with his money. He didn't even trust the accountant and chose to keep one copy of the documents with him. They weren't found on him, at his old house, or the hotel room, so they're probably here. Even if they aren't, a killer after the money would expect them to be."

"But why tonight?"

Sett tilted his head to meet my gaze. The slate gray of his shining eyes reminded me of a full moon's glow just behind a puff of fog. "Because Cliff's memorial is tomorrow, and his will is still unlocated."

"So why didn't you pull strings as a cop and go in to find it?" I shot him a side-eye glance. "Let me guess; the rules say you can't do that?"

He pursed his lips, likely suppressing an overwhelming desire to lecture me on the importance of following the law. To my surprise, he smirked, and the smell of confidence and happiness filled the air. The sandalwood and citrus combination drowned out the sweet scent of my contraband.

"Actually, I already went inside," he said. "I didn't find it, but nobody else knows that."

I shared how I'd learned about Cliff and Piper's potential elopement, and he spoke of a new recipe he'd invented. We chatted easily. Before I knew it, we were knee-deep in a discussion of which was the better movie: *Independence Day* or *Stargate*.

Movement caught my eye. A figure moved in the darkness, slowly approaching the beach house. I swatted Sett's arm and then yanked my hand back, shaking off the sudden pain in my fingers. I'd misjudged how solid his stony bicep was.

We each held our breath, waiting for the lighthouse's spinning shine to illuminate the mysterious figure. In the dark, all I could make out was their exceptional height, too tall to be Piper, though they didn't look wide enough to be Dr. Pitt. Was this person the killer that roamed Bewitcher's Beach? Did they murder Cliff in cold blood, all for a slice of inheritance money?

Why not run a shop or capitalize on the fall festival like the rest of us?

The figure froze, but it was too dark to see if the killer was facing us or the house. A shiver stole down my spine and my ears involuntarily folded back. If this were a horror movie, I'd scream. My imagination went wild, picturing a villain with a chainsaw and a clown mask, and I almost reached for Sett's hand for a reassuring squeeze.

Finally, though only seconds passed, the lighthouse's white light flooded the house. It partially illuminated the street and the figure. In a flash, I recognized neon-colored roller skates and shiny jet black hair.

"Cordelia," we both said at the same time.

The shiver from earlier seemed to trickle its way back up my spine, and my ears popped up. Sett and I dared to tear our eyes from the suspect and meet one another's gaze in a wide-eyed exchange. I swallowed the lump in my throat and slowly shook my head.

"She's not...no way...I don't—"

"Shh." He raised his finger to his lips and whispered. "Patience. Let's see what she does."

Patience? A frustrated breath blew from my nose. *Not while my friend is under silent accusation.* I squirmed in the seat, suddenly uncomfortable in the car's small space. I couldn't imagine how Sett felt, squished into the sedan between the steering wheel and his heavy folded wings.

Cordelia rolled toward the beach house. The sandy front yard made it difficult to skate, and she stopped. She bent, unlaced the skates, and stepped down, now significantly shorter without the wheels. What would Cordelia want with Cliff's inheritance? It made no sense. They weren't related, and she'd have no claim to the money whether he was alive or not.

"My love!" A man's voice broke through the distant crash of waves and our tenuous breathing.

In sync, Sett and I snapped our necks to the left. Another figure approached, one who appeared two-headed and menacingly tall in the darkness. My breath caught in my throat and I grabbed Sett's forearm.

When the lighthouse brightened the street, I suddenly felt silly for being afraid. Roman, Cordelia's boyfriend, carried their five year-old son on his shoulders. The little boy beamed, exposing his tiny fangs. Each vampire looked bright-eyed and bushy-tailed in the late evening darkness. Cordelia spun around, picked up her skates with one hand, and hurried toward her family.

"Stop worrying about it," Roman said. "It's my only night off this week. Let's just enjoy our walk."

Cordelia nodded but didn't follow as he kept walking. For a moment, she stood alone with the wind tossing her long hair around her waist. She tore her attention from the beach house and jogged after her family.

All of the tension in my muscles relaxed at once, and I suddenly felt ready for a nap. Sett glanced at my grip on his arm, and the hint of an awkward smile twitched his lips. I pulled away and casually flicked a lock of wavy hair from my face.

He opened his mouth, but I was saved by the bell. A little ring echoed through the night, and a bike rolled up. Light glinted against the shiny silver spokes as it rolled by. Vera hopped off the seat and bumped the kickstand out with her heel.

We watched as she confidently marched up to the beach house and pulled out a keychain with dozens of keys. I squinted, making out the shape of the similar keys, each appearing to belong to a house. Vera easily unlocked the door.

She didn't so much as glance around before disappearing inside. A light blinked on and flooded the downstairs window with a yellow glow.

"Do you think?" My voice trailed off.

Sett sucked in a breath and twitched his wings. It seemed he'd tried to expand them like a shrug but the car offered no room for extra muscular limbs. "It could be as simple as she's just doing her job. When she sold me my house, she'd made a couple of trips out for me to sign last minute contracts. She even came in the evening for my own convenience. The difference was my new home wasn't empty because I was alive."

"But he's not there to sign anything," I said.

"Right, so it's odd. Or she's preparing the house to go back on the market," he said. I mulled this over. Who else might show up tonight?"

"Does Cliff have any living relatives?" I asked.

"His parents recently passed away, and there's an estranged half-sibling presumed dead according to the accountant. Cliff's ex-wife doesn't want or need anything from Cliff—"

"But the new wife..." I said, getting excited. "Piper."

Sett tried to shrug his wings again and then shifted to get more comfortable in the confined space. "If it's his new girl, and if they were really married, then I'm almost positive we'll see her show up for the documents tonight."

I nodded and we turned our attention to the house. After an hour of no news and eating half the snacks, I drifted, waking only when I had a dream about drooling on Sett's shoulder. I straightened suddenly, realizing it wasn't a dream when I spotted the wet mark on the sheriff's blue shirt.

"Sorry," I said slowly, wiping the leftover drool from my chin. My cheeks burned, but Sett didn't seem to notice the wet spot.

"Vera left after you started snoozing," he said.

The car's clock read half past four in the morning in glowing green. I blinked and gasped. "I was asleep for six hours?"

"Seven," he corrected.

"Why didn't you wake me?"

Again with the attempted shrug. "You're a busy mom, I imagine rest doesn't come easily."

Had stony, serious Sett just said the most thoughtful thing I'd heard in a long time? I couldn't help the smile that snuck onto my face.

I licked my lips and sobered. "So, did anybody else show?"

"Actually, yeah, Piper—"

My palms slapped over my mouth, muffling my exclamation. "I knew it!"

"I'm not so sure," he said, in a tired, monotonous voice. "It looked suspicious when she peeked in the windows, but all she did was leave a bundle of flowers on the front porch. It was a little sad, actually."

I nodded, knowing Sett told the whole truth and nothing but the truth. None of the three women did anything exceptionally suspicious. A yawn overwhelmed me. I tried to stretch my long arms in the little space, but my fists bumped against the ceiling. Tomorrow, I had a full day of building props and getting ready for the play. I'd slept, but it wasn't enough for the amount of work ahead of me.

I suppressed a slip of the *curse* word. I was exhausted, and we hadn't come closer to identifying the killer. The curse and rumors still hovered over my business, out of my control. But I did have the play in my grip. I could throw myself into it to impress locals and tourists alike, proving to all that my scripts— like the VHS tapes I stocked at Mockbuster—were worth their time. Silly superstitious rumors or not.

My gaze fell to the unopened bag of Creme Savers. Maybe

he really didn't like the orange flavor, though I'd never seen him actually eat the strawberry ones either. Instead, Sett dunked a vanilla cookie into the Dunkaroo fudge sauce and popped it into his mouth. He gave me a slight smile with bulging cheeks.

I smiled back; at least the night wasn't a total loss. I'd successfully convinced Sett to give me information on the case, and it felt good to help. Even if it only lasted one night.

Tomorrow, I'd wake up and put the play as my first priority. I'd only hunt for clues if I had extra time. Satisfied with the plan, I yawned again and my eyelids grew heavy.

Before I knew it, I was waking to the shine of the sunrise and the cool morning breeze. Sett had let me rest more, keeping watch as the protector of Bewitcher's Beach.

The sleep was only more proof that last night wasn't a date. I'd never be that comfortable and relaxed on a date.

CHAPTER 20
ALIBIS AND GOODBYES

QUIET DAYS at Mockbuster gave me plenty of time to build sets, clean old props, and think. I sprayed cleaner on the window of a rolling door. The rag left streaks on the glass and I frowned. A growl escaped me.

Like Piper, the set pieces didn't come out as I'd expected. Not once in almost two weeks of rehearsals did I witness her behaving suspiciously. Instead, she nailed her performances, treated the other cast members kindly, always arrived early to help sweep the stage, and gathered the props from the fake gun to the faux gold.

While Vera's and Cordelia's acting didn't blow me out of the water, they too participated with the appropriate effort and worked well with the rest of the cast. The scent of frustration, not unlike the smoky smell of anger, rose around me. If both Sett and I found nothing, then someone would get away with murder—not to mention destroying my business, scaring the whole town, and...

I groaned and placed my hands on my hips with the rag crumpled in my fist. The store was a mess. A donated couch on wheels, the rolling door, and a pallet painted to look like a jail cell blocked aisles and leaned against movie stands. I missed the regular renters and the life of the once-busy shop.

Mockbuster had transformed from a movie shop to a storage unit for the upcoming performance.

Two pups and two kids dodged, leaped, painted, organized, and filmed every angle of the Mockbuster storage shed.

I sighed and wiped the rag over my forehead.

Stevie giggled and pointed to my face with a paintbrush. "It looks like you have four eyebrows." Red paint dripped into her lap from the brush. She'd paused on painting the fake bricks of a cardboard fireplace to stare up at me.

I rubbed my forehead again, but it only sparked more laughter. Halen, carrying the heavy camcorder on his shoulder, stepped up to me and tried to lift it into my face.

"Smile for the camera, Mom," he said.

I blocked the lens with my palm, but he dodged to the side.

"Say, 'I'm a momster with eyebrows that come alive and eat babies!'"

"Halen." I swatted the air in front of him. "Don't say things like that."

The haircut had grown to block his eyes now. He shook the shiny nutmeg hair from his face and looked through the lens again, almost tripping over his brother's wolf form. Jovi lay curled on a pile of costumes that never made it back to their hangers. The fluff of his tail wrapped to the front of his body and covered his snout.

I clucked my tongue and raked my fingers through my hair. "Jovi, you're going to shed on the outfits!"

In wolf form, Dio used his mouth to drag a heavier set piece through the door from the stage.

"No, no, no," I said, waving for him to take it back into the theater.

Dio barked in understanding then squeezed around the

piece and dragged it back to the other side. My artist, heavy lifter, cameraman, and boy genius all contributed to make my stories come to life. They enjoyed their individual roles in it, none of us having the desire to perform on stage.

The bell chimed, and I spun around. The tips of rough, leathery wings moved behind the rolling door.

Sett poked his head around the set pieces. "Noema?"

I hopped over Jovi and met Sett at the end of the row of romance movies. "I have *The Fifth Element* in stock." I darted past him and into the science fiction aisle. It took some rearranging, but I piled enough costumes on top of one another to uncover the racks of movies and grab the tape. "Noodle's mom returned it yesterday. It was the first time they never rented another movie after returning one..." I swiveled and offered him the VHS.

Sett took it and lifted it slightly. "Thanks."

I blinked at him. "I'm trying really hard not to ask about the investigation."

"I know," he said. "Actually, that's why I'm here." The sheriff's wings twitched as he rubbed the back of his neck. "I'm stuck."

My ears folded back. Did Sett actually come to me for help?

"I got the record proving a recent marriage between Cliff and Piper, but I've got nothing solid on her. Vera and Cordelia don't have motives. Cliff's first ex-wife said he had a half-sibling, but she'd presumed the half-sibling passed away since she'd never met them. And when I spoke with Piper, she said they'd separated. Cliff had no family left and two failed marriages."

"There's more to that story," I said. Piper also hated doctors after her botched surgery. Excitement bubbled inside of me. I lived to solve puzzles and write theories. And with a friend?

Even better. Without thinking, I grabbed Sett's wrist and dragged him through the obstacles of props to the front.

I whipped out my notebook and slapped it open on the desk.

"There," I said, jamming my finger against a scribbled note.

Sett squinted and cocked his head. Reading my hand-writing required a little extra effort. The longer it took for him to decipher it, the more my cheeks burned.

"It's a list of motives and suspects. See?" I pointed to Piper's name. "Money, anger over getting dumped, or revenge for her botched surgery. She has the longest list of reasons to hurt Cliff. It's clear; she eloped with him then killed him to get his inheritance."

"But she has an alibi."

"An alibi?" My gaze snapped to him. He shoved his hands into his coat's pockets.

"Mister Sett!" Stevie squealed. She hopped over her palette of colors and ran for the sheriff. With a dripping paintbrush and gray paint in her pigtails, she threw her arms around his torso for a big hug.

Sett crouched to give a high five at her level. "Hey, are you still talking to all the animals for me?"

Chocolate pigtails bounced up and down as she nodded. "The pigeons in the town square said they'll tell me if they ever see Halen steal a taffy again. Then you can arrest him and I'll get the video camera."

"I didn't do that!" Halen shouted from the other side of the shop.

Sett chuckled and shook his head. "You're just like Snow White with all your forest friends."

She stuck out her tongue and wrinkled her nose. Stevie wasn't a princess-loving girl. But she was a regular Cinderella with animals and the reason Squeaks communicated with us so well.

"So, what's her alibi?" I asked.

He nodded as he stood. "It's not solid, but her job shows she punched in for a shift at The Home Cheapo the night he was killed."

I tucked my hair up and over my ears. "No, I found the movie Cliff rented in the VHS case she returned. That puts them together that night."

"A swapped movie isn't proof of timeline. That could have happened at any point the day he died." Sett played devil's advocate.

"But Barney saw her arguing with Cliff that same night at the inn," I said, pointing out the large front windows as if we could see The Oyster Inn from here.

"I know, but Barney also refuses to wear the glasses Dr. Pitt prescribed him. If I'm more than a few feet away, he sees my wings and thinks I'm a fairy."

"I didn't know that." My ears folded back, and the lock of waves fell into my face again.

His wings expanded then contracted in a sort of shrug. "I only know because I had to take his driver's license away when he refused to wear them. Like I said, I've got nothing to go on and I wondered if you... heard anything."

My eyebrows shot to my hairline. Or unibrow, since I still had paint across my forehead. The burn in my cheeks returned with the smell of embarrassment. I rubbed at the smudge but it only drew Sett's gaze to my forehead.

If I mentioned Cordelia, he'd be forced to look into her. "I, uh, well." Since she had the strongest motive and the clearest record of being with Cliff that night, I feared the worst. Something told me Piper's alibi made little sense. But why?

"I know you're busy," Sett said. He scanned the donated couch. "I'll let you get back to work."

I nodded, relieved it'd give me more time to find an alibi for Cordelia. It had to exist. It *had* to.

His wings folded closer to his body as he pulled the door open. To fit through, he had to duck and squeeze his wings. Instead of walking through, he paused.

"If you're free this evening, would you like to discuss theories more?" He nodded toward the pile of pups. They harassed Jovi, wrestling and shedding all over the costumes. "We could all grab a milkshake at Roller Shakes—"

"No!" I licked my lips. Roller Shakes was too close to Cordelia. I needed more time to think, more time to expose Piper. No way did she go to work that night. But what made me so sure? "I mean, we don't drink... milkshakes." *Lame excuse.*

"Yes, we do!" Halen shouted.

Sett's brow twitched in a momentary furrow. The damp, earthy smell of rain filled my nose. But it didn't match the autumn sun that shone in through the windows and glass door.

Sett cleared his throat. "How about you just call me if you think of anything?"

Did the sheriff just try to ask me on a date? I gave my shoulders a little wiggle. He was the most confusing man I'd ever met, hinting at his interest and then getting frustrated with me for wanting to help and taking up Fitz's request.

"Wait." My eyes widened. The memory came rushing back. I glanced at my feet and patted the desktop, standing right where Cliff had been when he rented *The Swan Princess.* "It's a date!"

A side-smile flickered on his lips. "Yeah?"

"Definitely."

"Should I meet you here, or?"

I pointed to the carpet as if Sett could see the memory in

my mind's eye. "Cliff told me himself. He had a date that night, and it had to have been with Piper because her video case came with the movie he rented." I turned to face Sett with a huge smile. "I don't know how I forgot the date part."

Sett sighed. "A date makes sense with what the coroner found. Cliff had eaten popcorn and drunk wine that night. It's possible either of those were poisoned."

At the last word, Dio popped up on all fours from the wrestling match. He whimpered and released a deafening bark.

I dropped my voice to a whisper. "Don't say that around him. He thinks every food is poisoned because he doesn't like the taste of anything unless it's pizza-flavored."

"Sorry," he said, whispering back. "This might be helpful information. I'm going to verify with her job again."

"You don't have to keep whispering."

Sett straightened and rolled his shoulders back. "If nobody saw her at work that night, that's enough to bring her in and try to get a confession."

"I can get you a confession." It was a long shot, and I needed a sneaky way to ask. Asking about a date didn't sound like an accusation of murder, which meant I could catch her off guard. And with what we already knew, it put the puzzle pieces in place. I practiced the dialogue I'd use. *I'm just curious because you said you have personal experience with this character's backstory...*

Sett rubbed his chin. "I'm not so sure—"

"You came to me for help. I'm going to help. Tomorrow is the last rehearsal before the fall festival. If you arrive early and stay behind the curtain, you'll hear her."

The line of his pursed lips flattened. He nodded and offered me a hand.

"Deal," he said, "as long as you'll listen and wait for me."

I took his hand and shook it vigorously. "Of course; you're always my backup."

A bright citrusy scent freshened the room. The smell of mutual happiness mingled like lemon and lime.

It wasn't until Sett glanced down at our hands that I realized the shake had ended, and I hadn't let go.

CHAPTER 21
EVE OF OPENING
FRIGHT NIGHT

THE NEXT DAY arrived like a crashing wave as new information swept me right off my feet. Sett finalized the last detail, confirming that Piper had clocked in for her shift but didn't stay to work it. After cross referencing that with Barney's claim that he saw her arguing with Cliff in the lobby, Piper's alibi went down the drain.

Now there was only one thing left to do: tell Hattie we planned to get a confession from Piper tonight, and that our star actress would be arrested.

I downed the last fizzing bubbles of my Diet Pepsi and approached center stage. The worn floorboards creaked and groaned beneath my feet. Dozens of eyes stared up at us as Hattie belted out her night-before-the-show pep-talk.

Despite Sett's beliefs, I might find more safety hunting a murderer than hanging around Hattie. When rehearsals bombed and props got lost, she haunted more than the piece of jewelry that was tied to her soul. But with an actress arrested the night before opening day? Hattie might burn the whole theater down...

If I didn't grab her at the end of her speech, she'd be swarmed by cast members with questions. The chance to prepare her for what was coming would slip through my fingers if I didn't do it now.

It took every ounce of courage not to walk right through the ghost and into Mockbuster. There, I could hide from her wrath and wait for Sett's backup.

"Hattie." My voice came out as screechy as Squeaks' chatter.

Through her transparent head, I saw her angled brow and frown.

I swallowed. Time to take a hit for the team and prove Piper's crime, once and for all. I stepped up.

"You should know, Sett is on his way here." The words spilled over one another. Though Hattie's grimace exuded anger, I didn't have to suffer the smoky smell since a ghost had no body with which to create emotional scents.

"Pardon me?" Sequined fringe swayed as she crossed her arms.

I cleared my throat. "The Sheriff is coming to arrest Piper. *If* we can get a confession out of her during rehearsal."

Hattie held her palm out to my face. The faint glow of her manifestation made me squint.

"You just said so much insanity that I can't even begin to process it." She spoke so slowly it unnerved me.

"I know it's terrible timing, but the role has an understudy and Piper's a murderer, Hattie. She belongs in prison, not on stage."

The ghost pursed her lips, pulling the lines of her high cheekbones into sharper angles. "The curse is real, isn't it?"

"N-no?" I cocked my head.

"It is, I'm looking right at it," she snapped. "A curse with wolf's ears determined to ruin this performance!"

"Hattie—"

She vanished. In a blink, her ghostly form dropped through the floor. Hattie had worked to make herself solid enough to carry the object she haunted, which meant she no longer became entirely invisible. But that didn't stop her from disappearing. She easily walked through walls or would fall through the stage into the storage area below.

I sighed. Once she calmed, she'd agree that justice for murder trumped a solid performance. I took a cue from Dr. Pitt and pressed the cold soda can between my eyebrows.

Relaxation didn't last a minute. The distant chime of Mockbuster's bell caught my attention.

I hurried off the stage and greeted Sett in the aisle of romance films.

Thumping from upstairs told me Bette hadn't gotten the pups settled down yet. The muffled sounds of *The Lion King*'s song mingled with the kids' chatter.

The tips of Sett's wings towered over the wire shelves. With the rental shop closed, I kept the lights off. Only the dim illumination of the street lamps streamed in through the windows, and a light from the top of the stairs cast a scattered glow around the steps.

It was enough to see he wore a baseball cap with cutouts for his horns. I bit back a giggle at his incognito attempt. As if a navy hat with BBPD embroidered on the front made him unrecognizable.

I squeezed past set pieces and hopped over a luggage prop until I reached him.

"I confirmed the financials," he said, keeping his voice quiet. "Cliff stood to gain a lot of money from an inheritance once his parents' estate was settled. Piper must have known about it."

I nodded. A warm sense of safety filled my chest. Whether

it came from solving the crime or Sett's trust in me, I couldn't tell. Likely both.

"Ready?" he asked and nodded toward the theater.

"Let's wait until they run through all the scenes with Piper. Hattie started rehearsals early, so not everyone is here yet and they're running scenes out of order."

Sett raised his eyebrows. "You? Wait? I'm impressed. I thought Noema waited for no one."

I folded my ears back but ignored his cheeky comment. "That way the understudy gets one last look at how Piper plays the character. Plus, it'll give me a reason to pull her aside like I'm going to give her suggestions."

"Where do you want me?"

It was my turn to raise my eyebrows—both, now that I was smudge-free. "You're asking me? I'm not law enforcement, remember?"

Sett rolled his eyes. "That didn't stop you before."

And it wouldn't stop me now. Without thinking, I grabbed his wrist and guided him to the door.

"As soon as I open it, take a sharp right. You're entering stage right. Stay behind the curtain and I'll bring Piper over here. I'll discuss how her life experiences relate to the character's backstory to get her talking. If she figures it out and tries to bolt, you'll be here."

The door opened with a tenuous creak, and we slipped to the side before the cast saw us. A line of actors and actresses waited on the opposite side for a cue to enter the stage. Since it was the penultimate romantic scene, only two characters stood in the spotlight. The rest of the cast crowded in the shadows together, missing Piper, Vera, Cordelia, Chanel, Mae, and two background extras.

I peeked out from behind the curtain and spied Hattie standing in the main aisle between the rows of seats.

Triton's voice rang through the recesses of the theater. He'd come into his acting skills with Piper's help, though it was the pixie who co-starred opposite him.

I whispered and pointed for Sett to tuck himself in the folds of the curtain as much as possible. The fabric couldn't contain his massive wings and hulking shoulders, but the shadows still helped to obscure him. Hopefully, we wouldn't have to wait long for everyone to arrive and do a quick run-through.

I released my grip on his arm, though I didn't mind the cool touch of his stony skin. Werewolves run so hot that it took a downpour of chilly rain and wind to give me goosebumps.

Time to focus. I shook away thoughts of the sheriff's comforting touch.

Rough fingertips brushed my bare forearm.

"Hey," he said, "promise me you'll bring her close enough in case she gets aggressive."

"Sure, but I'll be fine," I said. "I'm just glad we're finally getting the killer and making Bewitcher's Beach safe again. Piper shouldn't get away with—"

A shrill scream interrupted me. The piercing wail shot through the scripted silence of the couple's stage kiss, muffled only by the distance.

It echoed from the open theater doors as Chanel burst through. The siren's song was a shriek that nearly split our eardrums.

"There's a body!" she screamed and pointed into the darkness beyond the doors. Thick blonde hair fell into her face as she huffed to catch her breath.

My heart leaped into my throat. Along with Sett, who'd untangled his wings from the curtain's fabric, I jumped off the stage and rushed outside, following Chanel's swinging hips.

Only feet away from Everland's doors lay a body, face

down on the cobblestone. Shock froze me—and everyone else who'd piled outside—in place. Shiny curls splayed out, covering the sides of the victim's face, and a thin, pointy object jutted from between her ribcage.

It was Piper, and she had been attacked.

"But she's..." My whispering voice died, just as the suspect had. I'd been so sure Piper had killed Cliff. Now she lay stabbed in the torso, her young life cut short. And over what?

Piper rolled to her uninjured side. The entire cast seemed to release a collective sigh at the sight of her movement. Everyone sprang into action, and chaos ensued while the rest of the cast either gawked, scrambled away, or tried to help—only getting in Sett's way.

The pixie screamed for someone to call Dr. Pitt. Triton shoved past me and into Mockbuster, presumably for the phone.

It took me a moment to process and for my hearing to return sharp and focused.

"Help is on the way," Sett said. He kneeled in front of the suspect-turned-victim and pulled out his pager, likely sending an emergency notification to Fitz.

Piper groaned and pressed her hands near the shallow injury. As she moved, the thin weapon caught the light that flooded out of the theater. The metal object looked like a broken off screwdriver, except that it was pink.

If this means she's not the killer, who else is left? A sick feeling bubbled in my stomach as I forced myself to look at Cordelia who'd just arrived, sipping on a cup of synthetic blood. The vampire white-knuckled her beverage. Had Cliff shared Cordelia's secret with Piper, sparking Cordelia to attack her too?

I just can't believe it would be her.

I spoke up, determined to get answers. "Did anyone see what happened?"

Chanel shook her head and plucked strands of hair from sticking to her glossy lips. The rest of the cast arrived, Mae, Vera, and the two young men who worked as extras slowly approaching the scene from different directions. They, too, shook their heads, and a few shrugs rippled through the group as murmurs started spreading.

Ammonia burned in my nose. I couldn't identify the smell of fish among all the fear. It seemed nobody was lying, or it was masked by the flood of other emotions.

"Please, give her space," Sett demanded with his arm stretched out.

Cast members backed away slowly, eyes still glued on the victim, until Hattie demanded their attention.

"Everybody back inside!" She raised her voice as best she could. "Let the professionals handle it." Unshaken, the ghost guided everybody. She instructed them to line up and calmly resume rehearsal.

I crouched beside Sett. "Piper, do you know who'd want to attack you?"

Her pale face wrinkled in concern. "No, I have no idea." She spoke between shuddering breaths. "Unless—" Her voice broke into a sob. "Unless they think I know something about Cliff's death. But I don't, I swear!"

"It's okay," Sett comforted her, slipping his open palm beneath her head. He exchanged a worried glance with me. We'd gotten it wrong, so wrong, and now a second victim lay on the ground only a few feet away from Mockbuster's doors.

"The curse has spread from her videos to her script!" A cast member's voice pricked my ears from inside. Mumbles of agreement rippled through the group. It sounded wrong, like the backward waves on Bewitcher's beach.

I shook off the prickly feeling of frustration and blinked at Piper. Her eyes lulled, rolling back into her head.

"We need answers," I said, standing.

"Noema, wait!" Sett met me upright. He stepped in my way and towered over me. "Once Dr. Pitt is here and gets the victim to safety, I'll be conducting this investigation."

"But Fitz—"

"It's too dangerous. I can't let anyone else get hurt. Especially—just, *no*."

I responded by side-stepping, but Sett's wings expanded.

"Please, don't." His slate eyes didn't blink, instead boring through me as if my head was transparent like Hattie's.

If I didn't question people and find the attacker, he'd have to blame Cordelia. Who else had motive and opportunity? She was with Cliff that night, and she'd admitted he knew a secret about her. Vera had no reason to kill a client, especially one whose home purchases could keep her business afloat. And the rest of the suspect list had been cleared. The evidence stacked up against Cordelia. But she was my friend and a fellow mom; I refused to believe her capable of poisoning someone.

"I need answers." I craned my neck to see past his wings.

Sett didn't budge. "I insist you back off. If you want to help, tell Hattie to keep everyone organized. I'll get statements as soon as possible and in an orderly fashion. Townspeople don't need more scares."

The earlier warmth of safety turned into a fiery rage. A low growl escaped me. I bit my lip to keep from baring my teeth at him.

"What about the half-sibling?" I offered a weak attempt at a theory, maybe a new suspect we never thought of. "If Cliff's girl didn't go after the inheritance, wouldn't his family?"

"I told you, they passed away. I don't care how impatient Fitz is, you'll let me handle this, Noema."

I wanted to shove his wings out of the way and run right into the middle of the investigation. Sett was always too slow, too methodical, and wasted too much time.

Someone followed Piper here and attacked her, and it was very likely the same person who'd killed her husband.

The dim light of the lamp posts illuminated Dr. Pitt's approaching frame.

I stood by, helpless, frustrated, and stewing in the stench of smoke and gasoline.

The doctor and a nurse he employed for emergencies got Piper onto a stretcher. With the victim safe, Sett approached Hattie.

The director waved for me to join them.

"The sheriff says we have to call off the performance," Hattie said, shooting daggers through her eyes at Sett. "But I say the show must go on. Did the Phantom's murder stop the opera? I think not. Right, Noema?"

I met Sett's stony gaze.

"The fall festival is our lifeblood. That's when we get all the money to keep the theater open," I said. "We can't call it off. And Fitz will have a cow if we let this ruin the festival and the performances."

"It's not safe."

I crossed my arms. "It is if we have backup. If you're there, we'll be fine. The murderer will either have to show up to perform, or we'll know who they are. It's safer than letting them run around town."

Sett's chest expanded, readying for a long exhale. "Fine. But I do the questioning."

I didn't stop him. I didn't even want to be around him. His painstakingly slow approach made me itch to transform into my wolf self. At least then I could threaten everyone with a snarl until the killer confessed.

Cast members took seats and waited to give their statements to the sheriff. Once he finished with one, Hattie insisted they return to the stage and run their lines before leaving.

I pricked my ears to catch the answers but kept my gaze turned away. If Sett caught me eavesdropping, it'd be the nail in my investigative coffin.

After several rounds of questions, it was clear nobody knew anything useful. Nobody except for Cordelia, it seemed. The vampire gnawed at her acrylic fingernails, ruining the polished design with her fangs.

Did I put people at risk if I didn't admit what I knew about Cordelia? Did she really have a secret that only Cliff knew?

The sudden earthy smell of rain overwhelmed me, and tears welled in my eyes. If I wanted the town to be safe, I'd have to confront one of my first friends in Bewitcher's Beach.

But I had to be sure before Sett barged in and dragged her through the long, painful process of interrogation, arrest, and trial. I blinked the tears back and resolved to do the right thing.

Tomorrow at the afternoon setup and when I had the courage, I'd speak with her.

CHAPTER 22
MYSTERY FIGURE

I HEATED PIZZA BAGELS, washed piles of pup clothes, and scrubbed the dishes as if today wasn't the day I'd confront my friend for murder. Today, the fall festival held its grand opening, and it'd run from Wednesday to Sunday evening. Vendors kept it short and sweet to make the demand higher.

I sat in front of the couch, folding piles of superhero underwear and hand-me-down jeans from Celeste's kids.

The thud of eight footsteps grew louder. Halen yelled at Dio, who shoved past him to reach the top of the staircase first. I turned from my folding spot on the rug to see the lens of Halen's camera.

"I got all the actors!" Halen announced, referring to his project to interview each cast member. After the last performance, we'd review the interviews as a thank you to Hattie for her hard work. And someday, if a movie director ever made it to Bewitcher's Beach's fall festival, we'd be ready with hours of footage about our process, actors, and recorded performances.

Dio shoved through, nearly knocking the camera from Halen's hands. The oversized eight-year-old dove onto the couch to cuddle the soft clothes. The neat piles tumbled onto the floor or suffered wrinkles from the weight of Dio's body.

Stevie walked carefully with Squeaks balanced on the crown of her head. She chattered, and the mouse lived up to his name, screeching softly. Finally, Jovi joined the group with his nose buried in a book about ancient Egypt.

"Mom, did you know the museum piece in your play is historically inaccurate?" he said without lowering the book.

"I should hire you to do research for my script next time," I said.

"Doesn't that ruin the plot of your story? The dude who steals the piece and falls in love with the lady doesn't make sense. He wouldn't even want to steal it because it wouldn't be in a museum in the first place..." Jovi rambled. While I appreciated his knowledge and suggestions, my mind wandered from the plot of the play to Cordelia's plot to murder. Did Piper find out whatever Cordelia had wanted to hide?

The question nagged at me the rest of the afternoon. It repeated in my head while I swept the stage. It continued when I unlocked the theater's double doors and let the laughter, music, and buzz of conversations float in from the fall festival. The question didn't go down with the sun and lingered instead until the cast arrived.

Each member dropped their bags and belongings in the small dressing rooms past stage left. Most emerged to check last-minute placements on the stage or run lines behind the curtains.

Bette posted up at one door to collect pre-purchased tickets while Mae manned the ticket sales at the other door.

I couldn't put it off any longer. Cordelia had yet to come out of the dressing room at the end of the hall.

I forced one foot in front of the other.

The door creaked as I pushed it open. The thin vampire

stood facing the large, round window at the opposite end of the room. She used the glass to see her reflection and apply another coat of lipstick since the old, silver-lined mirrors in each dressing room didn't work for vampires.

"Cordelia?" I said, opening the door wider. "Can I check-in with you really quick?"

Cordelia started braiding her dark hair as she turned. "Be my guest."

The urge to drop to all fours and run out in wolf form twitched at my muscles. I clenched my fingers and stood my ground. The mystery needed solving, once and for all.

"Mom to mom, I know you want your son to grow up in a safe town," I started. She furrowed her brows but continued twisting and tightening the second braid. "So I have to ask, was the secret Dr. Conflick knew worthy of murder?"

Her fingers froze mid-braid. "What? Noema, you don't think I..."

I furrowed my brow. The slight scent of rain emanated from her—sadness or disappointment over my suggestion. I hated the feeling that came with it, but I couldn't deny the rising smell of nerves.

"How bad is the secret?" I asked.

She shook her head, letting go of the braid. It unraveled while the first braid swayed side to side. "It's nothing. Honestly, no big deal at all."

Fish. The pungent, oily smell of fish overwhelmed both sadness and fear. Cordelia was lying.

I filled the silence between us. "I just want everybody in Bewitcher's Beach, especially our little ones, to feel safe. If you're hiding something dangerous, Sett will eventually find out."

Cordelia rubbed the back of her fingernails together like a

washboard. Fear wrinkled her forehead as she gnawed on her lower lip with sharp fangs.

After several moments of smelly silence, she collapsed into the chair in front of the mirror. She dropped her face into her palms.

"I can't tell you, I can't, but you have to believe me. I didn't hurt Dr. Conflick. I swear!" Her voice broke with sobs, though her body couldn't produce tears.

All smells resembling tuna and trout and salmon faded. Only ammonia remained. She'd lied about the scope of the secret, but not about murder.

I released a breath and stepped forward, crouching in front of her. "Does anyone else know your secret? If it's dangerous, I think you need to share it. Could it have been the reason Cliff got kill—" Movement caught my eye, and I gasped mid-sentence.

A shadow shifted in the window, and my heart skipped a beat. I shot to my feet at the sight of a hooded figure. The lights lining the mirror glinted off an object in the intruder's hand, nearly blinding me.

The silhouette darted from the window. My heart thudded against my ribcage.

Cordelia shrieked. I turned to see her standing, hands clamped over her mouth and eyes wide. "Who was that? They're coming to hurt me now too, aren't they? I told Dr. Conflick my secret and now the hunters want to kill me! But I didn't kidnap Henry. I promise, it's just an unofficial adoption. His parents begged me."

"What?"

She collapsed in the chair again, dry sobs wracking her body. "I don't want to be destroyed!"

Did a hunter really kill Cliff? And did that mean the last person left on my list was a hunter? I couldn't picture Vera, the professional, long-time resident and only realtor in Bewitcher's Beach, as an offbeat hunter who attacked supernaturals for sport. And who was the huge person in the window?

If I let the stalker get away, I'd never forgive myself. I grabbed the window frame and yanked it up. I left my human self behind in the dressing room, transforming as I jumped through.

Or so I thought. I hit the cobblestone on two feet. Instead of transforming, my body remained bipedal and without fur. My knees nearly buckled from the jarring impact but I caught my balance. Confronting Cordelia took too much emotional energy, and I needed either rest or focus to become my wolf self —neither of which I had right now.

I narrowed my gaze on the forest behind The Oyster Inn. Two feet would have to do. I ran after the figure, gaining on their slow, hulking form.

Was this a hitman? A hunter friend of Vera's?

The figure disappeared into the trees' shadows.

My feet pounded the cobblestone until I reached the edge of town. The slick mud and moss nearly knocked me on my butt. I slowed and listened for the rhythm of their footsteps, but the buzz of the fall festival, even out here, distracted me from focusing on one particular sound.

Instead, I followed the scent of shock as it shifted between smells. The sound of people faded, and I identified the snap of a twig.

I froze and listened. My heart pounded. If this person was a hunter, I'd put myself in the exact situation Sett had feared. I couldn't outrun a silver bullet. Even a regular bullet or knife would do while in my human form.

My muscles tensed but I still couldn't transform. I needed the power of my werewolf's nose to identify the person's unique scent. Where did they go?

Another footstep.

From behind me now.

The figure grabbed me, wrapping thick arms around me. This was it. I'd gotten myself into irretrievable trouble and without backup.

Son of a witch. I cursed at myself for impulsively chasing the attacker. Adrenaline flooded me, a temporary but useful source of energy. Hands became paws and my legs turned into hind legs. With my wolf strength, I was powerful enough to shove off of the attacker's hold and drop to all fours.

My clothes fell in a heap at their feet. I didn't pause to see who it was. For once, I resisted the impulse to return the attack, to rush at answers head-on. I ran. My paws squished into the forest floor as I covered the distance twice as fast as I ever could on two feet.

I glanced back to be sure the attacker didn't follow me, and if they did, that they couldn't keep up. The figure stood at their full height now, looking like a giant in the forest. A whimper escaped me at the thought of what'd just happened.

What was I thinking? I'd acted impatiently, again. At least I'd freed myself, but I'd also failed to identify the culprit.

I dared to look back again. Squinting, I tried to focus my vision while still running away at full speed. *Who is—*

A sudden whack stopped me. The pain of colliding with a solid, immovable object rippled through me. Dazed, I stumbled, and fell on my back against the wet moss. My legs scrambled as I tried to roll to all fours, but the shock and adrenaline had knocked me back into my human form. Paws became hands, and whimpering turned to gasps.

All at once I went from the modesty of a body fully covered in fur, to exposed—bare on the forest floor in front of another towering silhouette.

CHAPTER 23
BACKUP

THE FIGURE'S hands flew to his eyes as he turned his head away from me. Wings taller than a doorway surrounded me. The leathery muscles splayed out, creating a half-circle as if shielding my body.

I knew those wings.

"Sett?" I breathed as his reaction registered. He'd averted his gaze to give me privacy while also doing his best to block my bare body from the breeze.

I twisted to see if the attacker was still visible through the trees, but the glow of moonlight only illuminated tree trunks and bushes.

My heart thudded at an irregular pace until the slight scent of vanilla crept into my nose. Despite my terribly embarrassing state of exposure, relief flooded me at the sight of Sett. And the respect he afforded me helped slow my pulse.

"Here," he said, voice low. Sett kept his gaze tucked into the edge of his wing while he slipped off his coat. The heavy piece of fabric billowed out and nearly covered my whole body like a blanket.

I pulled my arms into the sleeves and stood to wrap it

around me. On him, the coat barely reached his waist, but it covered me to the middle of my thighs.

"Are you okay?" he asked. "Cordelia told me you went after a stalker."

I shook my head, stepping to where he could see me. "I know, it was stupid. They grabbed me and I ran." Still breathless, my voice faded.

Sett looked me up and down, but it didn't feel awkward. Instead, I recognized the concern that pulled his stony skin into wrinkles at his eyes.

"Who was it?"

"I didn't see their face." I frowned, apologetic. I smelled no judgment, but I couldn't meet his eyes after both losing the suspect and ending up naked on the ground in front of him. My gaze lingered at our feet. "I couldn't get a unique scent either, but they were huge and as tall as—"

"Dr. Pitt?" Sett asked.

The curiosity in his voice made me look up. Sett stared past me, and I spun around to follow his line of sight, pinching the coat tightly around me. A hulking figure emerged from between the trees and stepped out of the shadows.

The doctor shuffled toward us with his hands stretched out. He stopped in front of Sett and offered his wrists.

"I-It was m-me," Dr. Pitt said through a shaking voice. "Arrest me."

Sett and I exchanged gaping glances. The smell of lavender confirmed the truth but came with plenty of pungent fear too.

"But you were at Miss Raven's studio that night. How'd you get back in time to kill Cliff?" I asked. Words spilled out of my mouth before I could stop them and allow Sett to do his job in an orderly fashion. Maybe I needed to get comfortable with a little order and organization before I found myself naked in the woods again.

Dr. Pitt's head snapped up. His beady eyes bugged and a bead of sweat trickled down his temple.

"Kill Cliff? I didn't kill Cliff! Who said I k-killed Cliff?" The doctor heaved now, trying to catch his breath between desperate statements. He shoved his hand into his trench coat's pocket and produced an empty paper bag. The brown paper inflated like a balloon then and shrunk again. A shiny silver cross necklace fell from his pocket, but he didn't notice as he inhaled and exhaled into the bag.

"What were you doing outside Cordelia's window, and with a cross?" I pointed to the jewelry on the ground.

"That was just for precautions," he said, removing the bag from mouth. "I'm s-sorry that I grabbed you; I thought you were her boyfriend and had come to attack me. But when you changed into a wolf, I realized I was mistaken. It's dark, and I was just so scared!"

"Dr. Pitt," Sett started. He pulled out a small notepad and produced a pen from his back pocket, then clicked it and pressed the tip to the paper. "I'm going to need to take your full statement with an explanation."

The doctor dug into his other pocket and pulled out a crumpled envelope. "This was Cliff's. I knew he worried one of his patients had broken the law, but I didn't know who or how dire the situation was. When I located the envelope, I realized I needed to help right away."

Sett unfolded the envelope and scanned it.

When his eyes widened, I couldn't resist shuffling closer to get a glimpse at the contents of the letter.

The words *kidnapped* and *running from the law* caught my attention. A lump gathered in my throat.

"Why didn't you come to me?" Sett folded the letter and gave the doctor a stern glare.

"I was afraid Cordelia was in a domestic violence situation.

If I got the police involved, it could make matters more dangerous for her. I tried to be brave and offer to get her away from him while she was out of her house. But I-I'm not a brave man..." He dropped his head and stared at the ground. With the crumpled bag in his fist, he raised his wrists again, holding them for the sheriff to arrest him. "I shouldn't have acted outside the law."

"It's not her. This is about Cordelia's son, Henry." I pointed to the paper in Sett's hands "She said he's adopted, but it's not official. I don't know the full story, but it makes sense why she was getting plastic surgery to try to look like him. And why she was afraid Cliff would share her secret." I said. "It doesn't seem she's in any danger, other than from judgments and rumors."

Sett tucked the letter into his back pocket. "Go home, Dr. Pitt."

The doctor dared to look at us through his bushy brows. "C-can I watch the play?" He dug into his pocket for the third time and produced another piece of paper, a ticket that read *Everland Theater.*

Sett chuckled. "Of course. And I'll be sure to double-check Cordelia's safety and get the full story."

With that, the supposed stalker shuffled into the alley and headed for the theater's double doors.

We trailed several steps behind him, both deep in thought. Or so I guessed based on Sett's furrowed brow.

"Noema, Sett!" A cheerful voice greeted us. I looked up from the cobblestone at my feet to see the glow of the lamp posts reflecting off of Fitz's head. Though he was always positive, a line of concern creased his forehead. "Is everything okay?"

Sett filled him in on the events and asked him to check on Cordelia.

"Is Piper okay?" I asked.

Fitz swiped his palm over his bare head and turned. "Ask her yourself." He pointed to Everland's doors. I'd been so focused on the mayor, I didn't notice the woman lingering outside. "I'm her temporary bodyguard," he said. "Until this is solved, I'm escorting her to the performance. Hey, if I got you the weapon, do you think you could sniff out the owner?"

I shook my head. "It doesn't work like that. I smell emotions since emotions produce different reactions in people's bodies."

"But you smelled the paraquat in Cliff's stomach," he said, stroking his chin. "I recall you mentioning a salad or plants, and it turned out to be weed killer in his system."

"But weed killer has a smell," I explained. "A weapon doesn't. What was it, anyway?"

"A lock pick," Sett answered for him while Piper headed our way.

Her thick curls bounced with every step until she halted in front of us. "I hate to interrupt, but I've really got to get into costume." She smiled at Fitz. "Would you mind watching outside my dressing room door?"

Fitz nodded. "Sure thing!"

Slight ammonia filled the air, mingling with the scent of a seasonal bonfire blowing up from the beach. Poor Piper was nervous, and I couldn't blame her. But I admired her courage to live up to the phrase *the show must go on*. The only suspect left was Vera, but it still didn't make sense since she had no motive.

Piper marched to the double doors with Fitz trailing in her wake.

"Uh, Piper, wait," I called out. She and Fitz stopped and spun around as I caught up to them. A heavy shadow followed slowly behind.

"I don't want to be late," she said with a little laugh and then leaned in. "You know how Hattie is."

"Do I ever," I said. "This will be quick. Do you know who'd want to hurt you?"

Piper's big eyes shifted between me and Fitz and then landed on Sett, who'd ambled up beside me. "I already answered this. I have no idea." She shrugged. "I'm sorry."

The delightful scent of the truth's lavender filled my nose. Piper had nothing to lie about. Maybe it was time to ask about everything.

"You said you had business to settle in town." I thought back to the first time I'd met her. "Did anything change in your life recently that might have triggered an attack?"

Piper took a long breath through her nose and licked her lips. Her eyes searched the sidewalk until the lavender smell grew stronger and she blinked. "I'm trying to think of something, but I don't know."

"You mentioned trouble with the law," I said, "when you returned your late videos."

Her brow furrowed. "Yeah, I, uh..." A nervous look flickered over her face as her eyes trailed over the two cops. Finally, she sighed and her shoulders sagged. "Look, it's embarrassing, but Cliff and I had a volatile relationship. More than once, we had the police called on us when we'd get into fights and destroy one another's property. I'd gotten caught taking a bat to his sports car. He wanted to make up the night he died." Her voice cracked. "We got married just to spite each other, really, almost like a dare or playing chicken to see who'd give up first. We're both—*were* both—headstrong." Gingerly, she touched her lips. "We eloped but never had a real wedding. He wanted one and promised to win me again over a date with my favorite movie."

The Swan Princess.

She continued. "And I just wanted one last free surgery before I broke it off. He figured that out, we fought, and I left.

Once I found out he'd been attacked, I knew how that'd look, so I approached Dr. Pitt to fix my botched lips, and then I was going to stay out of Bewitcher's Beach forever."

The details swirled around in my mind. What was I missing? None of this explained a motive for Vera.

"And nothing else happened leading up to your attack?" I asked, pointing to my side where she'd been stabbed.

She shrugged again. "I got in trouble with my job when they found out I never returned for a shift I clocked in to. I wasn't supposed to stay out that long. I just popped into town to end things with Cliff, but then I accused him of purposely botching the procedure, and the fight blew up. Oh! And Cliff's accountant contacted me. I guess Cliff had a big inheritance coming in from his dad who'd just passed away, and I would get it as his wife. But I told them to donate it. I'm way too superstitious to take a dead man's money."

"Excuse me!" A screeching voice interrupted our conversation. Hattie materialized beside us and gave everyone a fright. My bones nearly leaped out of my skin. Even Sett flinched as the ghost appeared, pissed off expression and all. Fitz was the only one unbothered. In fact, he beamed at Hattie, his grin wider than I thought possible.

"Noema." Hattie's harsh voice grated me. "Piper begged me to still let her perform, and you're out here distracting her."

I reached out and patted Piper's arm. "Go. I'm sorry."

With that, they hurried into the theater's double doors, leaving Sett and me alone in the glow of the festival's lights.

I turned to face him, stepping perhaps a little too close, but the chilly feeling coming off of his skin drew me in and cooled my fiery burn.

"What did you say the weapon was?"

He blinked, shifting his gaze to meet my eyes. "A broken lock pick."

Where had I seen a lock pick? I couldn't put my finger on a specific memory, but it felt familiar. Citrusy smells rose around us. Happiness. We were two opposites, and yet we'd formed a friendship since I'd moved to Bewitcher's Beach. Maybe more...

"I'm sorry my actions dragged you away from the investigation," I said, mustering the courage to admit my mistake. Every day, I lived with the weight of turning my late husband into a werewolf. If I tried to carry more regret, I'd collapse, so the confession felt as freeing as shedding my heavy winter coat.

Sett looked at me and nodded. "It's no trouble. I was worried."

"Fair," I said. "I should have waited for..." I met his slate eyes and gnawed on my lip. If I ended by saying *you*, would he think I saw us as partners? I didn't want to overstep my boundaries, again. Twice now, I thought I'd found the murderer, and twice I was dead wrong.

"Backup?" He finished my sentence with a side smile.

I blinked away my thoughts and focused on him again.

The glittering festival lights shined against his stony skin and illuminated one side of his face. The rich yellow and orange glow warmed his natural shade of slate. Behind him, lights were strung between vendors and wrapped the trunks of the park's red and brown trees.

"Yeah, backup." I returned the smile.

His wings expanded slightly, then retracted in a sort of shrug. "Although, it seems you didn't need it. You're just fine without protection, aren't you?"

"Well, I'm not wearing any pants in the middle of town. Again." I said, letting a little laugh escape me. "I definitely needed to borrow your coat. Again."

Joyful music followed an upbeat rhythm. The song floated from the town's square as vendors wrapped up. The festival came to a quiet end for the night. It paved the way for people to move from the outdoor celebration of kettle corn and balloon animals and into Everland for the performance.

"Maybe you could slow down a little," he said. "But I admire your determination, and I should have known you can hold your own."

It wasn't until his cool breath grazed my neck that I realized how close we stood. Lavender aroma surrounded us, blocking out the scent of fried festival food and bonfires.

Slow down. I considered the suggestion.

Despite the unsolved mystery and the fact that we'd yet to save Bewitcher's Beach from Cliff's murderer, I allowed myself an entire minute to bask in the scent of relaxation.

"Thank you," I said, "for having my back even when I get myself into a sticky situation."

"I'm your backup," he said, side-smirk stretching into a full grin. His eyes searched mine and I swear he leaned closer to me. The cool temperature of his stony skin soothed the burn of my feverish wolf's side.

My heart skipped a beat.

As much as I wanted to lean into him and let his cold melt my heat, I hadn't kissed anyone since Christopher. I'd hurt my husband, and though I couldn't turn a gargoyle into a werewolf, I didn't doubt I'd make a painful mistake with Sett, too.

My chin tilted back. Everything wrong within me wanted the kiss, to impulsively give in to the odd camaraderie we'd built over the past few weeks, and feel Sett on my lips.

The rough tips of his fingers brushed my chin to pull me closer.

I can't.

I stepped back. The comforting chill of his skin faded. Heat rose all over my body as I removed myself from his proximity.

Sett cleared his throat.

I opened my mouth to tell him it wasn't that I didn't dislike him. The opposite, really. Maybe. I wasn't sure how I felt, but he didn't deserve to think I was disgusted by the thought of kissing him or anything...

Wait. Where had I heard that before? A memory rushed back. When Mae had teased Vera about kissing Cliff, Vera gagged. How had the obvious slipped past me so easily? She was disgusted by the prospect because she was the long lost sibling! And the pink lock pick—that was where I'd seen one— on her keychain.

"Vera," I said. With the others crossed off the list, I thought I'd missed someone else, assuming she didn't have reason to attack Cliff. But with Piper's story, it all made sense. Piper was attacked after the accountant contacted her. Vera must have found out and gotten upset that she wasn't getting their parents' full inheritance.

"What?" Sett cocked his head.

"I thought she didn't have a motive, but I was wrong," I said, waving my hands in excitement. The words couldn't come out fast enough. Maybe we'd still close this mystery and ensure the town's safety tonight. "But she was disgusted when Mae suggested she dated Cliff."

"Disgusted?"

"Of course." I hurried to the theater. "Nobody dates their own brother."

"Slow down, Noema. You're not making sense." He followed in my wake.

I turned to walk backward and catch him up to speed. "Remember how you said Cliff's half-sibling was presumed dead?" I smirked. "I'm willing to bet he's the only half that's dead."

Vera was still very much alive, and about to take the stage.

CHAPTER 24
A NECESSARY CRIME

I MARCHED past the theater with my sights set on the other side of town. There, the realtor's office butted up to Dr. Pitt's clinic. With Vera busy performing, I had approximately two hours to put on pants and then gather all the evidence I could find.

Of course, I knew that Vera's distaste for Cliff wasn't proof of their relation or that she'd murdered him. But if I fit enough pieces of the puzzle together, she'd be forced to confess. I was willing to bet Mockbuster's future as a business that I'd find weed killer somewhere in Vera's home and office combination.

Sett's cool fingers gripped the crook of my arm. "Where are you going?"

"To find the murder weapon," I said. "The poison, I mean. And the rest of the broken lock pick."

The disarray of puzzle pieces only made me more excited to fit them together. The details were there, I just couldn't see the full picture yet.

"What's your plan?" he asked, following me into Mockbuster.

"To find the murder weapon." I repeated. "I said that. How

much do you want to bet that there's weed killer in her house?" We passed the rows of movies. If this were a film itself, we'd find the paraquat and go into the theater, guns blazing until Vera dropped to her knees and begged us to spare her life. Of course, we'd never do such a thing. But we *could* grab enough evidence to back her against a metaphorical wall.

"I can't get that information without a warrant—"

I paused halfway up the spiral staircase and looked down at him. "Right, *you* can't."

"Noema!"

I darted up the steps and through the small apartment. I hopped up and down to pull a tight pair of high-waisted pants over my hips and then threw on a jean jacket.

When I emerged, Sett was pacing at the bottom of the stairs. I tossed him the coat with another thank you and headed for the door.

He grabbed me before I pushed through. "There's no way am I letting you break into her house."

"She'll never confess if we don't prove to her that we have enough evidence stacked against her." I pulled my arm from his grip and went for the front desk.

I crouched and grabbed the notebook tucked by the base of Mockbuster's computer.

Sett leaned on the desktop until the table cracked. He straightened again, realizing his weight was too much for the table. "I'll double-check Vera's statements and speak with her again," he said. "But I'm stuck until I find a record of a Vera Conflick. She must have gotten rid of that name completely when paper documents updated to computers."

"Updated to computers?" I repeated as a thought formed. I glanced at the decade-old relic on the desktop that stored years of customer information, even from before I took over Mockbuster.

I plucked the pen from Sett's hand and circled the clues I had recorded relating to Vera.

Vera had a meeting with Cliff at the inn's bar before he died.

Poison, wine, and popcorn in his stomach.

Motive?

I reached for his notepad where he'd neatly written *inheritance—half-sibling* and overlapped it with the last question in my scribbles. Together the clues created a picture: opportunity, means, and motive. The mystery was complete.

I almost wished Halen stood by with his trusty camcorder. This moment would make a perfect movie scene if we clipped out the clues and lined them up for the image of a puzzle solved.

Sett sighed and scratched at his left horn. "It could take weeks to verify her relation to Cliff." His gaze flicked from the clues on the page to meet my eyes. "We can't spook her."

My foot tapped as I waited for the computer to boot up. "Just give me a second."

Several minutes passed while the screen loaded, blinking in its attempt to wake up. I typed *Conflick* into the keyboard as fast as my fingers allowed. Typically, I'd never waste time to type a customer's full name since the computer would populate and bring up the accounts matching the first half of the word.

This time, I wanted to be precise. The screen popped up with a tiny spinning graphic of an hourglass. Finally, the records filled in, and two accounts came up under the same last name.

Conflick, Cliff: account cleared. Conflick, Vera: one outstanding rental.

I gasped and patted the old computer for a job well done. Out of curiosity, I clicked her name, and it opened another layer. *Outstanding rental: Clue.*

"No way." I laughed. "It's here. This ancient computer is

actually good for something. And Vera even rented a murder mystery nine years ago and never returned it. Technically, she owes Mockbuster over three hundred dollars in late fees."

Sett bumped into the desk, nearly toppling the computer as he came around the other side.

"Then it's true," he said. "Vera is Cliff's half-sister."

"The human half." Even as I said it, a twinge twisted at the pit of my stomach. Bewitcher's Beach was once a safe place. A place where nobody, especially not a human, could hurt a supernatural. If the legend was true, as Dr. Pitt and many others had sworn, what changed? How did Vera, a human, bypass the witch's spell with something powerful enough to kill her half-troll brother?

"I'll work on getting a warrant to find her in possession of the poison or other evidence," he said, side-stepping out from behind the desk.

"How long will that take?" I asked. I couldn't help but glance around the dark, quiet shop. Only the sounds of the performance, rehearsals, and cast members had kept Mockbuster alive the past few weeks. Business wouldn't return until the murder was publicly solved. Not to mention, people deserved to feel safe again, despite the legend's change.

Sett pulled his jacket on as he paused in front of the door. "It's the weekend, so a few days, at least."

A few days? The fall festival would be over, visitors gone home, and the curse still scaring people away from rentals.

I shook my head. "I can't wait that long," I said, thinking of the dismal business and the coming cost of rent due the beginning of November. I needed customers back in the shop ASAP.

"I'll get started on the paperwork right now." The bell chimed as he tugged the door open. He twisted his neck to give me a stony glare. "Don't do anything illegal."

I let the door fall shut before I responded.

"No promises," I said, squinting at the office building across town.

BRITTLE LEAVES CRUNCHED beneath my Reeboks. The remains crumbled to red and yellow and brown dust and blew away in the wind.

While people enjoyed watching the crime I'd written into the script, I risked a minor transgression of my own.

"It's for a good cause," I muttered as I tried the front door. As expected, the doorknob didn't twist. A growl escaped me, but I didn't let frustration slow me down. I circled to the left of the building and into the alley where a high window was open, inviting the fresh breeze and scent of the festival inside.

I'd have to bypass the lock by climbing—if I could get that high without my head spinning. After a huff and a shake, I secured my foot on an uneven brick and scaled the wall, moving from brick to brick. I climbed through the window and dropped on the other side with a tuck and roll. It didn't work as I'd hoped. I fell to the side, banging my hip against the office's hardwood flooring. I hated heights.

If only I could break in while in wolf form, I'd have the balance of all four paws to keep me upright.

But I wasn't about to risk leaving shed fur behind or getting caught with no pants again.

I flicked on my flashlight and scanned the plain area with a desk, computer, filing cabinets, and chairs for clients. Minutes of searching passed like hours as I carefully opened drawers and rummaged through an indoor plant for evidence of fertilizer, only to find it was fake. I tiptoed to the back of the office and found a long closet under the staircase with a wall of organized cardboard boxes. Each was labeled with a permanent marker. *Christmas decorations, summer clothes, movies.*

Movies? I clucked my tongue. Who stored videos away in the closet? They were meant to be watched and rewatched. I resisted the urge to dig out the box from the bottom of a stack and find the old copy of *Clue.*

I swept the flashlight to the other side of the closet where folding chairs, a trash can, and a small table lined the wall. Under the table, a pile of dirt collected from a slumped bag of soil. Clay pots were stacked beside it, and tucked in the back sat a white jug of weed killer.

I crouched and dragged the jug out from its hiding place. The colorful font read *Weed Wilter, sure to kill every last one!*

"And everyone in the way of getting the family inheritance," I mumbled. Paraquat was listed as the first ingredient.

I pushed the jug back into place. Sett needed to see this for himself, and sooner rather than later. But I needed more evidence. I couldn't confront her the way I had Piper at Dr. Pitt's clinic. That was both impulsive and embarrassing on my behalf.

So I resolved to keep searching and did a second round of rummaging through cabinets and drawers for anything suspicious. The drawers were full of paperwork and... a gun.

My heart stopped. I shoved the papers aside to fully uncover the weapon. The familiar signal of Everland theater's cursive E marked the side. Vera had the prop gun in her office. Why had she removed it from the theater?

Ready to call the cops, I hurried to the front door. Without thinking, I grabbed the doorknob and twisted, yanking it open.

A blaring alarm exploded in my ears. I folded my ears back and slapped my hands over them, yelping at the painfully loud sound. Fearing the worst, I narrowed my gaze to see if anyone emerged from the theater on the other side of town. Surely, they could hear the powerful alarm that announced my crime to the whole town.

I needed to escape out the back or through the window I'd come in. I stumbled back into the office while the honking continued. Whimpers died in my throat. The sound felt like it'd rip my ear drums apart.

On the outside of the wall, I'd used the uneven brick to climb into the window. Inside, I couldn't scale a smooth wall. I grabbed a chair and shoved it against the wall under the window. I stretched and swept my elbow to the window frame where I could drag myself up. If only I'd planned an escape route before I dove inside.

Too late now.

I swung my leg up and into the window, then peered over the other side. It was only several feet high, but with the disorienting alarm and my heart already pounding, it suddenly looked like the edge of a cliff. Jumping to the cobblestone was too dangerous, especially if I miscalculated my balance.

I perched in the window with my feet on the windowsill and hands holding the frame above.

"Jump. Just jump," I said. I squeezed my eyes shut, but that only made me dizzier.

Heavy footsteps approached, and my eyes flew open. A thick-framed figure jogged down the sidewalk, passing by the alley between the clinic and realtor's office. Sett vaguely glanced at me as he ran by.

A moment later, he doubled-back and marched into the alley.

I tried to smile, but I was sure it looked more like a cringe.

Sett stopped below me. His head almost reached the window and that slowed my breathing. I wasn't as high up as my panicked mind had tricked me into believing.

The sheriff checked the watch on his wrist before crossing

his arms. "One hour. You almost made it one hour after I warned you not to do anything illegal."

"You can arrest Vera now," I said. "I found the weed killer brand with paraquat in it."

Sett offered his hand to help me out of the window. I slipped my fingers in his, and the solid feeling of his muscles gave me the courage to hop down.

When I landed on the ground, he didn't let go of my hand.

I tugged and looked up at him. Sett glanced at a dangling pair of handcuffs on his belt loop. Instead of reaching for them, he let me go.

"I won't use them if you'll walk with me down to the station."

"Excuse me?"

"Noema, you know I follow the rules. I have to arrest you for breaking and entering."

I bared my teeth, and a growl escaped me. A murderer ran around on the loose—performing on stage for the whole town to ooh and ahh at—and the sheriff wanted to arrest *me*?

"What about the weapon?" I asked as I froze in place and threw my thumb over my shoulder.

For a moment, Sett's gaze trailed to the office building, then flicked back to me. "I'll get a warrant—"

"A warrant?" My voice pitched higher than normal and the smell of frustration rose around me. I stank of campfire smoke and black pepper. "That'll take way too long!"

The sheriff folded his arms across his chest while his wings cupped his shoulders. "This is the order of operations."

"We're not doing math homework, we're catching a murderer!"

He knocked his fist against his open palm, letting the hand-cuffs dangle from his fist. "*I* am catching a murderer, and unfortunately, gardening supplies don't take the same priority as a smoking gun. Owning herbicide is perfectly normal," he said.

I thrust a finger in the air, ready to refute that. "True, but when you're a suspect, storing the same poison used to kill a man is basically fingerprints on a weapon. Plus, I found a gun."

His wings flexed.

"Well," I continued with the full truth, "it's a prop gun, from the play. What if she switched it with a real gun?" I thought of the scene I'd written where Vera's character confronts Piper's character with a weapon in hand. Shivers rippled through me. Had my script set Piper up for a deadly fate?

Sett turned, showing the back of his wings to me as he shuffled away. "When I get the warrant, we'll know more. Accidentally taking home a prop isn't enough for me to go after Vera." He stopped and glanced back at me. "Right now, I'm looking at another lawbreaker for a crime I witnessed."

"Who?" I asked, though I knew the answer. *Don't say it's me, don't say it's me, don't say—*

"You, Noema," he said with a tilt of his head. "Come along. I really don't want to have to cuff you."

Everything within me wanted to transform into a wolf and run from him. I could dart through the alley and make it to the beach before he blinked an eye. But that wouldn't solve anything.

I left my canine fangs exposed while I followed behind him. At least I'd take comfort in the one good decision I'd made tonight.

I didn't kiss Sett Lawrence.

CHAPTER 25
BEHIND BARS

A RESTLESS TWITCH jolted through my legs and I popped up from the little bench attached to the wall.

I'm in jail. Me, not the murderer. This is nuts! I shifted into my wolf form, letting my clothes drop to the floor. On all fours, I paced the length of the holding cell like the caged animal I was. It felt better to work through my frustrations as a wolf, where I could scratch at the floor with my claws. And for some reason, I deemed howling more appropriate than shouting in anger.

When Sett appeared with a paper cup in hand, I couldn't help but growl. The low rumbling sound bounced off the cell's stark walls. My lips trembled as I bore my canines at him.

"I'm sorry, Noema," he said, and his thick shoulders slouched. "If I let you break the law, then I'm breaking the law by association. A sheriff the people can't trust to be consistent is a sheriff who can't protect the town. I have Fitz ready to watch over Piper and the play, though, in case your speculations are right."

He offered the cup of water to me through the bars. I padded past it, letting my raised tail haphazardly swing into it and knock the cup to the ground. The water splashed across the cold, hard floor. Droplets clung to the tufts of fur between my toes.

If this were a movie, I'd say something witty like *I have a thirst for justice, not water*, and then he'd be so impressed by my determination to solve the murder, he'd unlock the cell and release me without the required bail. Then we'd exchange jokes like dialogue from a buddy cop film before apprehending the killer with teamwork and good-natured determination.

Of course, real life wasn't like the big screen, and Sett was no comedic cop. The frown on his stony face looked like a permanent mark in cement. I did my best to ignore him, but a tickle threatened my nose. I snuffled and pawed my snout before the dusty floor forced me to sneeze.

"I called Hattie to check in on the kids," he said. "But as you requested, I didn't mention...you know, this. Would you like to make your phone call now?"

Who did he think I could call to bail me out? If I didn't want him telling Hattie what happened, *I* certainly wouldn't be the one to tell her. Mae would happily loan me the money and take the opportunity to babysit, but she'd spoil the pups with candy and a trip to the toy shop. And just like Sett, I didn't have family around to back me up.

Since I didn't respond, he continued. "I think Hattie will understand the situation—"

An involuntary bark escaped me. I needed to calm down. I jumped on the little bench and circled twice, squishing myself down as small as possible to fit. When I plopped down with my front paws crossed and hanging over the bench's edge, I met Sett's gaze.

In his slow, roundabout way, he rambled. He shared that he'd found Cordelia after we parted ways. Once he'd explained the misunderstanding caused by Dr. Pitt's confusion and worry, she'd calmed, and the show proceeded as normal.

The show. I should be there for opening night. I should be confronting Vera right now.

Sett's sigh broke the silence, and it seemed he understood that I had no intention of making my phone call.

Instead, I worked through the clues and practiced how I'd convince Sett that my presence at the police station was a sign I was meant to help. Sure, I was on the inside of the bars, but my crime got answers. It was a risk I'd take again to get closer to the truth and get a murderer off the streets where my children rode their bikes.

I laid my chin on my paws and thought of all the movies with heroes who break the law in the name of justice. The first character to come to mind was Batman, whose story supported my side of the argument. He apprehended plenty of villains. Though his actions were not always within the law, they ultimately helped the city of Gotham.

Who else broke the law to save lives? When the thought of vigilantes led me to *Ghostbusters* and the illegal siren on their car, a shiver stole through me. I didn't want to be associated with characters who gave hunters a good name and made ghosts look bad.

It was time to swallow my pride. I'd found the paraquat-filled weed killer in Vera's possession, but as Sett said, owning an herbicide wasn't the same as fingerprints on a knife. Nor was it like any other type of weapon I'd seen in mystery movies. At least I knew I did the best I could to help. Getting home to my pups was now my priority.

Hattie can't watch them forever. And I didn't dare suffer the ghost's wrath and miss tomorrow's matinee performance too. With that decided, I shifted back into my human self and quickly slipped my clothes on. Once I shouted out to Sett and announced I'd like to make my phone call, footsteps thumped from the other room.

The buttery, cheesy smell of Alfredo sauce filled the cell with Sett's entry. It took my mind a moment to realize this scent wasn't attributed to any particular emotion. Instead, it wafted from a pile of steaming food. He balanced the giant container of creamy pasta in his hand.

"It's home-cooked," he said as he offered it to me with one hand and unlocked the cell with the other. "It's kind of a hobby of mine."

"I'm not hungry," I lied, still unsure of how to respond to the man who arrested me. My stomach grumbled in protest at my stubbornness. It must have been almost midnight now, and I hadn't eaten since lunch. Confronting Cordelia, chasing Dr. Pitt, and breaking into Vera's office only took a couple of hours, but it felt like weeks had passed, and my stomach agreed.

As we walked to the front of the station, I found myself repeatedly glancing at the pasta in all its creamy, cheesy goodness.

Sett shrugged, plopped into the seat behind his desk, and stabbed the pile of noodles with a fork. The small station had only two rooms, not including the small bathroom. The front of the station housed the sheriff's desk, a wall of filing cabinets, and a small TV propped on a folding table. The screen played reruns of *The Andy Griffith Show*.

Beyond that, two large chairs with cushioned leather seats faced the desk. To the right, a dull bulb hung in the center of the indented wall over a sink, a microwave, and a mini fridge. Beside it, a black phone clung to the wall, and the spiral cord hung low enough to brush the ground.

The rest of the station was modest, much like Sett himself. It was a place for paperwork and dealing with petty crimes. From what I knew, most illegal activity in Bewitcher's Beach involved selling crafts in the park without a permit, the occasional shoplifting incident, parking in tow zones, the rare public intoxication, and, apparently, trespassing.

I swallowed a lump in my throat and reached for the phone. What would Hattie say when she heard Sett cuffed me and tossed me in prison? Well, it wasn't so much a prison as a little local holding cell, and I didn't technically wear the handcuffs. In any case, she expected me to be assisting backstage, not running around doing what she'd insist was *flirting* with the town's police officer.

I punched in the phone number for Everland Theater and waited for several rings. I knew it'd take a few moments of effort for Hattie to manifest in a state solid enough to hold an object.

It rang and rang until her angry voice bellowed.

"Noema!" Hattie shouted. "We needed your help backstage, and moving props, and cueing the cast and—" She broke off with a pitchy groan. "I'm running around with my head cut off while I try to keep up. And you're taking a mini vacation? I should arrest you myself!"

And I almost believed she would when I saw the angle of her eyebrows and quivering scowl.

Wait... Hattie wasn't speaking to me on the phone. I blinked at the apparition who'd phased right through the wall. Hattie didn't so much as bother to use the front door, instead barging inside with her hands on her hips like a disappointed mother.

Slowly, I returned the phone to the receiver and silenced the endless ringing.

Hattie huffed a breath from her lower lip. The rush of air sent her bangs blowing away from her forehead. "I'm not mad," she said. "I'm envious. I'd love a break to enjoy the holiday, but there's too much riding on this performance." As much as

Hattie and I both loved Halloween, we never had enough time to enjoy it.

"I know," I said, feeling the full weight of my mistake now. We'd agreed to restore and run Everland Theater together—her with the vision of working in film again, and me wanting to realize my dream of screenwriting. "I'll focus on the play from now on, I promise. We have to sell out for tomorrow night."

"Oh, Honey," she said with a wince. It took all of her strength to lift up the canvas bag in her grip. "We already sold out both the matinee and evening performances."

My jaw nearly dropped to the thin gray carpet on the station's floor. "We...we sold out?" I'd been so engrossed in the murder investigation, I'd missed the success of the ticket sales.

A sparkling grin spread across her face. "I told you a romance would capture the hearts of locals and tourists alike." She turned and floated the two steps to Sett's desk. She flipped the bag upside down and dozens of bills fell out, decorating the desktop like expensive green confetti.

"Wait, Hattie, that money has to go to Everland."

"It will," she said confidently, "when you appear in court. Isn't that right, Sheriff?"

Sett nodded. "I hate to take this, but rules—"

"Are rules," I finished for him. "Got it." I wasn't trying to be rude, but I'd grown tired of his slow, paperwork-restricted ways. The pile of cash posted bail and gave me a chance to walk free again. I stared at the money, warmth filling my chest at Hattie's willingness to help. "Wait, Hattie, how did you know? I didn't even get a chance to call you yet." I frowned and flicked my gaze to the gargoyle in the chair behind the desk. "You said you didn't tell her. This is *my* business."

He opened his mouth, but it was Hattie's voice that responded. "He didn't need to tell me, Noema. It was what he didn't say that made it obvious. Plus, you'd never willingly miss an entire performance."

I sighed with nowhere for my frustration to go. This wasn't his fault, but I didn't have the energy to deal with his rules anymore.

I turned to my friend. "Who's with the kids?"

"Mae," she said casually.

I groaned, knowing the sugar rush and inevitable crash my pups were experiencing, if she'd let them stay up late. And knowing her, she did.

"We'd better hurry."

Hattie nodded, and we headed to the door. When she disappeared through it, Sett spoke up.

"I'll let you know when I get the warrant," he said.

I didn't turn, only nodding in response. I reached for the door handle and paused. Finally, I glanced back to see him taking another bite of pasta.

"That smells amazing, by the way," I said. "You must be a great cook."

Sett looked up with his cheeks full of noodles. Before he could respond, I opened the door and slipped out.

While I couldn't blame him for doing his job, I wasn't ready to forgive him. Maybe, someday, if I ever felt ready, I'd get a taste of his cooking. But before we took the time to nurture our friendship, I had a play to run and he had a killer to catch... hopefully, sooner rather than later.

CHAPTER 26
A STAGED CONFESSION

MUCH TO HATTIE'S DELIGHT, the entire cast made it to the last performance of the weekend with no understudies. Though we had to make do with a blue water gun toy to replace the missing prop. When Hattie and I asked Vera about it, she was honest, saying she accidentally brought it home one day and couldn't find it now. Then Vera had mentioned that her office was broken into, and I kept my mouth shut.

But the possibility of a real gun in Vera's possession nagged at me. I took a bit of comfort in the fact that Fitz was always close by and kept us safe.

Mockbuster livened up again as cast members invited family to come see them perform. Pride swelled within me at the sight of the success. Basing the script's characters on the people in town worked to pique interest.

The shop bustled with grandparents, siblings, and in-laws. Half-pixies came to see their sister star as the leading romance role and Triton's grandparents drove all the way from Southern California to watch him on stage.

Tonight, we'd sold out every seat.

I offered smiles to everyone who hugged and wished their actors good luck. They accepted the smile but carefully avoided the suggestion on the sign hanging at Mockbuster's front door.

Late fees waived for a fall festival discount. Rent today!

Not one video tape found a temporary home. Nobody wanted to risk the curse, especially not so close to Halloween. And rent was due in a week.

I closed my eyes and tried to breathe, but my chest only squeezed tighter.

The door's bell chimed, and I followed Squeak's gaze as he dropped to all fours and turned to the source of the sound.

The sight of Sett's wings startled me. I blinked, trying to determine if I'd imagined him. I'd expected another white-haired pixie or a half-dragon's cousin to come through that door, not the man who arrested me. Getting processed with a misdemeanor really solidified my choice not to kiss him. Before we'd even held hands, I'd already disappointed him. I didn't want to think about how much damage I could do if we dated.

"Can I talk to you?" Sett's voice was rough as he glanced around the crowded shop. His gaze landed on me and I caught the faint scent of citrus—excitement.

Odd, coming from the guy who'd arrested me.

"About what?" I asked. "Did you get the warrant?"

The twinkle in his slate eyes matched another surge of lemony aroma. "I didn't need to."

Sett nodded at the door. As soon as I stood, Squeaks dove for my arm and skittered up to my shoulder. I followed the sheriff, though I wasn't the guilty one this time.

He turned to me with a smirk on his face. Again, we stood outside, face to face with the scent of the fall festival's last night. Salty sea air whisked my hair away from the frame of my cheeks. Tomorrow, Monday returned, and the magic of Bewitcher's Beach's biggest event of the year would fade with the rising sun. Only the pumpkins and the promise of Halloween festivities tomorrow softened the blow of the event's end.

"What'd you do?" I asked, not expecting anything particularly grand. If I wanted to predict Sett's next moves, all I had to do was look inside a rule book.

The tip of the gargoyle's horns faced me as he twisted his neck. I followed his gaze. The brick building looked tiny from here, too small to house both a murderer and her choice of weapon.

Sett's wings rose and fell in a shrug. "I paid her a visit this morning—as a client, anyway."

I cocked my head. Sett already owned a seaside house with a bay window that faced the ocean. I only knew because the week I'd moved to Bewitcher's Beach was the same week the former sheriff retired and Sett got promoted. The town had celebrated his achievement with a surprise potluck at his own house, arranged by Mae. Did he plan on moving away?

An unexpected lump gathered in my throat. I swallowed despite the squeeze.

"How did that help?"

He laughed. "Accidentally on purpose, I may have seen the weed killer."

My ears turned forward, ready to hear how he'd legally accomplished that.

"I actually have a friend looking to move to Bewitcher's Beach, and I realized it was the perfect opportunity to stop by Vera's office. When I asked to use her bathroom, I purposely went to the closet where you said you'd seen the jug."

"And you couldn't take my word for it?"

Sett licked his lips. "I could have. But would a jury? Proof is better than speculation. It's more connection to Cliff's death."

"Okay," I said. It made sense, but I still exuded the smoky scent of frustration since he'd arrested me and let Vera go free for so long.

"It may have been a little dishonest, but you were right, I needed to speed up the process. It's wrong that Cliff's dead while Vera is enjoying the praise of viewers for her acting. Not to mention, she's attacking again...poor Piper." He rubbed the back of his neck with his palm. "If I'd moved a little quicker, she might have been spared that scar on her side. And I did more digging with her real name and found out Vera just bought a gun. Thankfully, Fitz is watching Piper's every move, so we know she's safe if Vera tries to come after her again."

My heart jumped and my ears folded back in mild disbelief. Sett had safely stretched the situation and gotten answers. I could respect that.

"But seeing the weed killer and owning a gun isn't evidence, is it?"

He shook his head. "It'd be best if we had something solid to seal this case once and for all."

"What about a keychain? What if I can get the other half of the broken lock pick?"

The wrinkles on his forehead deepened as he raised his brow. "How do you propose to do that?"

Without an explanation, I told him to wait here and hurried out in the alley behind Mockbuster. I slipped into Everland from the back door and inside Vera's dressing room. As expected, I spied her bag, snagged the giant keyring, and plucked the lock pick keychain. It was folded in so the broken piece was hidden, but it took only a flick to open it and reveal the weapon's other half. Shining gold caught my eye, and my heart slammed into my stomach. A bullet was right there in Vera's purse, but the gun next to it was a child's water toy.

She'd switched them. But would she go so far as to pull the trigger on stage?

Quickly, I returned to find Sett browsing the science fiction films and held up the evidence. "I found a bullet in her purse and the prop. Now, we just need a confession."

With his brows furrowed, Sett tilted his horns across the shop and then rushed for the theater where the killer was about to take the stage. I hurried after him and opened the door between the rental shop and the theater's backstage.

I spied Vera's glossy hair wrapped in a half bun among a sea of other cast members yet to step out from behind the curtain. Sett hung back in the shadow of Mockbuster, lingering just before the doorway.

"We need to do this calmly," he whispered in a hoarse voice.

I nodded.

"Vera." I crooked my finger when she turned. "I need to go over a line change with you," I lied.

"At the last performance?" She asked, echoing my whispers in a harsh voice.

"Just come here." I waved her over.

Vera rolled her eyes and quietly marched closer to Mockbuster. "I'm about to go on."

"Don't worry about it." I just needed her close enough to see if the real gun was in her costume's holster at her waist.

"Excuse me?" The pale skin of her forehead wrinkled and her thin eyebrows furrowed. "My cue is coming up." She glanced at the doorway and tossed a thumb over her shoulder. The faint sting of ammonia rose around her. Nerves sent her emotions in overdrive while mine settled slightly.

The holster was empty. I narrowed my eyes and spied the piles of props across the stage and behind the other side of the curtain. There the gun lay, as it was supposed to for this scene

— the scene I'd thankfully written where Vera's character didn't need a weapon.

Still, I kept Sett's mention of moving faster in mind and dove into the meat of the accusation. It was now or never to get a confession, before Vera realized what was happening and ran for the gun. "I know, it's bad timing. But it was bad timing for Cliff to move to Bewitcher's Beach too, wasn't it?"

"My client?" She shook her head. "I'm not following."

"With his dad just dying, I guess he wanted a change of scenery. Is that true?"

"I...don't know." She laughed nervously, matching the scent of her awkwardness.

"I thought I'd ask, since he was your client and all. Did he say anything about it? I'm just trying to get my facts right because of the rumor of the curse. If you just answer this, I'll let you get back." I lied. "You had a meeting at Roller Shakes with Cliff the night he died, right?"

"No," she said. The smell of truth filtered through her fear for a moment. "We met at the bar at The Oyster Inn."

"Oh, right. Cliff bought popcorn and soda to eat that night, but it was the wine that was poisoned, right?"

Vera shrugged. "What? Can I go on now?" She took a step back. "My family is expecting to see me perform."

"What family?" I asked. "I don't think we sold any tickets to the *Conflick* family."

Vera's jaw dropped, and a gasp escaped her. "That's not—"

"Your brother isn't in the audience, is he?" I interrupted her.

The ammonia was pungent now, burning the inside of my nose.

"I–I don't have a brother."

"Not anymore," I said. "Dead people don't watch plays. Or receive their inheritance." Maybe I needed to think before I spoke, considering Hattie had been dead for decades and watched dozens of plays every year. Impatience got my tongue. "You said your business was struggling. You wanted both your half and your brother's half of your father's inheritance, didn't you?"

Vera frowned, and the ammonia faded to the rising scent of smoke. Anger turned her cheeks a rosy shade. She knew we'd caught her.

"No." She shook her head and stepped back again, bumping into a set piece. The door rolled an inch. She shifted to the side.

I stepped forward, anticipating that she'd step back.

"You have a nice stash of gardening supplies, don't you? For fixing clients' yards and getting better prices? I seem to remember you mentioning that. But one thing I can't figure out is, why attack Piper?" I goaded her, knowing she didn't like *Viper* and hoping she'd spill over like a shaken can of Diet Pepsi.

I stepped forward again, silently pressuring Vera to move backward and into the stage's full light.

"I did nothing of the sort," she spat.

With that, I held up the broken lock pick. The evidence. "I found this dropped on the ground outside your dressing room," I fibbed. "I went to return it to you when I noticed it's the same shade of pink as the weapon used to stab Piper. And you didn't lose the prop gun; you switched it with a real one. Were you going to shoot her and try to blame someone else for a prop mishap?"

Her jaw slid side to side as she gritted her teeth. Finally, the scent of lavender emanated from her, mixed with anger's smoke. "She was only married to him for a few weeks, and they spent half that time separated. That little creep doesn't deserve the Conflick inheritance!"

The last piece of the puzzle fit into place. Piper had relished Hattie's praises over her villainous acting, calling on her experience as 'the other woman' before she eloped with Cliff. That mention of their marriage had earned Piper a stab to the stomach. Still, I couldn't determine how Vera knew supernaturals didn't have the protection that everyone else believed in.

I stepped forward again, and Vera mirrored it with a backward shuffle into the middle section of the stage where the acoustics caught every little sound. Despite the sudden quiet, even from the actors, Vera kept her gaze fixed on me while all eyes watched her.

"How did you know the legend wasn't true?" The question slipped out of my mouth.

She responded with a scoff. "I never believed in that crap, and it looks like I was right. But this town is full of superstitious whacks. It was too easy to make everyone believe in a curse."

The audience joined for a collective gasp. Everybody, half-dragon and vampire, young and old, visitor and local, heard the truth. Mockbuster's curse was all a ruse invented by the murderer—the voice from the back of the crowd at the scene of the crime.

Vera startled at their reaction and snapped her gaze to the hundreds of eyes watching her confession.

I couldn't help the last question that slipped from my mouth. "Did you try to frame me when you told Cliff I curse people who don't rewind their VHS tapes?"

The twitch of her lip almost looked like a smile. "Don't flatter yourself, Noema," she said. "I told him that so he wouldn't run off to the doctor before the poison took effect. He was a superstitious chump, and I knew he'd run to the person he thought was a witch to undo the curse."

My pulse iced over and breath left my lungs.

Though I'd gotten the killer to confess in front of the entire town, Vera now stood closer to the gun. She spun around and tried to grab it, but Sett stepped from the shadows and met her with his own weapon drawn. Handcuffs dangled from his grip. The clink of the metal echoed throughout the theater.

"Vera Conflick, you're under arrest for the murder of Dr. Cliff Conflick."

Finally, the dizzying moment of intensity ended, and I was able to suck in sweet oxygen again.

Unfortunately for Hattie, the show would not go on.

CHAPTER 27
THE SPELL OF HOME

(2 WEEKS LATER)

SQUEAKS NIBBLED A PIECE OF POPCORN, dropping crumbs on the desk and over my new notebook. I wiped the crumbs off the page, but the words were still difficult to read.

My handwriting would never improve. At least I'd solved my procrastination problem by starting next year's play immediately after this year's performance closed.

Jovi leaned against the snack wall with his nose in a book. Halen and Dio raced each other down the stairs while Stevie climbed into my lap and tried sounding out the title I'd given the script.

"The witch's legion?" she said.

"Legend," I corrected. "It's based on a true story." *Maybe.* Would we ever know the truth about the protective spell? If it never existed, what had kept supernaturals safe in Bewitcher's Beach all those years? It couldn't be coincidence; not even a small-town was without the occasional hunter's attack every few years.

Stevie shrugged, uninterested now as she slid off my legs and hurried to greet Mae's poodle. The puppy wagged its entire behind at the sight of her. Stevie scratched the curly fur and asked if the poodle wanted to play with her.

Without so much as a bark, the dog seemed to agree. The poodle pranced after her and to the coloring book she'd left splayed on the floor in the middle of the rental shop. The evening rush came and went, leaving the back wall empty of new releases. People were hungry for entertainment after the festival ended and because they'd refrained from renting videos during the rumors. The rush of cash had given me just enough to pay rent and keep the shop open.

Mae's visit came as unexpected.

"A puppy, huh?" I asked, nodding toward her new pet.

"Yes, a puppy. If the protection spell is broken, I'll need an attack dog for extra precautions now that hunters can hurt us here."

I watched the poodle wiggle his tail and pick up the crayon Stevie requested.

"I don't think he'll be doing any attacking," I muttered. When I faced Mae, I raised my voice. "Hey, I should ask you more about the legend. I'm basing the next play on it."

Mae waved her hand before slapping her palm to her chest. The sharp tips of her claws snagged the knitted sweater. "Oh, Honey, I'm no expert."

"But you felt it was real. I mean, Cliff wasn't an expert on curses, but he believed I was a witch. Those beliefs must come from somewhere."

"Of course they do. They come from the spell book," she said.

"What spell book?"

Mae sighed and stared at the back wall. "*The Book of Prophecies*. But it's missing—has been for years. Some witches who've passed through Bewitcher's Beach said they've felt remnants of its magic near the library. But I say, pish posh. Some delinquent probably stole it decades ago."

After Mae shared a bit of juicy gossip—something about Triton accepting a duel with Chanel's boyfriend for her attention—she scooped up her poodle and left. Whatever it was, it didn't sound like it had much truth to it, considering nobody had ever seen the siren's boyfriend.

And of course, she didn't leave without mentioning another *love triangle*. Her words. Mae shared her condolences as she explained that Sett's ex-girlfriend was moving to Bewitcher's Beach.

My stomach did a cartwheel.

I slapped the notebook shut and tucked it under my arm. Determined to complete next year's script months early, I decided I needed to dive into research right away... and get my mind off of Sett Lawrence.

If I sniffed out that old book, I'd be able to make the play as accurate as possible.

"Pups, get your coats. We're going to the library."

THE SMELL of old books filled my nose. Rows of tall shelves felt like home. Instead of video tape cases, there were worn, well-loved book covers on each shelf. I brushed my fingertips along the spines.

The pups huddled in a small corner with colorful picture books and children's chapter stories. Jovi quickly gathered a stack of books he wanted to borrow. The others browsed through joke books, stories about adventures, and a textbook comparing science and magic.

A strange smell pricked my nose. The combination of sugar

and spice pulled me to the opposite end of the library. Dust covered the bookshelf in the shadowed corner. I pulled out books and scanned the titles, but nothing looked like information on witch prophecies.

The aroma grew stronger until I sneezed. I sniffed for the source, finding it came directly from the bookshelf itself. The smell rose as I dipped my head and inspected a dark rectangle on the bottom shelf. I touched a strange shadow at the back of the bookshelf.

It gave way to nothing, and I reached further, twisting my wrist to feel around in the darkness. My fingers bumped something, and it fell with a thud. I felt for the hard spine of a book and gripped it. *No way.* My pulse whooshed like erratic waves in my ears.

When I pulled back, I produced a dusty, worn book. In plain black lettering, a small font decorated the cover.

The Book of Prophecies.

My heart skipped a beat. If it'd been missing for decades, how in the world did I find it in minutes?

The spine cracked with disuse as I laid it on the carpet and opened it. I crisscrossed my legs and scanned the pages. Illustrations depicted different spells, and the deeper I got, the more the images showed prophecies.

Knitted Protection. I scanned the spell described underneath.

Though the lettering was messy, I deciphered it after years of reading my own disastrous handwriting. The author wrote her J's with the same squiggly loops and her S's tilted sideways like mine.

I brushed my fingertips over the words, and the smell returned, stronger than ever. It filled me with a sense of peace, but the smell of rain mingled with it as sadness seeped in. Where did I recognize the smell from? It felt like... home. Not the scent of pups and plastic VHS cases, but a different, distant home.

I breathed the words aloud, giving them life for the first time in decades.

"My magic is tendrils and I've come to contain it the way I roll a ball of yarn," I read the witch's record. "Once contained, I'm able to pull out strips and weave them together, just as I do when I crochet. Like a sweater or a blanket, the magic offers protection from the elements. It only works with supernatural elements. Hunters can't attack us here, supernaturals cannot be targeted within the boundaries of this beach."

The page almost ripped with how quickly I turned to continue reading. Something about the words felt so familiar.

"With enough power the spell can be laid over an entire town. Thanks to crocheted magic, here, on this beach, we've found a safe place to raise our girls. I'm afraid the magic reverses a few things, like the tide of the ocean flowing in the wrong direction. The spell can only be undone by one who can unravel weaved magic, or a curse can temporarily drop the defenses."

My throat squeezed with emotion but I didn't know why. Who was this witch and what had happened to her spell?

"It was real," I whispered.

Sadness and peace melted away as the smell of smoke over-powered rain and lavender.

If the legend was real, who had unraveled it, and why did they want to bring danger to the supernaturals at Bewitcher's Beach?

I thought I'd finish the script before next year's play. But with a mystery this important and oddly familiar, writing fiction was the last thing on my mind.

If this were a movie, I'd be the heroine who can do both— write and find the culprit at the same time.

Join Noema for another enchanting mystery in *Summoning, Skating, and Skulls: Book 2 of the Bewitcher's Beach Paranormal Cozy Mysteries!* Why does the Book of Prophecies smell so familiar?

If this suspect-sniffing werewolf is lucky, the next crime will lead her to the family she can't remember - or will it destroy the 'pack' she has now? When Sett's former girlfriend, Hattie, and more of Noema's friends are accused of murder, her life only gets trickier. To top it off, the spell book goes missing and the town votes to cancel the next festival, just when a mysterious patron offers to fund Everland Theater's transformation to the big screen.

It's enough to make a gal throw in the sleuth towel and howl at the moon.

BEWITCHER'S BEACH
RECIPES

NOEMA'S S'MORES FLAVORED POPCORN

When to eat: at movie night, preferably with a 1980s-2000s film. Some of Noema's recommendations include but are not limited to: *Clue, Stargate, Hook, Clueless,* and *The Swan Princess.* Be sure to check if your VHS tape is rewound before you start cooking! Share with your 'pack', AKA beloved family, especially children.

Ingredients:

- 2 cups mini marshmallows
- 2 cups of chocolate chips (milk chocolate, or dark, depending on what you prefer)
- 1 bag of popcorn (not buttered), or ⅕ cup of unpopped popcorn kernels
- 2 cups graham cracker crumbs

Instructions:

1. Line a cookie sheet with parchment paper. Depending on the type of popcorn you're using, microwave, or air-pop the kernels then scatter across the cookie sheet.
2. Seal graham crackers in a bag to smash with a rolling pin or crush inside a bowl with a spoon.
3. Melt 1 cup of chocolate on the stove or in the microwave (Noema opts for the microwave on everything because it's easier and faster!). Use a spoon or scoop into a plastic bag while hot to drizzle over popcorn.
4. Sprinkle mini marshmallows (or chop smaller to balance taste) over popcorn while the chocolate is still wet.
5. Repeat the process with the second cup of chocolate and marshmallows.
6. Cool, pop in a movie, and devour!

MAE'S FAMOUS MOZZARELLA MEATLOAF

When to eat: over dinner with family, friends, and neighbors. Or, if you've got a mystery to solve, bring a loaf to the suspects in exchange for a chat, just be careful! You don't have to be a half-dragon to enjoy this meaty delight.

Ingredients:

- 1 pound ground beef
- 1 onion chopped
- 1 stalk of celery chopped
- ½ green pepper chopped
- 1 egg
- 4 tablespoons breadcrumbs
- Sprinkle parsley
- 1 teaspoon mustard
- 2 teaspoons Italian seasoning
- ½ teaspoon salt
- ½ teaspoon ground paprika

- Top with ½ cup ketchup, if desired
- Stuff with 4 ounces of mozzarella cheese, shredded

Instructions:

1. Preheat the oven to 350 degrees F and grease or spread foil across a pan or cookie sheet.
2. Mix all ingredients in a large bowl.
3. Form the mix into a loaf and create a cut down the middle to fill with cheese. Sprinkle in cheese and enclose by squeezing the top together.
4. Top with sauce, if desired and bake for 30 minutes. Spread more sauce and finish baking for 25-30 minutes, or until the internal temperature of the meat reaches 160 degrees F.
5. Let it cool slightly (unless you're a half-dragon and prefer your food burning hot!), and enjoy!

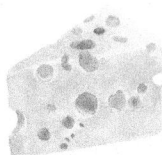

CREAMSICLE COOKIES

When to eat: whenever you're hankering for orange Creme Savers and can't find them. Enjoy these delicious cookies on the beach, after a soccer game, or share with the cast of your local theater's next play!

Ingredients:

- 1 cup granulated sugar
- 1 and ¾ cups all-purpose flour
- ¼ teaspoon salt
- ¼ teaspoon baking soda
- ¼ teaspoon baking powder
- ½ cup unsalted butter
- 1 egg
- 1 tablespoon orange juice
- 1 and ½ teaspoons vanilla extract

- Zest of an orange
- ½ cup powdered sugar

Instructions:

1. Whisk salt, baking powder, baking soda, and flour together.
2. In a separate bowl cream together butter and sugar for 2-3 minutes, or until fluffy. Beat in vanilla extract, orange juice, egg, and zest.
3. Combine both mixtures in one bowl, and mix. Cover the dough and chill in the refrigerator for 1 hour or up to 1 day.
4. Preheat the oven to 350 degrees F, and line the baking sheet with parchment paper.
5. Roll balled sections of dough into powdered sugar and bake for 11-13 minutes.
6. Cool and share!

PIPER'S APPLE CINNAMON MUFFINS

When to eat: absolutely *not* after they've fallen on the floor of a doctor's office, unless you're as brave as Sett. Not recommended to be used as payment to your medical provider for helping with post-plastic-surgery swelling. Instead, bake these and bring them to sell or share at the local fall festival!

Ingredients:

For topping~

- 1 tablespoon granulated sugar
- ⅓ cup brown sugar
- 1 teaspoon ground cinnamon
- ¼ cup unsalted butter, melted
- ⅔ cup all-purpose flour

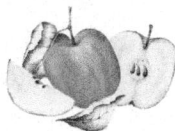

For the muffins~

- 1 and ¾ cups all-purpose flour
- 1 teaspoon baking powder
- 1 teaspoon baking soda
- 1 teaspoon ground cinnamon
- ½ teaspoon salt
- ½ cup unsalted butter
- ½ cup brown sugar
- ¼ cup granulated sugar
- 2 eggs
- ½ cup yogurt or sour cream
- 2 teaspoons vanilla extract
- ¼ cup milk
- 1 and ½ cups chopped and peeled apples

Instructions:

1. Preheat the oven to 425 degrees F. Grease a muffin pan or use cupcake liners.
2. For the topping: mix the brown sugar, granulated sugar, and cinnamon together. Stir in melted butter and flour until it forms large crumbles.
3. For the muffins: whisk together the flour, baking soda, baking powder, cinnamon, and salt.
4. Beat the butter, granulated sugar, and brown sugar together for 2 minutes. Add eggs, yogurt, and vanilla extract. Beat until creamy. Mix together the dry and wet ingredients and milk. Add apple pieces.

5. Scoop mixture into muffin pan and spoon topping on each muffin.
6. Bake for 5 minutes at 425 degrees F and then reduce oven temperature to 350 degrees F. Bake for additional 15-18 minutes or until a toothpick inserted in the middle comes out clean. Total time in the oven is approximately 20-23 minutes.
7. Let muffins cool and enjoy plain, with butter, or add icing for an extra treat!

SETT'S HOMEMADE ALFREDO SAUCE

When to eat: on a date, with a mate, or after a day on roller skates! Okay, that's enough Dr. Seuss—speaking of which, did you know Sett Lawrence volunteers hours at the local library reading similar rhyming books to children?

Ingredients:

- ½ cup butter
- 1 and ½ cups heavy whipping cream
- 2 teaspoons minced garlic
- ½ teaspoon salt
- ½ teaspoon Italian seasoning
- ¼ teaspoon pepper
- 2 cups grated parmesan cheese

Instructions:

1. Combine butter and cream in a skillet/large pan.
2. Simmer over low heat for 2 minutes.
3. Whisk in garlic, Italian seasoning, pepper, and salt for one minute
4. Drizzle over choice of noodles, chicken, or across garlic bread and enjoy immediately! (This is the only time Sett moves faster than molasses—when food is meant to be served right away.)

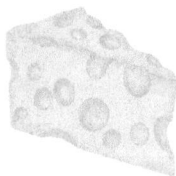

ABOUT THE AUTHOR

Congenital Heart Defect survivor, Emily Fluke, finds joy and peace through the expression of writing. She is a firm believer that all stories need a little magic and a lot of excitement. Emily and her husband spend their free time wrangling two children and playing video games in their busy California lifestyle. Otherwise, you'll find Emily solving an escape room, running, or writing Magic the Gathering-based poetry.

To stay up to date on new releases and connect with me, visit my website at Emilyfluke.com or follow me on social media under Author Emily Fluke, or @emilyflukefairytales.

Printed in Great Britain
by Amazon